A FAMILY AFFAIR: THE PROPOSAL

MARY CAMPISI

MARY CAMPISI BOOKS, LLC

EBOOK ISBN: 978-1-942158-54-7

PRINT ISBN: 978-1-942158-60-8

❀ Created with Vellum

DEDICATION

To Jim, my husband and best friend. You are my one constant in this crazy life we share and I am so very grateful for every moment of it!

A special thank you:

I often correspond with readers and we "chat" about any number of things: dogs, flowers, food. Robyn is one such reader friend. When I lost Cooper in February 2018, she reached out to me and expressed her sympathies. (Many other reader friends did as well, and I am truly grateful. Thank you!) Robyn also told me about the river rocks she painted and how some of them were of animals. She shared a few pictures of these rock paintings and they were just beautiful and so full of emotion. I remembered how I felt when I looked at those rocks and when I began to write A Family Affair: The Proposal, I decided to make Ava Marie Ventori a river rock painter. Robyn was kind enough to answer several questions about the process of

river rock painting, and that's all I needed for my imagination to take off...
Thank you, Robyn!

Best always,

Mary

INTRODUCTION

It was only supposed to be a simple arrangement—until emotions got in the way. Now lies and secrets could destroy everything.

Lawson Carlisle, the ostracized black sheep of the wealthy Carlisle family, is back in Magdalena. It's been sixteen years since he left, vanishing one night amidst speculations that included detention homes and jail time. Those were serious claims against one of the wealthiest families in town, and whether those stories were true or not, they fueled many a conversation and served as a lesson to the community: no person is invincible, no matter how much money his family has.

Ava Marie Ventori used to believe that doing good and following rules would gift her with the life she wanted, the man she loved, the dreams she didn't even know she craved. But her eagerness to find that perfect life landed her with the wrong man, the wrong career path, and the wrong dreams. At thirty-three, the jobs are meaningless, the relationships nonexistent, and the dreams are gone. Her one joy is painting river rocks with inspirational messages, but she's not about to share their existence, especially with the parents she continues to disappoint.

After a chance encounter with former classmate, good-girl Ava Marie Ventori, Law offers her the use of his cabin—no strings attached—so she can work on the mystery art she obviously doesn't want to share. But his "no strings" good intentions are no match for old-fashioned attraction... As Law and Ava spend time together, she discovers there's so much more to the former bad boy than a questionable past and he starts to believe that maybe Ava isn't too good for him. In fact, maybe she's perfect for him.

When lies and old secrets threaten the couple's happiness, will their love be strong enough to fight for a life together?

CHAPTER 1

"Law, it's time to head home and face the past."

Lawson Carlisle sipped his whiskey, considered his uncle's words. Calvin Eugene Beaumont had been doling out bits of wisdom for the past sixteen years, pretty much since the day Law got dumped at his uncle's farm in Logan's Creek, Pennsylvania, otherwise known as Nowhere town. At sixty-four, the man had a straight-shooter attitude and a gruff delivery that didn't cater to hurt feelings or been-done-wrong commentary. Cal said it didn't matter what misfortune befell a man. What mattered was how the man handled the misfortune; that's what marked character.

Back in the day, when Law was so busy fueling the anger that landed him in Nowhere town with a "hick" uncle who believed in hard work, 5:00 a.m. wake-up calls, and the notion of respecting one's elders, he fought the man's dribbles of wisdom that pounded him like raindrops on a window. Fought them hard, until one day, two months into his "sentence," one of his uncle's tidbits clung to him like a briar on a dog's hindquarters.

If a man doesn't honor his word, he's good for nothing.

Meaning, if you say you're going to do something, do it. No

excuses, no changing the terms, no trying to con or buy your way out of it.

For a kid who'd been raised to believe money was the universal currency that could buy happiness, love, *and* respect, this was an eye-opener. Of course, Law had suspected this truth long before he got booted to Logan's Creek, Pennsylvania, but watching someone live it? Well, that made a person take a hard look at himself and sometimes the deeper he looked, the more he wished he hadn't. But there was no going back because he'd seen the inside of his soul, and it was dark there, and shameful. That's when a person realized he had a choice: follow the path of a rich-punk-ass teenager who boosted cars, stole cigarettes, and got wasted every weekend, or find a purpose and a passion to believe in, starting with himself. The answers would come if he had someone to guide him, someone like Cal Beaumont, the uncle he refused to call uncle.

"Law?" Cal rubbed his stubbled jaw with callused fingers. "I know that look. What's rattling around in that head of yours?"

Law lifted his glass, saluted the man who'd been more of a father than the one who claimed the title. "Can't a man enjoy his whiskey without conversation? You're the one who told me words shouldn't be wasted."

Cal nodded his shaggy gray head, his thin lips stretching into an almost smile. "I did say that, didn't I? Measure your words and use them with respect and caution, because once spoken, they can't be unspoken." The almost smile shifted, spread. "I also said it takes a strong person to talk about things that make him uncomfortable." Pause, another nod. "Like heading back to Magdalena and seeing your father again."

And there it was, tossed between the reason for Law's current bad mood and his uncle's philosophical commentary. Well, Cal was not going to convince him that returning to Magdalena was a good idea on any level. "I've seen my father three times in the last sixteen years, and those wouldn't have happened if my mother hadn't insisted *and* made the arrangements. We won't count the fourth visit, since that was her funeral."

His uncle's eyes turned bright against the weather-beaten skin on his face, a testament to years of sun and outdoor work. "Evelyn's been gone four years, long enough for you to honor her final wishes." When Law didn't respond, his uncle continued. "It's time to move past the anger you've been carrying around since the day you arrived. You need to let it go, but you haven't done it, son. You've buried it behind polite words, a carefree attitude, and too much damn pretense."

Pretense? What did he mean by *that*? Law had earned every ounce of distaste he had for his father, and no one had a right to tell him how he should feel, not even his uncle. "All I ever wanted was the reason he hated me so much. The *real* reason, not the half-cocked one about disgracing the family because I stole a car..." And he hadn't really stolen the car; he'd merely *relocated* it for Harriet Schuster. "It's been sixteen years, Cal. Forget an apology from him, what about a let's-sit-down-and-work-this-out conversation or even a why-the-hell-are-you-avoiding-me question? But I've gotten nothing. He doesn't even know what I do for a living." He studied his uncle, waited. "Now why do you think that is?"

His uncle's answer slipped out smoother than the whiskey in Law's glass. "That's a question you need to ask him."

"Right." Montrose Carlisle was a dangerous subject, because the man *and* his intentions were stuffed with ill will and self-serving agendas that would sacrifice anything—even a child—to achieve a goal. "The man doesn't deserve my time, and I sure as hell don't plan on giving it to him."

"Your mother always hoped that one day you and your father might reconcile." Cal paused, blew out a long breath. "She never had any illusions you'd become best friends, but she thought you might come to respect one another in some measure, though not until you were grown and had your own sense about you."

That made Law laugh. "Respect? Interesting word. How does a son respect the father who disowned him?"

His uncle met his gaze head on. Calm, steady, burrowing deep enough to ferret out the rough spots in Law's character. "A big man knows how to set aside past disappointments and move on. You haven't done that, son. Not even close." The gaze narrowed, the voice thinned. "And your father *didn't* disown you. He sent you away to grow up and keep you out of trouble because, Lord knows, you knew how to find it."

Law fidgeted in his chair, studied his empty whiskey glass. He could use two more of these to ease the rawness his uncle's words created. The man was no fool. Cal Beaumont might not have advanced degrees, but he could read a person, a situation, and a financial statement in the time it took most people to say hello. Over time and with keen observation, he'd taught Law to do the same. "What's really going on, Cal? Since when did you care so much about my nonexistent relationship with my father?"

The older man's gray brows pinched together, the brackets around his mouth deepened. At just over six feet, he was lean and weather-beaten, his skin the color of an animal hide left out in the sun too long. He prided himself on the fact that he could still fit into the only suit he'd ever owned, the one he'd worn at his wedding over four decades ago. It hung in his closet next to his dead wife's wedding gown. Madeline Beaumont had passed away eight years ago, taken by a bout of pneumonia one February morning, just shy of their thirty-eighth anniversary. There'd been no sons or daughters to share the grief, but Law had been there, watched as the light in Cal's eyes dimmed for a solid year. They'd never quite regained their brightness, but his uncle said when desperation claimed a man's soul, he should stand taller, take his best shot, and never quit.

"You want the truth?" Cal asked, his voice raw, husky. "That requires another whiskey." He reached for the bottle, uncapped it and poured two fingers into each glass. Then he nudged Law's glass toward him. "Drink up, son. You're gonna need it."

Son. Law eased the glass to his lips, took a healthy swallow.

Cal set the bottle on the table between them, tossed back his drink. "The day your mother brought you here was the second-best day of my life. Marrying your aunt was the first." His voice dipped, his eyes clouded with remembering. "You were so angry and hell-bent on being a rebel, but I knew all you needed was time and hard work to wear the anger out of you. Maddie and I used to lie awake at night, talking about all the good things life had in store for you, and how we hoped we'd be here to share them." He leaned forward, planted both elbows on the desk, and cleared his throat. "Your aunt always said you had a kind heart and a big soul, and all you needed was room to grow and love to help you find your way."

Law stifled a sigh. Yes, his aunt had mentioned his kind heart and big soul many times, too many times, especially to the young women trying to capture both. Maddie Beaumont had taken up the challenge to find Law *his destiny*, meaning, a woman, but she'd never quite succeeded. Not that he needed her help because he had a knack for attracting women all on his own. The problem became what to do with them once the *attraction* cooled. And it always cooled. "I tried to tell her not everybody needed a special someone—" Law worked up a smile, held his uncle's gaze "—but she wouldn't buy it, not when she'd transformed the orneriest cuss in the state."

His uncle's laugh held a hint of sadness and when he spoke, there was no mistaking the pain. "I *was* an ornery cuss, and she should have dumped my sorry behind in a cornfield the second I gave her the I'm-too-busy-to-talk-to-you nonsense. But she didn't. Nope. Maddie spotted something in me that I didn't even know was there. That's what you need, son." Another sip of whiskey, a nod. "I've watched you turn into a fine young man, but you're stuck like a truck in a pile of mud. If you don't go back to Magdalena and deal with what happened there, you're going to keep spinning your tires just like that truck, and one day, there won't be any getting out."

Law plowed through his uncle's words, intent on making him understand why his father would never have his time *or* his respect. "I could care less about my father or his reasons for kicking me out. He gave up on me, Cal. Who quits on their own kid? Aren't parents supposed to stand by their child, no matter what?" He did not want to have this conversation, but the words tumbled out hard and fast, pushed by a truth that simmered with pain and sadness. "And what about my brother and sister? They're no better than my old man."

"There's a lot of hurt in those words. That tells me you've got unfinished business. I'm not particularly fond of your father, and I've got my reasons that go beyond how he treated you. As for your brother and sister, they're the product of a mother and father giving too much and expecting nothing in return, not even common decency or respect. I don't care about them, Law. I care about *you*, and the way you shut people out of your life." He dragged a hand over his face, said in a quiet voice, "You've never had a relationship with a woman that lasted longer than six weeks."

"So, now you're keeping track of my love life?" And it hadn't been six weeks; it had been eight. Hadn't it? Law tried to remember, but the faces and the bodies all ran together after a while—blonde, tall, big-busted, leggy: Teresa, Sydney, Lauren, Marjorie, Giselle...

"I'm keeping track of a life that's falling apart and you're

6

only thirty-three. Don't you want to find someone who means something to you for longer than a few weeks?" His uncle's eyes misted. "Maybe start a family?"

"Not really." Finding someone and starting a family meant opening up and letting her see the hurt boy inside, the one whose father didn't want him. If his own father had pushed him away, it would only be a matter of time before a wife would do the same.

"If you don't deal with this situation, you'll never be able to move on, and I can't turn over my company to someone who's stuck in a past filled with anger and resentment. It would cloud your judgment, destroy you *and* the company. I can't let that happen." Cal homed in on him, his words sneaking past Law's defenses. "You do care, and telling yourself you don't doesn't make it so."

Law dragged a hand through his hair, fell back sixteen years to the backseat of the fancy sedan as it drove him out of town to a new life and an aunt and uncle he'd never met. *He didn't care. He didn't care. He didn't—*

"Law." The voice that had guided him to adulthood with a firm hand, an open mind, and a kind heart saturated his brain. "You *do* care, and that's why you have to go back."

CHAPTER 2

Growing up in a small town with a larger-than-life older brother, a father who couldn't accept that gray areas existed in everyone's life, and a mother who spent more time keeping the peace than encouraging independence did not support free thinking or fulfilling one's passion.

Ava Marie Ventori read philosophical essays in her high school Humanities class on how life was meant to be lived: full-out, arms wide open, no boundaries. And there were class discussions on how words like *must* and *should* damaged the soul, but they were nothing more than a way to land her an *A* for participation and later, another *A* for the essays she'd write. It wouldn't be until years later, after her brother had been banished from town and she'd suffered her own downfall, that she'd realize the power of those classes, the lessons that lay dormant until she grew desperate, angry, and in need of revival.

And that's when Ava Marie Ventori found herself.

Of course, there were the years in between when she'd believed doing good and following rules would land her the life she wanted, the man she loved, the dreams she didn't even know she craved. In her eagerness to find her destiny, sixteen-year-old Ava chose the career *and* the man, believing dreams would follow, but by twenty-two, they were all gone.

At thirty-three, there was no career, definitely no man, and the dreams that flitted in and out of her brain were best kept there. Oh, she put on a good show, acted like she loved the carefree existence that answered to no one and did whatever she liked. Who wouldn't want to move to a new town every ten months or so? It saved coming up with a story about why she was quitting her current job—usually some retail position—and made her look like a true free spirit bent on wandering the country.

That was such a lie. Ava didn't quit because she was bored with the lack of cerebral challenge and the monotony of showing up at a place she didn't care about to perform tasks that meant nothing to her. She quit because she didn't want to get close to anyone or start to think of the local coffee shop as *her* coffee shop, the next-door neighbor with the golden retriever as *her* friend. There was only so much room in a closed heart, and she reserved that space for her family. No one else. What was the point? The love she'd yearned for and the life she'd planned had passed her over in one giant tsunami of betrayal, leaving behind wounds so deep they still hurt.

Who needed that kind of pain?

But the more she visited her brother and his wife, the more she wondered what it might be like to trust another person like that, to love him enough to share a child, dreams, a future. She'd never pictured Roman washing dishes or changing diapers, and yet, he did it, and didn't seem to mind. And Angie? Ava didn't miss the way her sister-in-law looked at Roman, those dark eyes shining with a brightness that made a person long for that sort of connection.

What would that kind of love feel like?

Ava doubted she'd ever know because it involved letting the other person peek inside, uncover the insecurities, the flaws, the *doubt* that lived in her heart. It would give him too much power, enough to destroy her. That had almost happened once, and she'd never let it happen again. She couldn't. Let people think she didn't care about anything but the next good time, the next job, the next adventure. The next whatever... So what if they thought her selfish and self-absorbed? Let them believe whatever they wanted.

At least she'd be safe. And if she told herself this enough times, maybe one day she'd believe that protecting herself from opening up to a man again would keep her safe and help her live a full life.

But probably not.

Ava's life turned upside down the night she got the phone call from her brother telling her their mother had tripped over a crate of oranges and sprained her ankle.

I'd pack up Angie and Dominic if I could, but we can't leave right now. Angie's pregnant.

Pregnant! Congrats! If she'd listened more closely, she would have heard the concern in his voice, the hesitancy that said this wasn't a time to celebrate. But Ava had been so busy making sure her brother knew how happy she was for him, despite her own mateless and childless state, that she hadn't listened to the emotion between the words.

Until he told her the rest. He'd faltered, his voice cracking and splitting open through the phone lines. *There've been complications with the pregnancy. It's called placenta something or other... She has to stay close to home for now...maybe for the whole pregnancy.*

Will the baby be okay? When Ava was younger, she'd believed pregnancies equaled babies. But as she grew older and people she knew got pregnant, she learned that wasn't always so. The dreaded and heartbreaking miscarriage could steal a couple's hopes, crush their dreams, and sometimes, harm the marriage. *Roman?* she'd asked. *Will the baby be okay?* Please, let their baby be strong and healthy. Please, dear God, let their baby live.

I don't know. All we can do is wait. Pause. A deep breath filling the lines before he continued. *Can you help out Mom and Dad? Please? I can't leave Angie right now and if one of us isn't there, you know Dad will try to take over at the grocery store.*

And probably risk another heart attack. *I'll be there in two days.* Heading to Magdalena for more than a few days was worse than attempting to give up carbs. There'd been a time when she and Roman were the type of children their parents called blessed and a godsend. Until the accusations started about Roman getting Paula Morrisen pregnant. Ava knew they weren't true, but she'd been too naïve to understand how greed could force a person to say anything. Bad enough most of the town sided with the Morrisens, but when their father believed the lies? Salvatore Ventori's refusal to stand by his son had created a divide that would take fourteen years and Angie Sorrento to fill.

When Roman left for college, Ava tried to repair the damage to their once-close family by living according to Sal and Lorraine Ventori's rules: not creating concern or worry, going to Mass every Sunday, and respecting her elders. She didn't take risks or dream too big because that might create uneasiness for the parents who needed calm after her brother's disaster. While she loved drawing and artwork, Ava decided nursing would be a career where she'd help others and gain praise for her lack of selfishness. Too bad she couldn't stand the smell of hospitals and gagged when someone threw up. None of that mattered but being a good and loyal daughter, and one day, a good and loyal wife who took care of the sick and worked part time so she could raise the children she and her almost fiancé would have.

Right. Too bad nobody told the almost fiancé it wasn't okay to sleep around. If she hadn't discovered the lacy underwear in the glove compartment of his car, would he ever have confessed? Or would he have continued cheating while she planned their perfect life in the suburbs with children, a dog, and a swing set in the backyard? Something broke inside Ava that day, stole her trust as rage seeped through her, settled in her soul, and smothered hope. Two days after the betrayal, she quit the nursing program and signed up for art classes because good intentions did not always keep a girl safe.

Her father didn't speak to her for three weeks, saying she'd chosen a foolish path that wouldn't earn enough to pay for a cup of coffee. Ava fought back, telling him she didn't drink coffee, so what did it matter? The battle continued until her mother stepped in and set her father straight; their daughter didn't want to be a nurse and had chosen that career to please them. If Lorraine Ventori had left it at that, Ava might have been able to bluff her way through the breakup with her almost fiancé and call the split mutual, but small towns had a knack for uncovering secrets, and that was Magdalena's specialty. Lorraine said she'd heard Ava's boyfriend had a new girlfriend, but if that were true, why were there bridal magazines in Ava's bedroom?

Good question.

Sal wanted to limp to O'Reilly's bar and find out who was telling tales about their daughter's boyfriend and why, but Ava couldn't let him do that. Not when the tales were true. The news that her father had misjudged the young man he'd taught to make homemade wine and shared stories of the old country devastated him. *This is my fault. How did I miss it?* And then, because he'd failed to protect her, he said, *Don't trust men, Ava. They'll only break your heart.*

Her mother *tsk-tsked* him, but Ava gathered those words,

repeated them in the dark until they became her mantra. *Don't trust men. They will only break your heart.*

And now she was back in Magdalena, sleeping in her old bedroom, working at the grocery store, and wondering how she'd ended up in a life she didn't recognize.

CHAPTER 3

Law Carlisle figured the town would have something to say when he returned, most of it not good, but he hadn't planned on them not recognizing him. That was as sad as it was entertaining, and Law hadn't enjoyed a laugh in three weeks, since the day Cal laid out the ultimatum: head back to Magdalena and settle things with your father or forget inheriting my company.

Law considered refusing for all of two seconds. The only positives in the whole mess were seeing the town again in the fall and his uncle's interpretation of the word *settle*, which he'd explained in his no-nonsense manner. *Say what needs saying, listen to his reasons, and the minute his past actions don't affect you any longer, you can leave. Dang it all, you can even tell him to burn in hell. That's when you know you're free of your past, Law, and that's when you'll get the company.*

Law arrived three nights ago, settled in the rundown log cabin his uncle purchased years ago on the outskirts of town, close to Boone's Peak. *Because I figured one day you'd end up back there and you'd need a project to keep you busy and a quiet place to sort things out.* Yeah, he'd guessed that right. The Carlisle homestead didn't exactly provide an atmosphere for contemplation or a place to pound a nail or two. Nope, that place was more like a showcase for the rich and richer.

He knew people were talking about him, guessed what they might be saying or not saying by the sideways glances and the second-too-long stares. Most erred on the side of discretion, but there were a few who didn't try to hide their curiosity or their comments.

Who's the guy in the ponytail roaming the streets?

Huh? What guy? What ponytail?

Can't miss him. Tall drink of water, suntanned, tattoos.

Oooh, did you say tattoos? What kind of tattoos? And where?

The ones that go down your arm, and maybe there was a skull.

I bet he rides a motorcycle...

I bet he's got tattoos all over his body...

He's a hoodlum, no doubt about it.

But Phyllis said when he ordered apple pie he had real manners. And a smile to boot.

Lily Desantro said she liked his eyes... Green as clover.

He's a bad boy, no doubt about it.

But why is he here?

And how long is he staying?

Where is he staying is what I want to know. Mimi would have told us if he was at the Heart Sent.

We better find out more, and we better find out fast.

You just never know what kind of riffraff comes into this town and what they intend to do.

Riffraff, tattoos, or ponytail, he's going to steal more than a few hearts in this town, no matter how long or short his stay is...

Law heard some of the chatter, ignored most of it, and

decided to work on the cabin for a few days while he devised a plan to confront his father. The cabin would definitely provide a challenge during his stay: kitchen cupboard doors that didn't close, cracked floorboards, dings and gouges in the walls. And then there was the deck that hadn't seen a power washing in too many years and the front porch that had a section of the railing gone. He had no idea how long he'd be in Magdalena, but he looked forward to working with his hands again. He hadn't used a circular saw or a nail gun in a year, and when was the last time he'd repaired drywall or worked on plumbing? Probably not since before he stepped in to help Cal run the business, a business that required more knowledge of spreadsheets and data analysis than working a table saw. Still, that didn't mean he'd forgotten the manual labor skills his uncle had introduced him to early on that taught the value of a hard day's work. Right now he wanted to dig in so he could forget the real reason he was in this damn town.

Law spent the first day making a repair list, and the second writing out supplies. By day three, he decided the cabin could be an on-going project, even if he reached some sort of resolution regarding his old man. Why not commit to staying and renovating this place? It didn't need marble or high-end floors, but working lights and floors without splinters would make it comfortable. If he had to head back to Pennsylvania for a meeting, his uncle's place was only four hours away, and once he got Internet up and running, it would be easy enough to make conference calls and conduct business from here. Cal hadn't seemed surprised by the idea. In fact, he'd acted as if he'd *expected* Law to come to that conclusion.

Boone's Peak had always been a place to get away and be by himself. Sure, kids came here to make out, party, and take advantage of the fact that their parents wouldn't venture up here. On occasion, he'd been one of those kids, too. But the main reason he headed to the lake was the quiet. In all of the places he'd traveled, he'd never found the kind of peace he'd found at Boone's Peak.

Tomorrow he'd drive to the local hardware store and see what he could pick up. His uncle had the foresight to send Law off with hand tools and a pair of sawhorses. Law stuffed the list in his back pocket, opened the front door, and walked down the path leading to the lake. He thought about putting a spotlight at the end of the road and wanted to measure the height of the post. He made it to the end of the gravel driveway, his thoughts still on measurements when he spotted the woman. Head bent, dark curls shielding her face, she sat cross-legged on a large rock with a sketchpad and a pencil. Who was she? He moved closer, careful not to disturb her. Law studied the slender curve of her back, the long legs...the graceful hands... He moved closer.

Who was she?

A crow cawed nearby and the woman glanced up, saw him. "Oh...I thought I was alone..."

Law held her gaze, stepped closer. "So did I." He glanced at the sketchpad, noted the shape of a leaf, a blade of grass, a raindrop. Not pictures, but bits and pieces of nature. "You're...an artist?"

Pink smeared her cheeks seconds before she flipped the page, hiding her work. "No, just enjoying the fall colors."

Those dark eyes turned darker. They were the color of slate with tiny flecks of gold in the center. High cheekbones, full lips, slender neck. And her complexion? He detected an olive hue beneath the tan. Beautiful. Natural. Unenhanced. Most of the women he knew wouldn't step outside without face armor, but this one didn't seem to care.

She cleared her throat. "Are you from around here? I don't think I've seen you before."

That comment made him smile. "And I'm sure I haven't seen

you before," he said, avoiding her question. But there *was* something about her that looked familiar... Law narrowed his gaze on the woman, tried to remember, but sixteen years away was a long time and the few random visits he'd made to Magdalena had not included socializing.

"I grew up in this town, but I've been gone a long time." She stood, held out a hand. "I'm Ava."

Law shook her hand, noted the firm grip, the direct gaze. "Nice to meet you, Ava." *Ava?* He'd known a girl by that name in high school: pretty, smart, a real do-gooder with big plans that would never include a loser like him. But there had been that one night—

"And you?" That voice turned soft and curious, the way it had all those years ago. "I swear you look familiar." A smile pulled out the dimple in her left cheek, made her eyes sparkle. "Have we met before?"

In high school, girls like Ava didn't talk to guys like him. *But they weren't in high school any more...* "Ava Marie Ventori. Or would you prefer Saint Ava?" He held her gaze, waited for the exact instant she recognized who he was. It took all of three seconds, four if he counted the confusion that slipped into shock and disbelief.

"Law Carlisle?"

She said his name as though he'd turned into a rattlesnake. Law stepped back, shoved his hands in his back pockets. "That's me."

Those storm-cloud eyes stared back at him, smothered with an emotion he couldn't identify. Or maybe he *could* identify it if he thought about it hard enough. Apprehension? Fear? Disgust? Probably all of them.

"It's been a long time." She licked her lips, inched to what she might think was a safe distance. "I haven't seen you since..."

Since the summer before her senior year when he'd caught

her trying to sneak into a party where she didn't belong. He'd spotted her from the shadows of an old oak tree as he was about to light up. He didn't recognize fresh-faced-next-to-sainthood Ava Marie Ventori at first because the young woman making her way up the long driveway didn't look innocent or saintly. The tangle of long hair, extra-tight mini, and red stilettos said wild and hot, but the unsteady gait and the dress-yanking with each movement told him she wasn't used to the outfit.

That had made him curious enough to toss the cigarette he'd been about to light and approach her. He was four feet away when the moon illuminated a scrap of her face and there, beneath the red lips and eyeliner, Law recognized Roman Ventori's kid sister.

"So, where've you been all these years?"

Her question sliced through his thoughts, cut off memories of that night—the confrontation, the anger...the kiss. Oh yeah, the kiss that scorched him, made him wonder just how innocent she was. Law shrugged, slid his gaze to meet hers. "Here and there."

Those gray eyes turned three shades darker. "More here, or more there?"

He didn't miss the judgment or the wariness in her tone. Yeah, Ava Marie Ventori would believe the stories that landed him in juvenile detention for "behavior unbecoming a Carlisle." Then again, she might have bought into the runaway tale, or even the jail sentence. He'd like to ask her what he was supposed to have done to end up in jail, but he kept quiet. What did it matter when his father was the one spreading the tales? Law blew out a long breath, shrugged. "Just because someone tells a story doesn't make it true, no matter who's doing the telling." He kept his gaze trained on her, his voice even. "People lie all the time, Ava. Haven't you learned that yet?"

Those small nostrils flared and the full lips pinched. "If you believe that, Lawson Carlisle, then you've been hanging around the wrong people." Pause, a sniff. "Or the wrong places."

He crossed his arms over his chest, forced a smile. "Or I've been paying attention. You'd be surprised what you can find out when you block the chatter and start listening to your gut."

CHAPTER 4

The man was as elusive as he'd been as a teenager, and just as intimidating. What was it about him that put her on edge? Ava thought of what her brother had once told her when she'd been afraid to talk to boys. *Go on the offensive; it's the best way to diffuse any situation.* According to Roman's wife, he hadn't followed that advice when they first met and that landed him in a huge mess. Ava narrowed her gaze on the "situation" standing in front of her and took her brother's advice. "Why did you come back to Magdalena?" There must be a reason to pull him back to the town that considered him a hoodlum and a liability. Whispers said his own family hadn't wanted him.

Sal and Lorraine Ventori were the opposite of disinterested parents: they wanted to control their youngest, see that she did right by family and church, by the husband she would one day have and the children she would nurture. But what they hadn't counted on was Ava herself and her own wishes. They wanted her to have the life *they* chose, the one *they* understood, and she'd tried. Oh, how she had tried. When it fell apart and she was left uncertain, confused, and lost, they didn't know how to help her. No one did. That's why all these years later, she was still floundering, still trying to find herself, still trying to gain her parents' respect.

"Do you know how many people will ask me why I came back?" His green eyes turned darker than the grassy bank next to him. "None. Not a single person."

"What about your father? Or your brother and sister?" Surely, someone would ask.

A faint smile flitted over his lips, disappeared. "They won't ask why I'm home. They'll only want to know when I'm leaving."

"Oh." What to say to that? Maybe she could offer him a bit of her own truth, a tale that would not make him seem so alone. "My parents *did* ask why I came home, even when they knew why. That's one thing about my family; they ask questions they already know the answers to, and if you don't spit it out the way they think you should, interrogations follow, and they're not pretty." Her father had done this to Roman years ago when Paula Morrisen accused him of getting her pregnant. So many questions, so many attempts to make him confess to an offense Ava knew he hadn't committed. It would take years of avoiding one another before Roman and their father reconciled, and though she didn't know the particulars, Roman's wife had a lot to do with it.

Law Carlisle kicked at the ground with a booted foot, let out a long sigh. "I was always intimidated by your father. Old-school tough, gruff-speaking, hard-nosed." Another sigh. "Does he still wear those white shirts and suspenders?"

Ava tried to hide a smile, failed. Her voice gentled as she pictured her father in his uniform: short-sleeved white shirt, suspenders, black pants, steel-toed black shoes. White socks. "Of course. You don't think he's progressed to jeans now, do you?" The man had a way of getting her to open up and talk before she realized what she was saying. That could be dangerous, if he chose to use anything against her. But for all of his bad-boy history, he didn't seem the type. Still, how did she know what Lawson Carlisle was capable of...?

"So, why are *you* back in Magdalena?"

The gentleness in his voice said he'd guessed it wasn't by choice. No sense pretending around the truth. Ava sucked in a breath, blew it out nice and slow. "My mother tripped over a crate of oranges and sprained her ankle."

"Ah. Sorry about that." He cleared his throat. "I mean sorry about your mom, not sorry you landed back in Magdalena." A swirl of pink inched up his neck, settled on his cheeks.

"I know what you meant. Still, you wouldn't be too far off to extend condolences for my return. It's not on my top ten to-do list, except for holidays and the occasional drop-in."

He nodded, his expression serious. "I get it."

"Figured you would."

A few seconds passed before Law Carlisle spoke. "You know, we're not that different." He must have seen the shock on her face because he held up a tanned hand, continued. "Think about it. We're both here out of obligation, not because we really want to be. And we're trying our damnedest just to get through it." His voice dipped, covered her. "Though I have to admit, you are the nicest surprise of all."

Heat swirled through her, settled in her belly. Why would she care about this man's compliments? They were probably an act, pulled out of his arsenal of smooth-talking lines for occasions when he needed one-on-one banter. "We are *nothing* alike. Trust me on that one." The glitter in those eyes said he didn't agree, but he didn't try to argue. "Why are *you* here, Law?"

He toyed with a gold and red leaf he'd picked up, twirled it between his fingers. "Obligation." The word settled between them, sat there like a boulder before he added, "My uncle seems to think I have issues I need to deal with in Magdalena. Called it unfinished business." His gaze slid over her, settled on her lips. "He might be right about that one."

Oh, no, this was not good. Her silly body tingled and burned. Not good. Ava stepped back, away from the sensations that threatened her common sense. "I...I should go." *Get out now, turn and run.* But she couldn't move fast enough; in fact, she couldn't move at all.

"You know, I don't *own* Boone's Peak," Law said in a gentle tone. "It's free property, and you're welcome to visit anytime and work on your drawings."

"I know that. You don't own the world, Law, even if you think you do." His laughter annoyed her, but not as much as the uneasy knowledge that she didn't *want* to leave. Why would she want to stay and talk to a hoodlum like Lawson Carlisle? She'd never been into long hair, tattoos, or bad boys, and it was so obvious he was a bad boy. He probably had three girlfriends at a time. Probably didn't even call them girlfriends. Hookups, that's what they would be...maybe he didn't even know their last name. Or their first. But when he looked at her like he was now, she didn't think of him as a bad boy or a hoodlum. He was all-male, all-consuming, and it was that last that annoyed her most.

And then there was the nanosecond of shared history all those years ago that included a smoking-hot kiss and a scolding that sent her running home to shimmy out of her too-tight dress and scrub her face. Three days later, Lawson Carlisle was gone. Rumors painted him with all sorts of less-than-desirable scenarios: jail, detention, boys' home. Wherever he went, he must have kept the night of her "party crashing" attempt between them quiet because rumors about *her* never surfaced. Maybe even bad boys had scruples.

"In case you haven't heard, I own the cabin down the road.

Remember the old rundown one where that mountain man lived?"

"Jacob Gunderson? 'Step on my property and I'll string you up'? That guy's house?" People said there were bodies buried on that property—lots of them.

Law nodded, and darn if he didn't smile like he was almost proud of the place. "That's me. Working on a renovation, as the fancy people call it."

Apparently no one told him about the buried bodies tale...or maybe they had and that added to the appeal. Ava raised a brow, couldn't resist a snipe. "Ever hear of a lost cause?"

The smile spread, made his eyes sparkle. "I'm a sucker for lost causes."

"Of course you are." That was another way of saying he couldn't afford a new place and wanted to make a heap of junk look like a renovation treasure.

"It's got potential."

"Potential." Right. Not in this world. But maybe the man needed something to hold onto and revive. Maybe that's all he had left. Maybe he really had been in prison...

"Let's keep this between us, okay? Our secret." He didn't give her a chance to respond before he added, "By the way you slammed that sketchbook closed, my guess is you don't show a lot of people your work. Does anyone even know you draw? Hmm," he mused. "I'll keep your secret, if you keep mine."

Oh, so now the man wanted them to keep secrets for each other. This should be interesting. "Just because I don't want to share my work does not mean people don't know it exists." Of course, they didn't have any idea, but she wasn't telling him that.

"Do your parents know you'd rather draw than be a nurse?" He must've seen her surprise because his eyes sparked and he said in a low voice, "You know how the townspeople love to talk. They'll tell you anything, even if it's not their business to tell."

She could only imagine what they'd told him. Dread covered her next words, though she tried to hide it. "And did you find it all amusing?" No doubt someone in town couldn't wait to tell him about her ex's betrayal and the almost engagement that didn't happen.

He shook his head, his long hair sweeping about his shoulders. "I didn't find any of it amusing, but then I don't like people judging others based on what they think they know." His next words puzzled her. "You can work at my place and I won't bother you or tell a soul we know each other. All I ask is that you don't mention you know who I am or that you've seen me."

"How do you know you can trust me to keep quiet? I could run to Lina's Café and make an announcement that the man everybody's been wondering about has a name and we all know it."

He crossed his broad arms over his chest, studied her. "You could, but I'm guessing you don't want anyone to know you've spoken a word to me, let alone had an entire conversation. Bad-boy reputation and all that wouldn't be good for you now, would it?"

She bit her lip, did not respond. She'd expected him to comment about the kiss all those years ago, waited, but he said nothing. "So, I keep quiet about you and you offer me a place to sketch?"

He nodded. "Call it that or call it a place to get away."

"Ah, a getaway. Is that why you're staying at the cabin instead of your family home?" She'd thought a Carlisle would never suffer the inconvenience of "roughing it" in a cabin unless said cabin were located at a high-end resort. Jacob Gunderson's place was definitely not high-end and Boone's Peak was not a resort.

He eyed her. "Something like that."

"Okay, you've got a deal. My silence for your cabin." He nodded, held out a hand: tanned, strong, capable. She shook it, tried to ignore the tingle that shot through her. "Do you have a phone number so I can call you before I stop by? I wouldn't want to intrude…" Rumors of Law Carlisle's past exploits with women once filled the halls at school and she did *not* want to walk in on a surprise.

"You can have my number and text or call whenever you want but trust me, you won't be intruding." And then he gave her a real smile, one that spread to his eyes, covered her and made her think that maybe those tales about Lawson Carlisle's exploits were not just tales.

CHAPTER 5

Law decided it was time to "meet" his family and there was no easy or desirable way to do it. The Carlisles were known for their extravagance: parties, cars, jewelry, trips. He'd done a little research before coming to town because a lot could change in four years. Apparently, his brother, Brett, was still married to Katrina, the frail blonde with a skittish disposition he'd met at the funeral four years ago. They had two children, a girl and a boy, Ursula and William. Brett ran the car dealership with their father. His sister, Cynthia, was obsessed with her dogs, and did some sort of fundraising, though he couldn't quite say what that was. There were maids, a cook or two, gardeners, but he doubted any remained from the old days when he'd lived at the house. Who could stand to be ignored or treated like you didn't know your right hand from your left, just because those hands didn't glitter with diamonds?

He'd been ticked when Cal told him about the required trip to Magdalena but the cabin was a godsend, and a great relaxer. *Contemplate*, his uncle had said. *I remember you telling me how much you liked the area, so enjoy it; sit by the lake and try to forget what brought you there... Let it give you clarity. You'll be surprised what you learn about yourself.*

Law didn't appreciate the attempted psychological exercise, or the people attached to it—his family—but he'd do it because he wanted to run Cal's company, had wanted to run the place for a long time now. Calvin Eugene Beaumont wasn't just a farmer but a businessman who knew how to make a buck, keep a buck, and turn that buck into a whole lot more. Farming was only a small part of his enterprise. It was the land that brought in the money: acres and acres of undeveloped real estate. Cal had taught Law how to study the market, wait for the right time, and negotiate with enough skill to minimize losses and maximize profits.

So what if Law had to stomach his way through conversations and meet-and-greets with the Carlisles of Magdalena—he refused to think of them as family—to get a chance at that company? He could do it; he *would* do it.

Cal taught Law that the best way to confront an enemy—and his family was the enemy right now—was to come at them sideways. *They'll never see it coming*, he said. That's why Law decided on the car dealership as the initial meeting, the perfect place to keep tempers calm, voices even, and enjoy a surprise attack. Law parked the old pickup he'd borrowed from his uncle for the trip, hopped out and made his way to the glass double doors. No salesman scurried toward him in hopes of eliciting interest in a new car. They'd probably written him off as a low-life struggling from paycheck to paycheck the second they spotted the truck. What would they say if they knew about the convertible and the vintage Aston Martin sitting in a climate-controlled garage a few hundred miles away?

"May I help you?" A twenty-something man with a tousle of blonde hair hanging over his forehead and a too-bright smile eyed him.

"I'm looking for your boss."

That seemed to confuse him. The smile faded, the pale blue eyes shifted from curious to judgmental as he moved his weight from one shiny loafer to the other before responding. "Mr. Carlisle is unavailable."

Law waited until the young salesman pulled at the collar of his starched shirt and darted a glance toward the back, where the offices were located. "I'll wait."

"If you're looking for work, we're not hiring any more mechanics. Lawn care's covered by a service, and we have cleaning people."

"Good to know. What about if I'm looking for Montrose Carlisle? My father?" This time it was Law who worked up the too-bright smile, thrust a hand at the dumbfounded salesman. "Lawson Carlisle, black sheep of the Carlisle family. And you are?"

The fumbling turned to stuttering, simmered to an almost inaudible "Seth Winters." The young man's face matched the cherry sedan in the showroom. "*You're* Law Carlisle?"

He said it as if he'd witnessed the devil firsthand. Law pasted that damn smile on his face, followed it with a shrug. "That's me. I'm sure you've heard a lot about me...or not." People wanted to know about outcasts, even if it wasn't polite to inquire. They found it exciting and while it might not be acceptable to share a beer, information gathered when no one was looking was a real high.

"I...let me check... Just a moment... " The young man held up a finger, hesitated.

"Sure, no problem." Law shoved his hands into the back pockets of his faded jeans, nodded toward the red car. "I'll just peruse while you go find him."

Law had thought about what a meeting with his father would look like since his mother's funeral four years ago, when the old man refused to acknowledge him. While he might not have straight-out told Law he wanted nothing to do with him, his actions and silence said it all. Interesting, that when Law showed up at the funeral service, he didn't have a seat in the front pew with the rest of the Carlisles. Nope, he was sequestered ten rows back with the locals. No problem. Didn't matter. So what? But while he could tell himself he didn't care, didn't mind being shunned by his own flesh and blood, he *did* care, because he wanted the right to tell his father to go to hell. Yet the old man hadn't even permitted him that.

And now, Law was supposed to make amends? Pretend it hadn't happened? No, that's not what Cal had said. What the hell had he meant by *Say what needs said, listen to his reasons, and the minute his past actions don't affect you any longer, you can leave?* Law pondered this as he studied the reflection in the car window and spotted his father approaching.

"Lawson? What are you doing here?"

No *nice to see you, how have you been*, nothing but hesitation smothered in excellent diction. Law turned, eyed the man who'd shaped his childhood and fueled his desire to prove he was *not* good for nothing, not a waste or a throwaway. "Hello, Dad. It's been a while."

The man did not attempt to approach him: no hug, no clap on the back, not even a handshake. "Four years."

The pause at the end of those words made Law wonder if his father hadn't intended to add *four years and it should be another forty-four*. Montrose Carlisle believed in appearances, especially in his business, and he would not want a scene. Law scrubbed the emotion from his voice and stared down the man who'd discarded him years ago. "We have a lot to settle, and I figured it was time."

~

As a young man, Montrose Carlisle had a reputation as a smooth talker who could convince a person to change his religion, political affiliation, or place of employment. That silver tongue had landed him in the same charity event as Evelyn Beaumont, and while the wealth associated with her name had drawn him to her, it was the woman who stole his heart. For a boy who'd grown up in the mountains of Pennsylvania, hungry and cold more days than not, with an on-again-off-again father and a demanding mother, Montrose vowed early on he would *not* repeat his parents' lives. At eighteen, he borrowed a cheap suit from his mother's "friend" and began selling vacuums door to door. Within three months, he was the top seller in the area and had earned enough money to buy his own suit—and two ties.

But Montrose wanted more money, and he longed for the prestige and admiration that went with it. As a boy, he'd tried to ignore the cruel words and sneers when classmates talked about the tears in his pants, the grime on his shirt and neck...the mother who had a boyfriend *and* a husband. At ten years old, he'd learned to wash and mend his own clothes and became obsessed with cleanliness, so much so, his sister dubbed him Mr. Sanitary. It was the need to be seen as more than a pathetic excuse for humanity that pushed him on, earned him another sales position and then another and with each job, better clothes, nicer shoes, fancier handkerchiefs, and most important of all, confidence.

It was this inflated confidence that first propelled Montrose to approach the young brunette with the ruby pendant dangling from her neck as she sipped champagne and chatted with three other socialites at the Logan's Creek Country Club. Montrose had finagled an invitation from his boss, the fourth in as many weeks, and his intention was single-minded: find a rich wife. The socialite with the ruby pendant was movie-star beautiful with a regal disposition. Delicate as a rose petal. More entrancing than the most glorious sunset. Just as untouchable.

Still, that didn't stop Montrose from approaching her for a better look. He offered a smile and an introduction with precise grammar and calculated inflection, the perfect cover to hide his meager upbringing and thin wallet. In less than five minutes, he had her laughing; ten minutes more, and they were on the dance floor. Her skin was soft, the scent a faint floral that reminded him of the peonies in his grandmother's garden. He was so enraptured with the woman that he barely noticed the jewelry or the linen dress that claimed old money and lots of it.

She told him that night her parents would not approve of a salesman who peddled vacuums. Then she'd smiled and those beautiful lips whispered, *And I don't care. Not. One. Bit.* Evelyn Beaumont wanted to see him but it would have to be their secret. Montrose knew all about keeping secrets; hadn't he lived one in the creation of his fictional self these past four years? He agreed and for the next several months they met, they talked, they held hands and dreamed of a life that can only be imagined by those who have no concept of reality. After the third month, they did more than hold hands and dream, and it was the "more" that landed her pregnant.

Evelyn's father wanted to send her away but her mother refused, demanding a wedding *and* a respectable occupation for her daughter's future husband and father of their grandchild. For a man who'd chased respect and money his whole life, Montrose believed *this* was his destiny and never considered he might not be suited or capable for the position.

He certainly never thought he'd grow weary of it, torn up, used, and cast aside like a beaten man. But that's exactly what had happened as he tried to fulfill his wife's every wish and sacrificed a son in the process. That son glared at him now with undisguised animosity as Montrose sank into a leather chair behind the massive cherry desk that had been the setting for business deals, side deals, and everything in between. "Law, I never wanted to send you away, but your mother insisted, said it was the only way to protect you. It all came at a bad time... There was that issue with Brett..." He dragged a hand over his face, tried to settle his breathing, but it was no use. The memories hit him head on: glaring, accusatory, too painful.

"What issue?"

A half-second hesitation before Montrose shook his head. "That's in the past and better to leave it there." How could he tell one son what he'd done to protect another? If he told Lawson the truth now, it would betray the other promise he'd made to his wife. There had never been a right or easy way to handle the situations he found himself in, but he'd chosen his side according to Evelyn's wishes. It was *always* about his beloved wife and *her* wishes. If only he'd stood strong that one time, he might still have a relationship with his younger son. But he'd not been able to do it, not because he didn't love his son. No, that was not the reason at all. It was pure and honest fear that gripped him, held tight and made him agree with a wife who had learned long ago that the greatest power in a marriage was loving the other person less. He did not *want* to lose his son, but he *could not* lose his wife. And so he had agreed, and she'd patted his cheek, squeezed his hand, and told him she was proud of him, even though they both knew he'd forfeited his choice the moment he fell in love with her.

Montrose slid a gaze to the son with the tattoos, long hair, and a nose like his mother's. He'd never understood the boy, never grasped the reasons for the perpetual scowl, school suspensions, or the need to defy everyone.

Law crossed his arms over his chest, shifted in his chair. "There's a lot in the past that's shaped where we are today."

If he only knew the truth in those words. *We have to send him away*, Evelyn had told him. *It's the only way to save him. He'll hate you for it, but he needs this*. She'd paused, eyes bright. *I need this for our son.* Apparently, his wife had been right on both counts: the boy had been saved and he'd ended up hating Montrose. He'd once asked Evelyn why they couldn't form a united front and tell Law it was *their* idea to send him to his uncle's, but she'd merely shook her head and murmured, *I can't because he's my son.*

But now Evelyn was gone and their son was alive. If the boy were going to continue despising him, at least he'd know the whole story. "I never planned to send you away, Law. The threat of jail or juvenile detention was just that: a threat with no intent. We didn't like the drinking, the staying out all hours, or the school suspensions, but we told ourselves you'd grow out of it, given enough time. But when you hotwired Harriet Schuster's car and wrecked it on Elderberry Road, that was the end. The blasted woman would not leave it alone. She didn't want a simple apology, and she didn't want money either, though I tried both." Memories of the woman's tirades sifted through his brain: relentless, harsh, demanding action be taken. *You think you're better than everyone else because you have money. You think the law doesn't apply to you, but I will show you that it does. Just watch.* Those words told him she planned to use his son as payment for every unjust action that had ever happened to her.

"You sent me away...gave up on me." Law cleared his throat, his gaze homed in on Montrose. "What kind of father does that?"

"One who's trying to save his son. Your mother insisted we give you an opportunity to straighten up and the only way to do that was to send you away. She said if we didn't, you'd end up in jail, or worse." Regret filled him as more of the past spilled out. "I could never say no to your mother, no matter what she asked. But I should have." He didn't try to hide the anguish or the sadness in his words. "Damn it, I should have told her no."

"Why would she do that?"

"Because she loved you. Because she didn't trust Harriet

Schuster not to create trouble… Because she thought you'd continue with your behavior until you ended up dead like Mimi Pendergrass's son. He was a wild one, died in a car crash before he made it to eighteen. Your mother couldn't stand to see you or your siblings in 'situations,' as she called them, even if they were of your own making." His voice dipped, clogged with guilt. "I should have said no to her...I should have just said no." More guilt smothered him, made it hard to take in a clear breath. He'd done what Evelyn wanted, even when he knew it was wrong, knew it would ruin lives. But she hadn't cared about anyone but saving her own children—and using him to do it.

CHAPTER 6

L awson Carlisle's the guy with the ponytail and tattoos?
Now what do you think about that?
He's a hunk. Pure 100% grade A male.
Oh, yes indeed.
And dangerous.
Do you think he was in jail? I heard manslaughter.
My sources say a jewelry heist.
Who knows? Maybe both?
What's he doing back in town?
Exactly. Why is he here?
Lawson Carlisle, well, I'll be darned.
We should have looked closer; he's got Carlisle eyes.
We weren't looking at his eyes. Snicker. Snicker.
I heard he got disinherited.
No, he lost his money at the track.
Does he have a job?
Probably not. Those kinds are drifters.
Yup, no money, no job, no prospects.
Bet that's why he's back home.
Heard he's working on Jacob Gunderson's old cabin.

That's what happens when you blow your inheritance and have a jail record.

Sounds about right.

I think I'll bake him a tray of brownies, check out that cabin.

You want to check out Lawson Carlisle. Titter. Titter.

Oh, that I do. That I do.

You're not the only one. I'm going to make him an apple pie and deliver it in my new low-cut sweater.

Hmm... I'll wear my tightest jeans and red stilettos. Something tells me he's a leg man.

Titter. Titter. *Something tells me he likes it all...*

Pop Benito heard the talk about town heating up like oil in a frying pan. If a body would have stopped staring for half a second and paid attention, they would have seen the eyes and nose, the cleft in the chin that said Lawson Carlisle with as much boldness as those tattoos he favored. What was the big fuss about a tattoo here and there? And didn't Jesus Christ have hair past his shoulders? Yes, if the artists had guessed that one right, then the Man wore his hair long and loose.

Certain people in this town loved their stories and Pop was one of them, but when they were flat-out fanciful notions based on nothing but guesswork and nosy curiosity, then it was time to stop the tongue-wagging and listen. It was one thing to study and surmise based on actions, reactions, *and* observations, but to toss out comments willy-nilly like you were writing a book? Now that was what he called pure fiction, and it wasn't right, and he was going to stop it. Darn right he was, if he had to set up camp at Lina's Café and listen for the chatter. Pop still had two good ears and thanks to the cataract surgery, two good eyes. Nobody was going to start telling stories about a boy that got booted out of town by his own father.

Or did he?

Now that was the interesting part of rediscovering history, no matter how long ago it happened. Stories and reasons didn't always match, and if you lived long enough and the history happened in your lifetime, you might get a chance to pick it apart. Like why did Montrose Carlisle pay Pop and Lucy a visit four days after his son got shipped to some undisclosed location? It wasn't like the big-shot car dealer spoke more than three sentences to them in all the years they'd lived in Magdalena. But sure enough, he'd trudged up the front steps in his fancy three-piece suit and shiny wing-tip shoes, sweat beading his forehead, a bouquet of pink sweetheart roses in his hands. The man didn't look angry or annoyed, not even exhausted. Nope, he looked downright heartbroken, and when he spilled out words like *saving my son, had no choice, second chance*, those were the words of a father who loved his son.

Pop and Lucy would wonder about that strange visit for years to come, and it would prove interesting conversation many a night over a bowl of pasta or a glass of Chianti. Why had Montrose Carlisle visited their home? What was he after? Forgiveness? Absolution? *From them?* It made no sense and yet, the more they talked, the more they surmised that maybe he'd heard of Lucy and Angelo Benito and how troubled souls found comfort with them. His wife could always poke a hole in the middle of an issue and pull out the answer. Oh, how he wished Lucy were sitting beside him so he could ask her what she thought.

The return of Lawson Carlisle was another piece of this curious puzzle. Why had the boy come home and why wasn't he staying at the family residence? His pizzelle-eating, Chianti-drinking partner, Sal Ventori, didn't have the gift of figuring out the whys and such of a situation, but he knew how to ask questions that made Pop dig deeper for answers.

"So, what do you think about that Carlisle boy coming back to town?" Pop had the boy on his mind and the reasons for his leaving town skittering in his brain. Something was off, worse than too much oregano on a pizza, and he had a mind to figure out what.

Sal squinted at him, frowned like he'd tasted bad salami. "You mean that hoodlum with the ponytail and tattoos? I spotted him the second he headed to the produce department and started picking around the endive. Ha. You think he even knows what endive is? Then he poked around in the turmeric, lifting one out, studying it. I made sure he didn't stuff it in his jacket pocket."

Sal Ventori had come a long way since reconciling with his son, but he was still plenty old school in his thoughts. "Just because a body doesn't look like me or you or Nate Desantro and his men friends doesn't mean he's got bad intentions in his heart. I saw Lawson Carlisle at Lina's and he was very polite, used the proper utensils and his napkin, even left a ten-dollar tip, according to Phyllis."

Big sigh, followed by a huff and a snort. "Throwing money around, that's what the Carlisles do so everybody knows they have it." He balled his hand into a fist. "Don't think I'm ever going to forget what they did to Roman. Saved their son and sacrificed mine. No good thieves, and stealers of reputations."

It wouldn't do any good to remind Sal that he'd been one of the first to condemn his own son, so Pop shrugged and tried another tactic. "That boy had nothing to do with Roman's situation. The poor kid had his own issues, and I'm not talking about the time he stole Harriet Schuster's jalopy."

Sal nodded. "That old biddy would report her own relative for taking that car to fill it up. I'm not saying joyriding is okay but she didn't have to raise such a commotion for a foolish prank. Not that I agree, and not that I don't think that Carlisle boy is a hoodlum who doesn't bear watching when he comes in the grocery store, but he got served up a bad deal."

"Yup, and I'm thinking whatever happened was about a lot more than a car."

Sal shot him a look, leaned forward, brows pinched together like a caterpillar. "You don't say?"

"I do say." That was as much as he could tell his friend without divulging the long-ago visit from Montrose Carlisle. Best to collect information and see what shook out.

"Huh. Wonder what's going on. I liked the Carlisle woman… She was a real lady; used to come in the store wearing white gloves and carrying a pocketbook that matched her outfit. Shoes, too, not the flat ones all the women wear today, but high heels." He smiled and shook his head. "Lorraine used to stick up her nose when Mrs. Carlisle came in and asked about artichokes or shallots; said a woman who dressed like that didn't know the first thing about what went on in the kitchen. I think she did, though, because a woman who handles produce and vegetables like they're newborn babies understands what to do with them."

Pop grinned, handed Sal a pizzelle from the batch he made this morning. "That says something about her, doesn't it? Just because she had hired help doesn't mean she wasn't in the kitchen. My Lucy would have done the same." He rubbed his jaw, thought about his wife and the hours she'd spent cooking and baking. If he added them up, he bet he'd have two decade's worth. "I bet Lucy wouldn't have minded a clean-up crew, but all she got was me, and that was only part-time."

"Lorraine thinks *I'm* her cleanup crew, but I told Ava she's on dish duty. Lot of good that does because the girl never learned how to scour a pot or set a proper table. It's all mishmash, but she says it doesn't matter how the napkin's folded; triangle or rectangle. But it does matter, don't you think so, Angelo? Don't you think the triangle is fancier than the rectangle and more appropriate for Sunday gravy?"

Sal sure did have some strange notions. "I don't think it

matters if you fold a napkin into a bird like they do at those fancy hotels, as long as you know how to use it." He'd been waiting for Sal to mention his daughter, which he hadn't done since last week's visit when the man said he could see why Ava still didn't have a husband. *She flits around from job to job like a butterfly that can't find the right flower*, he'd said. *How's she ever gonna settle on a man? And how's a man gonna settle on her when she can't fry up a good meatball?*

If Sal taught his daughter the key to finding the right partner was in a meatball, then no wonder that poor girl was single. Pop guessed it was a lot more complicated than that, even if Sal didn't see it. As for flitting from job to job, well, that bore some investigation and Pop knew just where to start. He poured Sal more Chianti, refilled his own glass, and settled back in his chair. "How's Ava doing at the grocery store? Has she gone from being a hindrance to a help?" Sal had been on a roll about Ava's inability to tell the difference between escarole and endive. He said Roman could spot escarole from across the room, but Ava had no clue, not even if it was in her mouth.

Sal sipped the Chianti, eased back in his chair, and said in a pitiful voice, "I got nothing to say about that because, according to Lorraine, I'm supposed to keep my mouth shut. She's not the one people will complain to when the greens are marked wrong or the sale price doesn't get counted. And what about the pickles? Ava was rotating stock and broke three jars." He shook his head, made the sign of the cross. "Lorraine said we have to be thankful she came home to help. What should I say to that? Thank you, dear Lord, for sending my daughter home so she could break the inventory, mess up the produce department, and then give me fifty excuses why it happened? As soon as Lorraine gets out of that boot and moving around on her own, we're sending Ava home. Wherever that might be," he muttered.

Well, that sure sounded like a hornet's nest about to break

open and swarm the room. Sal wasn't really upset about broken pickle jars or his daughter confusing escarole and endive. He didn't even care about the mess with the price reductions. What still nagged at him was the fact that Ava had had plans to become a nurse and then dropped out. Pop tried to tell him it wasn't like when they were young; kids changed their minds about careers all the time, but Sal didn't want to hear it and his next words proved Pop's point.

"A nurse is one of the most selfless and rewarding professions in the world. And it pays. She could work part-time and have a family... But did she consider that? Of course, she'd have to get a husband first, but knowing Ava there'll be no husband, first or second."

"Ava will find her way, just like Roman did, and just like my Anthony did."

That comment brought a snarl and a huff from Sal. "Her clock's running out, Angelo, and she's got nothing to show for the wasted time, not even a career." He grunted, scratched his jaw. "I'll bet this house and everything in it that Roman loaned her money more than once. And if I know my son, he's even offered her a job at his firm in Chicago, whether she's qualified or not."

That sounded like Roman Ventori. Good-hearted, kind, champion of the underdog, and his sister had always been considered the underdog. How was the girl supposed to match up to her all-star brother? It had been a cakewalk after the scandal, but before that and after Roman and Angie got together? Comparing the two siblings was like comparing a slice of tiramisu to a puny vanilla wafer. "Why don't you go easy on Ava and let her be? Maybe she's the artsy type or one of those late bloomers that take forever to figure out life, and once they do, they explode like a tomato in the heat?"

Sal made another sign of the cross, followed it with a pitiful groan. "She's going to burst all right, and it's going to be a mess, and guess who's going to have to clean it all up?" He jabbed a stubby thumb at his chest. "Her senior citizen parents. All I wanted was to see my children settled before I went to the good Lord, but now I wonder if I won't get my final wish."

"We need to love our children for who they are, even if it's not what we want them to be." It had taken Pop years to understand this and another several to accept it. Anthony was not the son he thought he'd have or wanted, but in the end, he was the son Pop needed. You couldn't tell a parent this because they had to live it: the hurt, the pain, the sadness. Once they did, acceptance could settle in, create peace and harmony with the child, and that's what Sal needed now. "Ava's a good girl, Sal. Don't give up on her."

His friend's eyes grew wet behind his glasses. "When we asked her to come home and help out at the store, she was a little too quick to agree. That tells us her life isn't so great, and that worries us, because Ava's a gadabout and a restless soul. We even talked about having her run the grocery store for good, but how could that ever happen? We can't turn over our legacy to someone who doesn't know how to ring up produce or pack a grocery bag." Sal cleared his throat, said in a voice that wobbled, "I'm going to tell you a secret that won't be a secret for much longer."

The pain on Sal's face said whatever he was about to share was a doozy. "What is it? You know you can tell me anything."

His friend took a deep breath, closed his eyes and spilled a whopper that would shock the town. "We're going to sell the store."

CHAPTER 7

Law spotted Ava Ventori stacking cans of tomato products on the shelf of Sal's Market, her slender neck bent forward, hair pulled into a high ponytail. It had been two days since they met at Boone's Peak, and he'd been thinking about her, curious if she'd show up at his door with her sketchpad and whatever she kept hidden inside it. He bet there was a lot he could discover from the contents of that sketchpad, if she wanted to share it. Law moved toward her, the small grocery basket dangling from his right hand, and spoke to her back. "Do you have any crushed tomatoes?"

Ava spun around, squinted up at him, a can of tomato sauce in her hand. "Crushed, puréed, diced." She eyed him from her kneeling position. "What are you making?"

Did he detect a hint of curiosity in that voice? The raised brow made him wonder if she were poking fun, teasing, or really wanted to know. He shrugged, pointed to the shelf of tomato products. "I plan to make a marinara sauce and I'm out of crushed tomatoes."

"So, you cook?"

That was definite curiosity. He slid her a smile, nodded. "I do. Cooking relaxes me."

She stood, placed the can on the shelf, and brushed her hands on her jeans. "Cooking never relaxed me." Her lips pulled into a faint smile. "But eating does. Sometimes a bit too much."

Hmm. A crazy idea shot through his head, flew out of his mouth before he could consider the wisdom of saying it out loud. "Since I like to cook and you like to eat, why don't you join me tonight?" The look she gave him said *Forget it, Buster,* and the scowl said, *No way.* Law ignored both and tossed out the bait a true food lover would not be able to resist. "Linguine with marinara sauce, garlic toast, arugula salad with my secret balsamic vinaigrette… Coconut cream pie for dessert. I can't claim the pie; that's coming from the bakery."

She bit her bottom lip, shifted from one foot to the other. "It's probably not a good idea."

"Why? Because you think I'm asking for more than a meal?" The look she gave him said that was exactly what she thought. "An invitation to dinner sometimes is just that, especially if the invitation comes from me." She didn't trust him, no question there, but maybe she didn't trust any man—other than her father and brother. Yeah, he'd lay money on that last one.

A splash of red covered her cheeks as she cleared her throat, stumbled with an apology. "I'm sorry, I didn't mean it to come out like that. I wasn't accusing you of anything. It's just… I don't know… I don't know what it is."

"Then come for dinner, no strings. How's seven o'clock?" He ignored the ridiculous thump in his chest when she nodded. It was just a dinner…maybe a little conversation that didn't start and end with an accusation. He liked that idea—probably more than he should.

"See you at seven." A tiny smile flitted across her face. "I'll bring the wine."

At seven-eighteen, Law realized Ava Ventori wasn't coming. He'd been a fool to invite her and he still couldn't quite understand why he'd opened his big mouth and done it. It's not like he minded being alone or needed companionship to get through a meal. In fact, he'd eaten alone plenty of times, enjoyed it, too. There were no awkward pauses, forced comments, or scrambling for the next topic. Nope, none of that but the sound of chewing, crunching, savoring. He poured a glass of wine—the merlot he'd bought yesterday before Ava offered to bring wine. The water was about to boil and once it started, he'd toss in the linguine, his choice for tonight. His aunt taught him that the shape of pasta changed the taste of it. Spaghetti did not taste like rigatoni, rigatoni was not the same as rotini, and fettucine in no way resembled pappardelle.

He'd planned to have this discussion with Ava, figured she might enjoy arguing a few points and he'd have welcomed the verbal sparring. But that wasn't going to happen because Ava Marie Ventori wasn't coming. When the water reached a rolling boil, Law tossed in the linguine, stirred. Nope, she wasn't coming. *He'd been stood up.* Had that ever happened to him before, on any level, even as a teenager? No, he couldn't say it had. He drank more wine, stirred the linguine, added salt. Why couldn't she just say *Thank you for the offer, but no?* And then let the unspoken meaning in the words say the rest: *I don't trust you. You're dangerous. I don't like you. You're dangerous...*

Law polished off his wine, poured another glass. Guess he shouldn't have made another pit stop at the bakery and picked up a four-pack of double-fudge brownies in case she was a chocolate lover. Oh well. He'd dump them off at Lina's Café tomorrow, tell Phyllis to take them home to her grandkids. Phyllis was a good source of information and town enlightenment. The other day, she'd told him about the guy who moved from Chicago with his family, built some big mansion and opened an Italian restaurant. She said he had young kids but had been a confirmed bachelor for a lot of years until he met his wife. Hadn't she said he was related to somebody in town? He couldn't remember, but tomorrow when he dropped off the brownies, he'd ask her about him. What was his name? Henry? Hal? Harry? Yeah, Harry, that was it.

He thought about the guy and the life he must have had in Chicago while he drained the pasta, mixed it in the sauce with a sprinkle of pecorino Romano cheese, and scooped it onto his plate. The working section of the kitchen was tiny, but the breakfast nook in the far corner served as an eating and reading area. The oak table needed a heavy-duty refinish and he'd put it on his "to-do" list along with the two chairs. Law plunked the plate on the table, eyed the empty place setting, the empty wine glass, the bouquet of pink sweetheart roses. *Fool.* He sank into his chair, tossed his napkin on his lap, and leafed through a woodworking magazine while he dove into his pasta.

The knock came while he was reading about mortise and tenon joints and considering a second helping of linguine. Another knock, quiet, almost timid. He paused, fork midair. At first, he'd thought it might be the wind, but when the *rap, rap, rap* came a third time, he understood it for what it was: someone was at his door. Law wiped his mouth, pushed back his chair, and made his way to the front door. One glance at his watch told him if it were his dinner guest, she was an hour late. It wouldn't be Ava; he'd counted her out forty-five minutes ago and spent the rest of the time trying to stay distracted with "Table Saw Tips and Tricks." Law sucked in a breath and opened the door.

Ava Marie Ventori stared back at him, small hands clutching a bottle of red wine, a cabernet. She offered a weak smile and a soft, "Would you believe it if I told you I took a wrong turn?"

He didn't smile back, didn't step aside to let her in, didn't even say hello. What was the point? "I don't like games, Ava. Just tell me you changed your mind and we'll let it go at that."

She opened her mouth to answer, closed it. "Can I come in for a minute?"

Law straightened his shoulders, blocking more of the door. "I think you said what you wanted to say—" he glanced at his watch, calculated how late she was "—about an hour and ten minutes ago."

"I'm sorry." She tucked a lock of hair behind her ear, bit her bottom lip. "I was on my way out the door when my mother asked where I was going. She spotted the wine and I saw the way her face lit up, like she was hoping it was a date." More lip biting, followed by "I tried to tell her it was dinner with a friend, but then my dad started in with the questions: who's the friend, male or female, do we know him? And then, the one that sent me flying out the door. *Is it serious*? What they meant was are you going to marry the guy and spit out babies." Her eyes glittered with anger and frustration. "I got in the car and didn't stop until I was in Renova." She shrugged, inched her gaze up to meet his. "There's a candy shop there that specializes in dark chocolate with nuts. I favor the pecan bits." She reached in her jacket pocket, pulled out a crumpled bag. "I think there are a few pieces left if you want a sample."

Law tried to hold onto his anger, but one look at the meager peace offering and he couldn't do it. He reached for the bag, opened it and peeked inside. Resting at the bottom of the crumpled bag, amidst salt and pecan bits sat a lone hunk of dark chocolate with pecans. Law eased it out of the bag, studied it.

"I saved it for you," she said.

He popped the chocolate in his mouth, savored the taste of salt, nut, and sweetness. Milk chocolate had always been his favorite, but something told him that might have changed the second Ava held out the crumpled peace offering. In some ways, he guessed her family considered her as much an outcast as his did him. "Thanks." Law stepped aside, nodded toward the living room. "Come in before you freeze." He scanned her light jacket and T-shirt. "There's supposed to be a frost tonight. You definitely didn't dress for the weather."

"I wasn't thinking about the weather when I ran out the door." She moved past him, her scent reminding him of warm nights and lilacs.

"You hungry?"

Pink shot from her neck to her cheeks, spread to her forehead. "I've been thinking about that pasta dish for hours." She paused, her lips pulling into a faint smile. "And the garlic toast, plus the salad with the special balsamic vinaigrette...."

He raised a brow, his mood shifting. Ava Ventori would no doubt prove a constant challenge: annoying, confusing, mercurial, but beneath it all he sensed honesty and a desire to follow her own path, whatever that might be. He understood this last one, had believed in it even when he didn't know where he was heading. Maybe they really weren't so different after all. His lips twitched once, twice, before he tossed out a comment that made her blush again. "And here I thought you came to apologize."

"I did," she blustered. "I am...I mean..."

He laughed, a real laugh that filled his chest and spun through the room. "Come on, I always make too much food." Law grabbed the wine and pointed to the kitchen. "This way. Careful, I've got a lot of work to do and tons of sanding." He eyed her slender, graceful fingers. "I don't want you to get splinters or cuts."

That comment made her shake her head. "Obviously, you don't know about the Sal Ventori weeding program that involves pulling weeds minus gloves or tools. Makes you strong and sturdy, according to my father." She rolled her eyes and slid into the wooden chair next to the extra place setting. "And I doubt you've heard about the Sal Ventori clean-up-minus-gloves mantra that says no person needs gloves to scrub a floor or a toilet. Gross, on so many levels." Ava sipped the wine he handed her, sighed. "If a woman wants to wear heavy-duty gloves to scour, so what?" More wine sipping, another sigh. "In fact, why does my father think cleaning is relegated to the woman? Ha! I'll bet Roman cleans the toilet if his wife asks him to...no doubt about it. He's so head over heels, he'd do anything for Angie."

Roman Ventori, head over heels. Interesting visual. The guy had always seemed way too cool to let emotion cloud common sense, but that was a long time ago, and before the accusation that pretty much screwed the guy. Better avoid that whole topic, especially when Law planned to find out more about the situation that made her blow off the dinner invitation. He set a plate of linguine in front of her along with the salad and a basket of garlic toast, then eased into the chair next to her and reached for the bottle of wine. "If we finish this bottle, we'll open yours," he said, filling his glass.

Ava munched on a slice of garlic toast, eyed her wine glass and nodded. "Trust me, we'll get into that second bottle."

Law sipped his wine and watched Ava attack her food. He had no idea how many dark chocolate pecan chunks she'd eaten, but the woman sure enjoyed her food. They chatted about too little versus too much garlic and how her mother grew her own in the backyard along with parsley and oregano. Then she offered to bring Law bunches of parsley and oregano. *If you have a use for it, say, on pizza?* A smile accompanied the comment and made him wonder if she wasn't asking if he knew how to make pizza, which he did. She finished another glass of wine, helped with the dishes—drying only so she didn't chap her hands in the water—and waited while he fixed her a cup of tea and sliced the coconut cream pie.

"I really am sorry I no-showed earlier," she said as she dried the pot he'd cooked the linguine in. "Coming home has been harder than I thought it would be." She set the pot on the counter and adjusted the comment. "That's not true. It's been *exactly* like I thought it would be."

"How so?" He guessed it had to do with parental expectations and getting pushed into a slot where you didn't belong. Yeah, he knew all about that. Still, he wanted to hear her version of why she avoided Magdalena.

Ava eyed him from his position at the sink as he scrubbed the saucepan, hesitated a few seconds before she spoke. "Why can't parents accept us for who we are? Why do they have to try and change us even when they know deep down we can't be changed? Don't they know how hard it is on us when we get compared to our perfect sibling?"

Ah, so she meant Roman. That, he understood. Law slid her a look, said in a gentle voice, "Because they expect us to be like that perfect sibling and when we aren't, they start to peck away at what they perceive are our shortcomings, and the only way to survive is to get out." His voice dipped further, "And stay away for good or at least until we can accept their inability to stop trying to change us."

"That's right!" Her face lit up, whether sparked by excitement or wine, it was hard to say. Law took in her beauty, pleased he might have had a small hand making those gray eyes shine, those full lips smile. Ava clutched his arm, squeezed. "The only guarantee in the pursuit of happiness is that it's random and fleeting."

Law narrowed his gaze on her. "Random and fleeting," he repeated, toying with the meaning of those words when accompanied by guarantees and happiness. They sounded an awful lot like *been hurt and don't want to get hurt again.* Other than his family, he'd never opened his heart enough to get hurt by anyone, especially a potential partner. But from the stories swirling through town about her past, Ava had bought into the happily-ever-after nonsense from a two-timing jerk with good manners and a boy-next-door smile.

Those gray eyes sparkled. "Exactly. They should not try to tell us how to define our own happiness or judge us when they don't agree with our choice."

Now that idea he liked. Choices, and the opportunity to find happiness, should be as unique as the individual and not boxed into a one-size-per-family. Ava got that, and she'd lived it, just like he had. He'd never met anyone who had, especially someone like her: spirited, honest, compassionate. It was damn attractive, probably a bit *too* attractive. *Be careful, be careful. Do not fall for this woman. She's not like the others.* But he wasn't listening because deep down he knew it was already too late.

CHAPTER 8

"What do you mean you're selling the store?" Ava stared at her mother, certain she hadn't heard right.

"It's time, Ava." Lorraine Ventori's dark eyes misted, her voice turned softer than the dough she kneaded once a week. "Probably past time if your father and I are honest about it." She rolled a meatball into a perfect circle, set it on the tray next to the others. "Since the heart attack, your father and I have been talking about a time when we'd be free of obligations and could just enjoy ourselves, our children—" her expression filled with joy "—and our grandchildren. Do you know little Dominic recognizes our faces when we video chat? Who would have ever thought your father would get so excited about electronic gadgets?" Laughter spilled from her, ended on a sigh. "What we don't do for those we love. If we didn't have a schedule to keep, we could talk to Dominic in person, maybe even attend a grand-parents' day at the preschool instead of being *those people* who live in another state." This time the sigh held sadness and a hint of misery. "No one knows how long the good Lord will give us, and your father and I want to know our grandchildren."

"Grandchildren?" Was her mother including the dog, or did

she mean the unborn one in Angie's belly? Of course, it *could* be wishful thinking in regard to the children Ava might have one day. The first and second were high probabilities, but with Sal and Lorraine Ventori, the third option could not be ruled out. They were sneaky when it came to their children's relationships. Well, if they were waiting for Ava to present them with a grand-child, they'd be waiting a long time—like maybe forever.

"Yes, grandchildren, dear, or did you forget Angie's pregnant?"

The raised brow implied Ava had been neglecting her brother and his family. Ha, if her mother knew she called Roman and Angie every week, had heard all about Dominic's latest ear infection and the short list of boys' and girls' names for the next baby, Lorraine might be miffed. *Ava, we only speak to you once every few weeks, and never with any regularity or purpose. Now why is that?* And her father would say, *Don't you care if we're still breathing? Daughters are supposed to look after their parents. It's God's rule and it's tradition.*

"Ava? Are you still upset they didn't ask you to be a godparent for Dominic? I hope not, but I feel confident you'll get asked for the new baby."

The only people who'd been upset that Rourke and Kate Flannigan were Dominic's godparents were Sal and Lorraine. Of course, they'd never flat out admit it, though they sure dropped hints at the service about how if Angie were more "family-oriented," Ava might have been asked. Right. Wasn't this exactly what she'd been spouting off to Law Carlisle about last night? The lack of acceptance and the judgment that sat at the center of her relationship with her parents? Ugh, wait until she told him this one. He would not believe it. Then again, he probably would.

Ava reached for a hunk of meatball mix, eyed the size of the meatballs lining the cookie sheet. Her mother claimed years of practice helped her become an expert, but that wasn't true. Lorraine had a gift in the kitchen, along with the desire to learn, improve, and perfect, unlike her daughter who possessed no such skills and less desire. She eased a hunk of mix from the bowl, rolled it into a ball, added more mix, subtracted it, added a bit more. The meatball looked sad and lumpy, and nothing like her mother's. She bet Law rolled a perfect meatball, pictured his long fingers working the mix with ease and confidence. Sal said nobody could make a meatball like an Italian, but she bet that wasn't true...

"Did you hear Lawson Carlisle's back in town?"

That comment pulled her straight back to the squishy mix and her mother's curiosity. "I heard that."

Lorraine continued to roll meatballs, plop them on the non-stick baking sheet, and deliver news of Law Carlisle's return. "I saw him the other day in the store."

"You mean the day you weren't supposed to be there?" Ava and her father had been after her to rest and stay away from the grocery store until she could get around better—as in no walking boot. But Lorraine Ventori had a mind of her own, and maybe that's where Ava got her strong-headedness, though nobody could claim Sal was a pushover.

Her mother raised a brow, huffed her annoyance. "I might be off work, but that doesn't mean I'm going to stop breathing. How long do you think I can sit in the house with your father's television shows and commentary about how the world is in sad shape? I swear those soap operas will be the end of me." She shook her head, scooped up more meatball mixture. "And don't let him tell you he fell asleep and didn't know they were on. That man tunes in to those shows every day and can tell you who's pregnant, who's cheating, and who's got amnesia."

Ava laughed. Her father enjoyed witnessing chaos and unrest as long as it was on television and not in his personal life. Unfortunately, she'd been the child to give him chaos, unrest, *and* indigestion on a somewhat regular basis. "Maybe you can get Dad back in the kitchen so he forgets about the television."

"Ha. You think I want that man pestering me about not adding enough basil to the sauce or cheating on the salt? No, thank you." A grumble, followed by another shake of her head. "Salvatore Ventori is not getting back in my kitchen, and that's that."

"So, if you and Dad sell the store, he'll own the television and you'll own the kitchen?" Ava placed an almost round meatball on the baking tray. "And every few months, you'll visit Roman, Angie, and the grandkids in Chicago?" That did not sound like a solid plan for people who claimed they wanted to enjoy a life that didn't revolve around checking inventory and cleaning produce.

"Of course not. Your father and I have plans." Her voice drifted, turned mellow. "We still have dreams and we want to fulfill them together." More mellowness, a hint of sadness. "I know I complain about his habits and that darn stubbornness, but I wouldn't have him any other way." She slid a glance at Ava, her eyes wet. "I only pray we have enough years together to share those dreams."

"You will, Mom, you'll see." For a woman who didn't admit to feelings like love and forever, that was a proclamation of both. Would Ava ever share that with a man? She'd thought she felt that way about Jordan but if she were honest, she'd have to say those emotions had been driven by a timetable and a wish list rather than the relationship or the man.

"Anyway," Lorraine heaved a long sigh, shrugged. "We wanted to tell you about the store before we meet with the attorney to discuss it. He's married to Bree Kinkaid. Remember her? She used to be Bree MacGregor before she married Brody Kinkaid? They were a few years ahead of you in high school.

She was the strawberry-blonde beauty queen; he was the big bruiser who played football."

"Bree and Brody? I remember them." Who wouldn't remember the sugar-sweet girl with the long legs and fake southern accent that had all the boys drooling for a second look? But she'd settled for Brody Kinkaid, the guy with more muscles than gray matter and proud of it. Ugh.

Lorraine leaned toward Ava, lowered her voice, "Not much in the brains area, but he did idolize Bree." *Tsk-tsk.* "Then he up and died one night. Heart attack. Left Bree and those baby girls all alone. Thank the good Lord her parents were there to help. We all thought it would be the end of her and for a while it was, but then she picked herself up and kept working at her father's place. Next thing you know, this handsome city boy named Adam Brandon comes to town and it's fireworks." The smile and the hushed voice said she'd been cheering for the couple. "Pop Benito filled me in, and let me tell you, your father's daytime soaps have nothing on that couple's story. Oh, but the misunderstandings and accusations that flitted between those two were something else. But there was no denying they were meant to be together." Another *tsk tsk* and a sigh that could melt butter. "They're married now and Pop thinks one day soon they'll announce another addition to the family."

Of course, her mother meant a child, but no way would Ava go along with it, so she said, "They're getting a dog?"

Lorraine shot her a don't-you-dare-start look and pinched her lips for all of three seconds before she commented, "No, not a dog. A baby. You know those tiny creatures that carry on long after we're gone? The ones that make sense of our lives and force us to grow up?"

Ava shook her head, homed in on the meatballs sitting on the tray in perfect order. "Babies aren't for everybody, Mom, no matter how many times you wish it."

"I know that. You think I don't know that? I'm sure if you had asked Bree back then if she thought she'd find love again, especially with a man like Adam Brandon, she would have sworn on her dead husband's grave that it could never happen. People come into our lives for a reason and if we're open to it, our lives can change in ways we never imagined. Look at your brother. Who would have thought he and Angie would end up together?" She laughed, her expression softening. "Those two were at odds from the very beginning, and it didn't help that your father had it in his head he wanted to see a grandchild before he left this earth. Oh, but he was relentless and the harder he pushed, the more those two pushed back, and not in a good way. But anybody who saw them together knew there were sparks, even if those two refused to admit it."

She scooped up the last of the meatball mixture, rolled it into a perfect ball and placed it on a second tray. "Love comes to us, whether we want it or not, but once we open our hearts, that's when the magic begins." Lorraine washed her hands, dried them on a towel, and turned to Ava, her dark eyes bright. "My only hope is that you don't let one wrong choice keep you from ever trusting a man again."

What to say to that? That one wrong choice had turned into a mess that still hurt when she let herself think about it. Add the bad career pick and the floundering to find her place in life, and it was a disaster of mega proportion. Not surprising that she avoided questions about her future *with or without* a man. Law Carlisle seemed to understand that. In fact, he seemed to share her issues and *that* surprised her. Other than that one steamy kiss, she would have sworn they would never share anything, least of all values.

But she'd been wrong, and it wasn't the first time.

"Ava? There will come a time when you're going to have to stop punishing yourself for the choices you've made and learn to live with them." Her mother placed a hand on Ava's, squeezed. "And maybe one day you'll even accept them."

Ava stared at her mother's strong hand clasping hers and let a snippet of truth sneak out. "Will you and Dad be able to accept my choices, even if they aren't ones you like?" She darted a glance at her mother, waited.

"I guess we'll have to if we want a relationship with you, now, won't we?"

"I guess you will." It was Ava who swiped at a tear, sniffed. "I don't want to disappoint you or Dad, but I have to figure out my own way, no matter where it takes me. I know I've disappointed you both and made choices you don't agree with and can't accept. Maybe one day I'll understand why it turned out this way." She sniffed again, placed a hand on top of her mother's. "Please don't give up on me. I'll never be as perfect as Roman, but I can be a better me. You'll see. Just don't give up."

CHAPTER 9

L aw hadn't seen his father in four days. Not that Montrose hadn't called him twice a day, invited him to dinner, lunch, *anywhere*, so they could talk, but it was too soon, and he wasn't interested. His uncle gave him space and time to adjust to being back in Magdalena, but the phone calls would start again soon, and with them there would be the underlying questions about Law's attempts to mend the relationship with his father. What to say to that?

There is no relationship?
There never was a relationship?
It's too late for that?
That wasn't the deal?

Montrose had offered a weak explanation that could be true but spoke of a soft character and an inability to stand by core values. Loving a woman didn't mean a person should cast aside what he believed in to make her happy, did it? No, a person couldn't do that or the relationship was doomed. Why would a man let himself become someone he didn't recognize? Didn't he see the destruction that could cause, to himself and everyone around him, especially his family? Law had been young and innocent in regard to marriage, commitment, and the lives parents shared. What did he know about the lies they told to get through the night?

Not a damn thing.

That's why he didn't have a wife *or* a relationship. That's why he didn't *want* one. Ava Ventori flashed through his mind: the dark eyes, the full lips, the husky laughter. But it was more than that. What stayed with him were Ava's thoughts and opinions on life, judgment, and accepting others. They were his opinions, too, rare and heartfelt. Did she realize this? The woman had been sneaking into his brain at random times when he should have been concentrating on other things like the tile in the shower, his current project. He wanted to see her again, hear her gentle laughter, watch her expression as she sampled another bowl of pasta or hunk of garlic bread.

He muttered a curse, shook his head, and turned back to spreading mortar. This was dangerous territory and he needed to avoid it. But how was he supposed to do that when he *liked* thinking about the woman, enjoyed the challenge and the exhilaration of her presence? He was contemplating this when he heard the knock. Had Ava decided to take him up on his offer and use the cabin to work on her sketchpad drawings, the ones whose significance she had yet to explain?

But when he answered the door, it was his father and brother who stood on the other side of the threshold. Law didn't want them here, but a scrap of civility forced him to invite them inside. Curiosity took over as his father shifted from one foot to the other, hands clasped in front of him, face the color of snow. Yeah, that was a definite *not comfortable* look. Maybe the old man realized he was trespassing as in *not welcome*. Brett didn't seem to know or didn't care if he were intruding and the tone in his next words proved it.

"So, this is the palace?"

Law brushed off the comment, moved into the living room, and gestured toward the couch. "This is it." No sense asking what either thought of it because the uncomfortable expression on his father's face said he'd rather *not* think about it, and the disdain on his brother's said he could *not* think about it. Law hadn't seen Brett since their mother's funeral four years ago, and yet his brother eyed him as though he wouldn't mind another four-year stretch between visits. How had he ever thought the guy was someone to admire and emulate?

"Dad said we should pay you a visit since it doesn't look like you're going to head to the house any time soon." Brett laughed and added, "Though what you find so appealing in the boonies is the real question."

"It's peaceful here." Law rubbed his jaw, studied his brother. "Quiet, simple, a good place to think."

"A good place to *think*? About what?" Another laugh, accompanied by a headshake that didn't budge a strand of hair. "No thanks. I'm not a fan of coyotes or black bears." He made a face, glanced around the room. "Bet you don't even have cable TV." His gaze darted to the corners of the living room. "Hey, where's the TV?"

"Don't have one, and yet somehow I still manage to breathe."

"Yeah, somehow…"

Their father jumped in, offered what he must have thought was a peace offering. "You've been busy. Care to show us what you've been working on?" He moved toward the kitchen, ran his hand along the railing. "I like what you've done with the finish. Very smooth."

Law followed him into the kitchen, placed a hand on the railing. "Thanks. There's a lot to do, but I'm enjoying it."

Brett scanned the kitchen, dismissed it, and pulled out his cell phone. He didn't bother to look at Law when he said, "Katrina thinks we should get together for dinner. Says you should meet your niece and nephew. Dad's going to pull it all together and let you know the date."

Interesting. Law met his sister-in-law at the funeral, a quiet, subdued blonde who didn't look at him head on or speak. Something was going on with those two, and he didn't doubt Brett was behind it. "Let me know the date and I'll make sure I'm available."

His brother laughed. "Sure, check and make sure you're available." Then he turned to their father and said, "You about ready? We need to head out so I can get to my appointment on time."

Montrose Carlisle nodded, extended a hand to Law. "I like the place. Good luck with it." His voice shifted. "Don't be a stranger." Law accepted his hand and when his father leaned in, he whispered, "Let me know if you want to grab a meal, whenever and wherever."

Law nodded, curious why his father did not want Brett to know what he'd said. Would his brother bully their father, try to weasel an invitation or maybe try to uninvite Law? He did not miss the screwed-up dynamics or the fractures that were part of the Carlisle family.

"Maybe one of these days you'll get to meet our sister, if she's ever done gallivanting. Cynthia's a real treat. Loves those dogs more than her own family." Brett shook his head, nodded. "Looks like she's not going to give our father grandkids either." And with that, he and Montrose headed toward the door, leaving Law with a lot of questions and no answers.

The next afternoon, Ava showed up on his doorstep with her sketchpad and artist's bag filled with pencils, pens, and whatever else she kept inside. He'd love to take a peek in that bag but until she trusted him enough to share, it was off limits. She settled at the kitchen table, sketchpad open, pencils to her right, and asked him the same question for the fifth time. "You're sure I'm not bothering you?"

What to say to that? *Of course, you're bothering me. Any flesh-and-blood guy with half a pulse would be bothered by you, but not in the way you think.* Law couldn't admit *that* so he shook his head, and said, "No problem. You're not bothering me." For the next two hours, they worked in silence except for the radio's old-school rock station and their occasional comments about a band or lyrics.

I saw the Rolling Stones back in the day.

I don't do concerts anymore, but I definitely would still see Fleetwood Mac if they were around.

How about Bob Seger? The Eagles?

She looked up, smiled. *Definitely.*

Ava returned the next day after work with a rotisserie chicken, a six-pack of dark ale, and two bunches of escarole. "I never can tell the difference between endive and escarole, so I just grabbed one."

Law opened the fridge and placed the six-pack on the shelf. "You did good. I'll sauté the escarole with a little garlic and oil, then add mushrooms and faro."

"Sounds delicious. I can do the prep and cleanup if you want."

Did she know her eyes sparkled when she talked about food and the dimple in her cheek deepened? Probably not. But Law knew; he'd started to pay close attention to Ava Ventori's mannerisms. "Your parents won't ask why you're not home for dinner?"

She made a face and gave him the answer he expected. "Of course, they'll ask, and of course I'll tell them I'm having dinner with a friend."

Friend.

Is that what they were to each other? Was that all she

wanted? Because when Law looked at her, he didn't see just a friend but a woman with gray eyes, dark hair, full lips, and a smile that teased and tormented. When she spoke, her voice turned husky and he wanted to get closer, hear more. And when she touched his hand, often by accident but sometimes on purpose, he couldn't deny the heat *or* his desire to feel more skin, more heat.

Bad idea, his brain warned. *Don't do it. Leave her alone. You'll ruin everything*. But his damn heart didn't listen. No, the damn thing beat out a different answer. *She understands you. She's the only woman who's ever made you feel something that went beyond sexual. You can't let her go. You can't lose her. You have to take a chance. No matter what.*

No matter what? What if I lose the only true friend I've ever had?

But what if you don't? What if you find the one woman who can change your life? Isn't it worth it? Isn't she worth it?

CHAPTER 10

Ava didn't like being the center of conversation, at home or around town, especially if the subject linked to her was a man. Past or present. That's why she visited Law at his cabin and nowhere else. What would people say if she and Law were spotted together? The guessing and the speculation would swarm through town and everyone would have an opinion about what was or wasn't happening. Ugh. Other than the one random meeting in the grocery store where he'd invited her to dinner, they hadn't seen each other around town, in the presence of onlookers and the curious. And that's exactly how she planned to keep it. No way was she going to subject herself or Law to opinions that were off base and ridiculous.

She could just hear it all now...

Did you see Ava Ventori and Lawson Carlisle together?

A little too close, and a look that said trying to get closer.

She was watching him, like he was a chocolate éclair and she wanted a taste.

Hmm. Yummy, no doubt about that.

I bet they're together.

Together? You think so?

No doubt about it. You can always tell.

Bet that will make her father happy.

You think Sal Ventori's going to jump up and down and cele-brate because his daughter's gone and fallen for a Carlisle? The reckless one nobody's heard about since he got kicked out of town?

Well...

Trust me, the old man will not be happy.

Doesn't matter. That girl does whatever she wants. Look at the way she flits in and out of town, can't land a real job or a husband, and she's not getting any younger.

How old is she now? Thirty-six? Thirty-seven?

Can't be that old, but she's getting there. Thirty-three, I think. Same age as my niece, and she's got three babies, a husband, and a dog.

Maybe this will be Ava's last chance before she gets the outdated stamp. Chuckle. Chuckle.

Ava Ventori and Lawson Carlisle. Interesting. Who would have thought?

She better enjoy him while she can because he doesn't look like the settling-down type.

Neither was the last one we knew about...at least not with her.

That was a shame, though...humiliating that everybody but Ava knew he was cheating on her, and all the while she's plan-ning this white-picket-fence life for them.

Goes to show, you can never tell the honest ones from the cheaters.

And Jordan Rogers was definitely a cheater.

Wonder if Lawson Carlisle will be a cheater, too?

Hmm. Good question. Time will tell.

Jordan Rogers was a name she'd rather forget, and she'd certainly like to erase the time spent with him planning their perfect future. Some future. She'd been such a naïve fool and he'd strung her along. Of course, most of the town knew the whole sad story down to the bridal magazines stacked in her bedroom and Ava's attempt to rework the truth about her two-timing almost fiancé. Humiliation at its grandest. No one dared bring up the man's name, at least not to her face, and she'd heard his parents were on an extended vacation in Texas, so she didn't have to worry about seeing them in the grocery store.

Still, if only the town could stay quiet, Law wouldn't hear the gossip.

Because she really, really did not want him to know about her idiocy with Jordan Rogers.

But she should have known that with Lawson Carlisle, nothing was safe, not even bad choices or secrets. With a man like Law, everything was fair game and it was the *everything* that caught up with her soon after she started visiting his cabin.

"Here you go." He slid a turkey Reuben sandwich on rye in front of her, eased into a chair and rubbed a stubbled jaw. "So...Jordan Rogers, huh?"

Ava had the sandwich halfway to her mouth when he spoke. She sucked in a breath and placed the sandwich back on the plate. She did not want to have this conversation, did not want to hear the jabs about trusting the wrong person. But the expression on his face wasn't judgmental or disgusted. What she saw was compassion laced with a hint of curiosity and that's what prompted her to speak. "I thought I could trust him...thought we were meant to be together."

The head shake said he didn't like her answer, but when he spoke, the disgust that surfaced was directed at her almost fiancé.

"The guy was a player, Ava. Girls loved to hear him tell them how special they were, and a few of them clung to his 'one-and-only' line. He knew exactly what to do with those words and how to get unsuspecting targets to believe he was more than a testosterone-fueled jerk bent on nailing—" he coughed, cleared his throat "—I mean, winning his next target."

So, the story Jordan gave her about making a mistake and a few seconds of bad choices was a lie? He wasn't the kind, sweet, attentive boyfriend he pretended to be, not even when they first started dating? The guy had always been a player who recycled sweet talk and I-care-about-you's to get what he wanted? As in sex or as close to it as girls like Ava would agree to...? She didn't want to believe it, didn't want to think that *nothing* about their relationship had been real or honest. She couldn't believe it. "How...how do you know this?" Maybe Law had been the one tossing out promises he never intended to fulfill, but even as the possibility flitted through her brain, she knew that wouldn't be true.

Lawson Carlisle wouldn't lie about what he wanted with a woman; they'd flock to him despite the lack of commitment or interest that wouldn't last more than ten minutes.

Law leaned forward, said in a voice filled with gentleness, "Ava, everybody knew."

"No..." Whatever had happened after, she'd always hung onto the belief that he'd once cared about her, maybe even loved her. *But what if it had all been a lie?* What if Jordan had never cared about her at all and had been cheating on her all along?

"Ava? I'm sorry." Law reached out and clasped her hand. "Maybe I should have kept my mouth shut." Regret covered his face, inched to his lips. "I'm sorry. You were way too good for him, and everybody knew that, too."

Who would have thought a guy like Law Carlisle would show more consideration for her feelings than most of the town?

It was this kindness that prompted her to ask the next question. "Do you think...was he the kind who would...?"

"Don't ask." His voice spilled over her, made her forget he was a rebel the town said was better off gone. "The guy was a jerk who didn't respect the person he was with or their privacy. Let it go at that." He cleared his throat, eased his hand from hers. "He never should have gone near you." More throat clearing. "He should have known better." Pause. "Even a fool like me knew to stay away from girls like you."

"Girls like me? What's that supposed to mean?" What *was* that supposed to mean? She didn't know, but she definitely didn't like the sound of it, as though she were in a class of—

"Untouchable." The word stretched over the space between them, snuffed out her thoughts. "Special." He lifted a shoulder, added in a soft voice, "Perfect."

What to say to that? She couldn't get upset about being associated with words like untouchable, special, or perfect, especially coming from someone who probably didn't offer compliments often. "Oh" was all she could muster.

"Yeah." He stared at her hard seconds before he worked up a smile and said, "Can we change the subject? This conversation is making me twitchy."

"Twitchy?"

"Twitchy," he repeated, then added, "Uncomfortable. Edgy."

"Sure." She stared at him, wondered what was going on in that brain of his. Obviously, he didn't like conversations that held too much emotion. Good, because neither did she. Still, there was one subject they'd both avoided—the kiss they'd shared one hot summer night—and while she'd have bet her reputation he'd broach the subject before she did, maybe even torment her with it, he'd done neither.

Why? Was the kiss so lackluster that he'd relegated it to better-forgotten or that-was-not-a-real-kiss territory? Maybe he was drunk or high and couldn't remember. He hadn't seemed either, though he had been angry, furious actually, with her outfit, her makeup, her plan to crash a party she'd definitely not been invited to... That anger had let her know what could happen the second she stepped inside the house.

You think you can handle those guys inside? he'd said, his voice shaking. *A few drinks and you won't know what you're doing or who you're doing it with.... Go home, Ava, now before somebody sees you.*

Or what? she'd tossed back. *What will you do?*

He'd backed her into the shadows, against a tree. *I'll find a way to keep you from the party.* He smelled of fresh air and tobacco. *No matter what I have to do...*

I'm not afraid of you, Law Carlisle. She'd stared back at him as he moved closer, her pulse tripling, her breath falling in little puffs. Closer still.

You should be.

And then he'd kissed her. Not a soft, gentle touch of lips to lips, but hard, greedy, desperate. His hands sifted through her hair, framed her face as his body pressed her against the tree, releasing an explosion of need. The tongue came next; oh, the deliciousness of that tongue, tasting, teasing... More. She wanted more. Ava squirmed, flung her hands around his neck, eased her legs apart. Law moved against her, fitted himself between her legs...

Shit! He'd jumped back, let out a shaky breath and flung a string of curses into the night. *Go home,* he'd said, his gaze fixed on the ground. *If you try to crash a party again, I'll be waiting for you. And next time, I won't stop.*

"Law? The summer you left...the party... Why did you...?"

He dragged his gaze to hers, his green eyes dark, intense. "Don't ask."

She'd wondered about that night for sixteen years, in

between the times she tried to forget it. But after Jordan's major betrayal, the wondering picked up again, escalated with the string of guys who followed, each more lackluster than the one before. Ava rationalized her fixation on that night with the belief that it could have been pivotal to her future.

If she'd been able to sneak into the party, she might have discovered Jordan inside with another girl and been saved from future humiliation. She would not have wasted years planning a life with him that included a house, children, a dog. Or, and this was the possibility she wondered about most, Law Carlisle would not have stopped kissing her and sent her home. No, he would have led her further into the shadows and shown her just how good a bad boy could be.

But the past was gone and still she had no answers about that night or the boy she thought she knew. "Law? I was furious with you for keeping me away from the party, but a few days later, I realized you were only looking out for me. I...appreciated it, and even thought about thanking you—"

He sliced her a look, his jaw twitching. "That would have been a bad idea. And impossible. I was gone, remember? Shipped off, courtesy of my old man."

"Where'd you go?" *There'd been so many stories...*

He shook his head. "Leave it alone."

Ava sipped in a breath. "Okay." Why did it matter where he went when the possibilities would be bad and worse? She steadied her voice, forced out the question she'd wondered about for too long. "Why did you kiss me?"

He stared at her, long and hard, his expression grim. "Because I couldn't help myself. I knew you were out of my league, but that didn't stop me, and the second I tasted you, I wanted more."

"But you stopped." She ignored the heat climbing up her neck, scorching her cheeks. For years, she'd wondered about that kiss, and now the flesh-and-blood answer sat right in front of her. All she had to do was ask. "Why did you stop?"

Law reached for a lock of her hair, let it slip through his fingers. "Because we wouldn't have stopped at a kiss, and I knew that, even if you didn't."

CHAPTER 11

Nate Desantro was the kind of guy who could intimidate a person from a hundred feet away. It wasn't just the guy's size, or the way he carried himself, like he'd homed in on a target and planned to squash it with one of those weapons people called hands. If a person were on the fringe taking it all in, maybe hoping to copy bits and pieces of the take-down, that was one thing. But when the person *was* the target? Well, that was a whole other level of how-the-hell-do-I-get-away-from-this guy?

"What are you doing with Ava Ventori?" Nate Desantro stood in Law's backyard, dark eyes burning into Law, fists clenched, *pissed off* written all over his face.

Law remembered the man from years ago and there'd been plenty of stories about him, all starting with *Stay away from the guy* and ending with *Do not cross him...and don't look him in the eye.*

Too late. Law clutched the hammer he'd been using to replace the back steps, squared his shoulders, and held Desantro's gaze, which proved a challenge, considering the heat in those eyes. "Ava and I went to school together. We've been catching up..." Yeah, that scowl said he wasn't buying it.

"Last I remember you were a punk-ass kid bent on causing a lot of trouble to your family and this town. I doubt you and Ava Ventori had *anything* in common." The scowl deepened. "And I sure as hell don't see you having anything in common now."

What to say to that? *We might be from different worlds and she might be too good for me, but we actually have a lot more in common than we want to admit?* Doubtful the guy would appreciate that confession, so Law appealed to what he remembered as the man's desire for fairness. "You know, you scared the crap out of me when I was a kid even though I never heard you say more than five words, but I never thought you judged people based on their background or town gossip."

Desantro didn't like that. His eyes turned to soot, flashed anger and annoyance. "I'm protecting Ava from getting mixed up with somebody like you who's only going to hurt her."

Now Law was the one who was pissed off. He might end up with a black eye and a bloody nose, but he was *not* going to sit back and let the man spout BS. "So, you aren't judging me by telling me I'll hurt her? Implying I'm incapable of not hurting her, because I'm what? A bum? A hoodlum? A convict?" There, let the guy stare his way out of that one.

"Those are your words, not mine, but..."

Meaning the guy thought he was all of the above and a few on top of that. "Huh." Law rubbed his jaw, forced out the next words before he lost his nerve...or Desantro's eyes burned him to the ground. "Aren't you friends with Cash Casherdon? The biggest bad-ass this town has ever seen?"

Desantro clenched and unclenched his fist like he was preparing for a blow. One connection to any part of Law's body and he'd be done. "My business is my business, you got that?

76

Mine, not yours. I know everybody in this town, know who I can trust and who I can't, and I can't trust you."

"But you can trust Cash, the guy who shot his fiancée's brother?" See what the guy had to say about that. Desantro might kick the crap out of him or he might just snarl and zing him with a stare, but Law and Cash weren't much different. Of course, Desantro wouldn't agree, but he didn't know about the multimillion-dollar business Law helped his uncle run or the hard work that filled his days.

Or the vision he had to grow the company...

Or how he liked being around Ava Ventori in a way that had nothing to do with sex...

Nope.

All the man saw was a punk who'd done his share of damage before he disappeared from town.

Desantro took a step closer, crossed his arms over his monster chest. "You sure seem to know a lot about Cash. Now why is that?" The scowl faded a bit, the tone bordering on curiosity, like he was trying to assess Law's reasons and coming up with answers that didn't add up.

What the hell? Why not just tell the truth? "Cash was my hero. A bad-ass who didn't care what other people said. Word had it his parents didn't want him and he didn't fit with nice society or follow the rules. That made him a rebel, and I understood it." Law shrugged, pushed out more of the truths he'd carried inside for too long. "There's nothing worse than knowing your own family doesn't want you. It makes you not care what you do or who you hurt—especially if you're hurting yourself."

Those dark eyes singed him, and then, the shoulders relaxed and the scowl disappeared. "Fair enough. But that doesn't explain why you're sniffing around Ava Ventori."

What to say to that? "Because I like her? Because she intrigues me? Or maybe because she can't stand me, and that makes her even more intriguing?" He could toss out a few more reasons, starting with those kissable lips he was dying to taste again or the satin skin he ached to touch, but that would land him with a busted nose, maybe a busted face.

"I don't like any of those answers because something tells me you're going to hurt her."

"That's not my intention." What exactly *was* his intention regarding Ava Marie Ventori? Hell if he knew, but the woman lived in his brain and he'd be a fool *and* a liar to deny it.

"I don't know your game, but I'm going to figure it out." He eyed Law like he'd just as soon squash him. "Just because you're a Carlisle doesn't give you free access to anything you want, including Ava."

Law squared his shoulders, spat out, "I know what it means to be a Carlisle; trust me on that one."

A curt nod, a narrowed gaze, and then "You hurt her, I'll come after you."

"I expect you will."

Three days later Law was in the backyard chopping wood when the living, breathing legend, Cash Casherdon, showed up, stood six feet away, larger than life, bolder than Law remembered.

"I hear you're talking about me."

Law set down his ax, squinted at the man he'd modeled his past life of recklessness and don't-give-a-damn after. "You heard right. Let me guess. You've been talking to Nate Desantro."

Cash laughed, moved closer. "Yeah, good old Nate. Don't want to cross that guy or he'll make you pay. I've been threatened a time or two and we're best friends."

The guy was cool *and* funny. "Guess he told you I used your past as a game plan for my teenage antics?"

Another laugh, followed by a grin. "He did, and he wasn't happy about it, but then I'm sure you could tell. That's one thing about Nate: you always know where you stand with him and he does it in three sentences or less."

"The guy doesn't waste words, does he?" Law worked up a smile, added, "I don't think he knows what an adjective is."

"Nope. Doesn't care that he doesn't know either."

"Sounds about right."

Cash shoved his hands in jacket pockets, let out a sigh. "Yeah, well, here's the thing. Nate's one of the best guys I know; a real straight shooter who's going to protect this whole town and the people he cares about. Doesn't matter if it'll cause him grief or a world of inconvenience—which it often does. Doesn't even matter if he'd rather *not* do it, which he often doesn't since he hates butting into another person's business. It's like he has to get involved because he's a champion of doing right, and if somebody's in danger, he'll help them, no matter what."

"So... A real modern-day hero."

Cash eyed him, said in a quiet voice, "He wouldn't like hearing that. He's just a good guy trying to live his life and keep his family safe. But he's seen a lot and been through a lot; we all have. Nate and I screwed up and made mistakes." Cash shook his head. "You do not even want to hear about the drama that swirled around us for too long, but we finally got it right, and we're not giving it up. What he was trying to tell you in the five-words-or-less Nate Desantro style is that if you're here for short-term and a good time, leave Ava alone. There are plenty of women who don't care about anything past the next good time." He paused, his gaze narrowing. "Ava's not one of those women."

Law removed his gloves, tossed them on the chopping block. "Why do I feel like I'm in Relationship 101 Meets the Family?"

Cash let out a laugh bordering on a howl, kicked his booted foot at a clump of dirt. "Because we're talking about the Ventoris: old school, Catholic, Italian. It can't help that she's got a near-perfect brother and parents who are keeping track of her biological clock. I don't know Ava very well but I hear there've been some not-so-good past relationships and now she's sworn off them." He shook his head again, rubbed his stubbled jaw. "Isn't that the way it always goes? You finally find somebody and she's not into relationships? Or, as in my case, I blew up the relationship and then suffered the aftermath for a whole lot of years. And just when I think Tess and I can finally take a breath and feel like a normal couple, another disaster lands in town, and I'm right in the middle of it."

He must be talking about the woman who brought her son to Magdalena a few years ago and claimed the kid was Cash's. Phyllis told him all about it, said it was a disaster that almost cost Cash his marriage. He'd done a little digging on Nate Desantro, too, and that was a whole other crazy and unbelievable situation. A secret family? A child with Down syndrome? Marrying his mother's lover's daughter? Way too bizarre. How had he missed all of that? And later, a pretend seduction starring Magdalena's very own sin girl—Natalie Servetti. Law was younger than this group, but every breathing male knew about *seduction and sin* Natalie. Phyllis spilled the dirt on her, too: told him Natalie had settled down, married, and had a kid. Got rid of the tight clothes and makeup, too. Now *that*, he would like to see.

"So, you got another ax? Chopping wood's a pain, but it works out a lot of frustrations." Cash slid Law a look, said in a curious voice, "Especially the unfulfilled physical ones...."

Law was not touching that one. "Don't know. Never been a problem."

The smile slipped from Cash's face and he advanced on Law, his expression grim, his voice low. "I could take that one of two ways. One, you're sleeping with Ava and if that's the case, you'd better have good intentions. Or, two, you're leading her on and getting something on the side. If it's the first—" the voice turned harder "— you'd better do right by her. If it's the second, you're going to have to answer to me, and I'm not as controlled as Nate."

"Hey, this is all premature… Nothing's happened between me and Ava…" Unless he counted a kiss years ago that scorched him and a need that kept him awake at night. "And I'm not the kind of guy to express interest in one woman and sleep with another."

Cash nodded. "Good to know." A slow smile crept over Cash Casherdon's face. "Now that we understand each other, you got any beer inside?"

CHAPTER 12

Ava spent two days dissecting every detail of Lawson Carlisle's confession: the words that fell from his full lips, the tone when he delivered those words, the expression on his too-compelling face. She'd even replayed the body language, before *and* after he'd delivered the shocker revelation, but what struck her most was his refusal to offer an extra inch of detail behind those comments. *Because I couldn't help myself. I knew you were out of my league, but that didn't stop me, and the second I tasted you, I wanted more.* He'd wanted more? Her recall of that night was an angry Lawson Carlisle who told her to go home, even when she would have stayed. *We wouldn't have stopped at a kiss, and I knew that, even if you didn't.*

Of course, she hadn't known it. She'd been so furious and agitated with him, she couldn't understand what had happened or why. Ava had attributed Law's upper-handed behavior and the kiss to arrogance and entitlement—and being a rebel, too. But that wasn't why he'd kept her from the party or why he'd kissed her. He'd done the first to keep her safe, and by his own admission, the second because he couldn't help himself. Every time she thought of those words and remembered the intensity in those green eyes, she had to gulp air. *We wouldn't have stopped at a kiss, and I knew that, even if you didn't.*

He'd been interested in her. Thought she was too good for him. Had called her untouchable. Special. Perfect. Well. Even her almost fiancé had never used those words. Okay, so maybe untouchable was a stretch when you were sleeping with the guy, but special and perfect? What woman didn't want to hear those words, even if they weren't one-hundred-percent accurate? All that mattered was being special and perfect in *his* eyes.

Well. Ava hadn't been able to get him to budge on more details the next day either and when she'd called to ask if she could stop over, he'd come up with a lame excuse about painting a room and not wanting to expose her to the fumes. Right. Did he think she was an idiot? Law Carlisle was avoiding her because he didn't want to talk about what he'd admitted, or what it really meant.

But he wasn't getting off that easy, and paint fumes or not, she was going to get answers.

And then what? Say, *Thank you for clearing this up; I'll be on my way?* She could play games with herself, but deep down she knew exactly why she wanted those answers, and the truth might not be pretty or appealing, but it was the truth.

Law Carlisle made her stomach jumpy, her head spin, her breath catch, and when she was near him, she wanted to get closer, touch him...listen to his voice...breathe in his scent. Ava had a thing for him and that *thing* was bubbling just below the surface, ready to explode...all he had to do was tell her the truth about that night and then add a few extra words.

I still want you; I've never stopped wanting you.

Was it really that difficult?

She grabbed the cookies her mother made that morning along with a bottle of wine and flew out of the house before her parents could interrogate her. What could she say? The truth? *I'm bringing these to the man I might sleep with tonight...you know him. Lawson Carlisle? Yes, he might have spent time in jail or juvenile detention, maybe both, but that was a long time ago. He's a really nice guy, and guess what? He could have taken advantage of me when we were in high school and he didn't. Isn't that something a gentleman would do? Yeah, so how about that?*

By the time she reached Law's cabin, it had started to drizzle and she'd had second and third thoughts on the wisdom of unearthing sixteen-year old desires. Maybe she *was* just pitiful and in need of attention. Maybe the guy had no interest in her now other than as a friend...though it didn't feel that way. What did she know about telling what a guy really meant? Still, somebody like Law wasn't long-term or serious, but he sure could supply heat and sizzle, and it had been so long since she'd had either.

Do it. Stop critiquing the moment. This doesn't have to be about tomorrow or next year. It only has to be about tonight. She slid out of the car, flipped up the hood of her jacket to protect herself from the rain, and hurried toward the cabin. Three knocks and a Hail Mary later, Law opened the door.

"Ava?" His dark brows pinched together, his lips pulled into a frown. "What are you doing here?"

Talk about tall, lean, and irresistible in jeans and a half-opened shirt. She thrust out the cookies and wine. "I brought these for you. Chocolate chip and merlot." *She could do this.* "Aren't you going to invite me in?"

He hesitated, his gaze darting from her offering to her face. "I'm not sure that's a good idea." His expression darkened, those green eyes sparked with something that could be warning—or desire.

"Well, I think it's a very good idea." She pushed away worries of rejection, snuffed out fear and nerves, and spoke. "Let me in, Law. It's cold out here."

Another second of hesitation before he stepped aside. "One glass of wine and a cookie, and then you're out of here."

Why the rush to get rid of her? She stepped inside, shrugged out of her jacket. Unless... "Are you expecting someone? Am I... intruding?" She glanced toward the far room where she guessed his bedroom would be. "Or is somebody already here?"

"What?"

She recognized the word for what it was—a stall tactic. Law didn't want her here because he already *had* a woman waiting for him. She cleared her throat, stumbled over an apology. "I'm sorry... I didn't know... I thought...I thought you'd be alone." It was useless to hide her intentions or her humiliation. "I'm sorry," she mumbled again, yanking on her jacket as she rushed to the door. *Stupid, stupid, stupid.* This was what she got for trying to play cool and carefree. She had her fingers on the handle, but his voice stopped her.

"Ava, nobody's here but you." She turned and watched as he closed the distance between them, the wine and cookies still in his very capable hands. "The only woman I want in this house is already here. Look, this could get complicated. I'm giving you one last chance to leave."

A normal person would take that message and run, but Ava had spent her whole life choosing logical and guaranteed, and she was tired of it. "Complicated? Definitely."

He set the wine and cookies on the table near the door, shoved his hands in the back pockets of his jeans. The action pulled his shirt open to reveal more chest, more springy hair —*more sexiness*.

"It would be a train wreck."

So, he'd thought about it too. "Or fireworks."

"Unforgettable," he tossed out.

"Earth-shattering," she whispered.

He blew out a long breath, his gaze singeing her soul. "Run, Ava. Fast. Don't look back."

She inched forward, reached out, stroked his cheek. "I'm not going anywhere unless you kick me out."

"I could never do that." Long pause. "But I should, damn it, that's exactly what I should do."

She leaned on tiptoe, placed the softest kiss on his mouth. "I'm not asking for a ring; I'm just asking for a night."

He pulled away, the brackets around his mouth, deep. "What happens when one night isn't enough?"

Another kiss, a gentle "Then we'll have another night...and another."

He tensed. "What if I want more than that?"

Lawson Carlisle wanted more than casual sex? "You mean, like a relationship?" She shook her head, confused. "You've never seemed the type for long-term, so don't say that for me because I'm not interested in long-term either." He opened his mouth to respond, closed it. For a split second, she saw something on his face that looked like sadness, maybe even despair, but then it shifted, smoothed out, leaving the cool and untouchable expression she'd come to associate with the man.

"That's what you want? Sex, no strings?"

"Not just sex, Law. Great sex. I'll-think-about-you-until-the-next-time sex." He didn't press for more of an explanation and she didn't offer it. What would be the point? The man could tell her anything, whether it was true or not, and what if she believed him? She could *not* do that again; she'd never survive. Better to enjoy their time together without promises or hopes of a future that could never exist.

The first time they made love, he took her hand, led her into the bedroom, and undressed her with such exquisite precision, she trembled. The tasting came next: the inside of her elbow, the column of her neck, behind her ear...along her belly...lower still...

It was pure torture and the sweetest agony she'd ever known. No man had ever touched her this way, brought out the ache of longing and the desperation for a touch she hadn't known she craved.

In the moments when she'd let herself imagine what it would be like to share such intimacy with Lawson Carlisle, she'd never dreamed it would be so overpowering. For a man who gained his reputation as an impulsive, selfish person, there was nothing selfish or impulsive in his lovemaking. His kisses scorched her soul. His hands and mouth claimed her body, made her wonder how she'd ever considered him worthless. Law was beautiful in his nakedness: lean, muscled, with a scar on his thigh...and making love with him was all-consuming, breath-stealing, perfect.

After, she would wonder if he felt the same pull, the same desperate need...the same peace.

And if he did, would he ever admit it?

CHAPTER 13

L aw brushed a lock of hair from Ava's face, tucked it behind her ear. There was something about having her so close, whether in bed, in the kitchen fixing dinner, or working side by side, that calmed him and eased the loneliness in his chest. It made him want to pull her closer. Protect her. Make her worries go away. She'd just told him about her parents' plan to sell the grocery store. "Is it because of health issues?" He'd heard about Sal's heart attack and everybody knew Lorraine's tumble over the orange crate had started an avalanche of worry about the present and the future.

Ava lifted a shoulder, traced the dragon tattoo on his right forearm. "Maybe, but they say they want to take time and visit their grandchildren. I guess that could be true. though I can't imagine my father spending too much time around kids with sticky fingers and runny noses, or listening to those repeating songs that land in your head and won't leave." Her lips pulled into a smile, and she met his gaze. "My father, in case you haven't guessed, was never the touchy-feely kind, though word has it he's turned into an old softy. I couldn't say because I've never witnessed it, but it would be a sight."

"I wouldn't mind seeing that." He'd never thought about children or what they meant, and other than a glimpse of his niece and nephew on rare occasions, he didn't think about it. In fact, he knew *nothing* about children... And what did he know about family other than they screwed up your life, implanted issues in your brain that lived with you for decades? "So, do your parents have any potential buyers?" He could offer to help, but what would he say? *I've been keeping a secret from you. I'm a businessman and I negotiate deals for my uncle's company. And I'm pretty good at it. Great, actually.*

Nope, he was not going to reveal that just yet, but he could offer support. "I'm happy to help any way I can, even if it's doing something at the store like stacking shelves or working the register. I can balance books, too." He let this one truth slip out. "I have a knack for numbers, balancing books and that sort of thing." *And an eye for which deals are worthwhile and which aren't.*

Her gray eyes sparkled. "Thank you. That is so very kind of you. I'll let them know." Law nodded, trailed a finger along her neck, traced the tender spot behind her ear. "Whatever you need," he murmured, "just let me know and I promise I'll give it to you."

Ava slid her hand under the covers, stroked his thigh and whispered, "Now that you mention it..."

Two hours later, Law slipped out of bed, showered, and pulled on jeans and a flannel shirt. He might not reveal his business skills just yet, but that didn't mean he couldn't utilize them to do a bit of investigation. There were always ways to research buyers and sellers, starting with the one person who knew all the business happenings in and around Magdalena: his brother.

Most of the time, Law couldn't stand Brett or his self-indulgent ways, but there were occasions when the man could be useful, like now. Law hopped into his pickup and drove to the dealership, intent on a conversation that involved finding out what his brother knew about local businesses for sale—including Sal's Market—and potential buyers.

When he entered the building, the young man with the mop of yellow hair who'd blown him off last time rushed toward him. "How do you do, Mr. Carlisle?" And was that a bow? Damn, but it sure looked like it. Law nodded, proceeded to his brother's office, and poked his head inside. "Got a minute?"

Brett looked up, his too-handsome face a mix of curiosity and awareness. "This is a surprise. Tired of pretending you aren't a Carlisle? Let me guess. You're looking for a job?" The raised brow and smirk said that's exactly why he thought Law was here. To grovel.

Law shook his head. "None of the above." He stepped into his brother's office, closed the door, and sank into a chair. "What do you know about businesses for sale in town?" He did not want to flat-out ask about Sal's Market because that might lead to questions he preferred not answering, like *Why are you asking?* Or, *What do you know about running a business?* Maybe even, *Would this have anything to do with Ava Ventori?*

"You want to know about businesses for sale?" His brother leaned back in his plush leather chair, crossed his hands behind his head, and sighed. "Do you have any idea how difficult it is to run a business?"

"Some." *Yeah, some.* Law bet Cal's company's net worth could outpace this dealership and any holdings Brett had several times over. And while Law's name wasn't on the business yet, he was included in all major decisions and handled most of the company's negotiations. Not bad for a guy everybody thought would end up in jail.

Brett's laugh revealed gleaming teeth and two dimples. "Some." Another laugh, this one louder and more obnoxious than the last. "You don't run a company on *some*. And where do you plan to get the capital? Dad? He's not as flush as you might think." He paused, said in a low voice, "The old man's made a few questionable business decisions that cost him a big chunk of change."

Law didn't want to hear about Montrose Carlisle's bad business decisions. He didn't care about any of it except making sure Sal Ventori got a good deal and no one took advantage of him. But first he had to find out what Brett knew. "So, maybe I'll get financing somewhere else. I don't even know if there's anything I'm interested in, or if I want to hang around here, but I can't decide unless I have the facts." He scratched his jaw, kept his gaze trained on his brother. "So, do you have information on the businesses for sale, or maybe ones coming for sale? I heard you were the guy to talk to about it."

"Oh?" Brett's eyes lit up. "Who's been talking?"

Hard to miss the air of self-importance in the puffed-out chest and slippery smile. Yeah, the guy thought he was Mr. Businessman of Magdalena. Fine, let him think he ruled the state. All Law wanted was a list of names: buyers and sellers. "The question you should really ask is who hasn't been talking. You've got a reputation." He worked up a smile, kept the lie in place until his brother's expression burst with pride. Law could deflate that look by telling him the only one chanting Brett's skill was their father and it had been a mediocre commentary.

"Okay, I'll give you the names." He turned to his computer, began typing, leaned in and studied the screen, finished with a dramatic punch of a key. "And print." Brett reached toward the credenza behind him and snagged a piece of paper from the printer. "Here," he said, sliding it across the desk. "Four companies for sale in a fifty-mile radius: a frozen yogurt shop, a drycleaners, a candy store, and a café."

Law scanned the short list of companies, their owners, and

contact information. No mention of Sal's Market. He glanced up, met his brother's steady gaze. "Is this it?"

"That's what you've got to choose from, and it's not much. The frozen yogurt shop couldn't make it because the owners insisted on taking a two-week vacation in July. Who can afford that? The drycleaners was a mom-and-pop business and the husband died of a heart attack three months ago. The kids are moving the mother to Florida." He rubbed his clean-shaven jaw, shook his head. "The candy store was a good idea, but you can't work from 10 a.m. to 2 p.m. and expect to make it."

"Not a solid business plan." Law zeroed in on the café, wondered if it could be Lina's and hoped it wasn't. He liked Phyllis, liked the food and the welcoming atmosphere and didn't want to think about someone coming in and changing it all around. "And the café? What's going on with that?"

"Penny's is a dive in Renova. The guy's been skating on his taxes and the feds caught him."

So, Lina's was safe. Law blew out a quiet sigh, glad Phyllis and the rest of the staff were okay. But what about Sal? How had Brett not heard about that? Or maybe he had... Why wouldn't he tell Law about it? He couldn't know about Law and Ava...could he? He decided to try one more time. "I'm not thrilled with any of these places. I eat ice cream, not frozen yogurt, I don't dry clean my jeans or flannel shirts, and I prefer cookies to candy."

"And the café?"

Was that sarcasm in his brother's voice, as though it didn't matter what business was for sale, Law would never be able to afford any of them? Right, if he only knew. "I'm not going to compete with Lina's Café."

"Really? You like that greasy spoon?" A scowl covered his face. "That waitress forgets her place *and* her manners. Where does she get off snapping her gum at me and rolling her eyes?

Don't think I didn't threaten to tell the manager about it. Damn right I did."

"Uh-huh." Law couldn't be sure, but he thought Phyllis was the head waitress *and* the manager at Lina's. "Guess I was hoping for something more diverse." He scanned the paper again, waited three seconds. "Like maybe a convenience place or even a grocery store." The swoosh of air made Law glance up, zero in on his brother's face, which had turned three shades paler. "Nothing available, huh?"

A glimmer of challenge swept over Brett's face, followed by a shake of his head and words that did not quite ring true. "Nope, sorry, nothing at all."

CHAPTER 14

"Ava, why are you cleaning a rock?" It had taken several nights in bed for her to share the secrets inside the bag. She'd shown him paints, brushes, a cloth, a few photos of leaves, and the sketchpad she dove into most times she visited. So where did the rock cleaning fit in? And why? That was just odd. He kept his voice even, tried to act as if cleaning rocks was something people did if they had a small obsession or quirk. But he must have failed because the look she gave him and the tone that followed said she didn't appreciate the comment.

"See, this is exactly why I didn't want to tell you. You're staring at me like you think I'm crazy." She clutched the darn thing so hard he wasn't sure if she planned to hurl it at him or hug it against her chest. Maybe both.

"I didn't mean anything by it; I'm just trying to understand." If she wanted to clean rocks, so what? As long as it made her happy and she trusted him enough to share it, he'd be okay about it. It was the trust and sharing that mattered most, and soon he'd have to do his own bit of trusting and sharing and that meant telling her he was more than an errand boy at his uncle's company. But not yet. He guessed he'd also have to tell her he'd never been in jail or any sort of detention center, though doing a stint there might actually sound better than the truth. *My family sent me to my uncle's because they didn't care enough to keep me here.*

She hesitated, eyed him with uncertainty, and continued to clutch the rock. "Cleaning the rock is the first step in a process of creation. The landscape doesn't matter, does it? Neither does the medium." When he nodded his understanding, she reached inside the bag and pulled out a flat rock with the word *Hope* scrawled over it alongside tiny designs that resembled peacock feathers and circles. Then she pulled out another, set it beside the *Hope* rock. This one was painted red, covered with white circles and dots and *Love* painted on the top in black.

Law leaned forward, one hand resting on her shoulder, the other gesturing toward the rocks. "May I?" When she nodded, he picked up the first one, turned it over, noted the delicate lines and intricacy of the pattern. "I like it." Smooth, delicate, beautiful, like the woman who'd painted it. He placed the rock on the table, picked up the next one, studied the precision and simplistic design. "Why don't you share these? They're beautiful."

She shook her head, frustration lacing her next words. "How would I ever explain them? My parents wanted me to be a nurse, not a rock painter. What would I tell them? I've given up the medical profession so I can paint rocks? Can't you see how beautiful they are and what they mean to me? Can't you appreciate the detail? Oh, you expect me to make *money* from these? Yeah, well, they probably won't make me a millionaire. In fact, they probably won't make me any money at all." Her voice rose, smothered him in frustration and sadness. "But I love them and I'm *not* going to stop creating because the world can't assign them a dollar amount worthy of paying my grocery bill. Do you think my parents could ever understand that?" Those gray eyes turned smoky. "Do you think anyone could understand this?" Her voice dipped, fell out whisper-soft. "Could you?"

Law understood doing something you loved irrespective of whether or not it provided economic support. "I can." He stroked her cheek, placed a kiss on her forehead and murmured, "I do understand. I think it's a courageous and honorable endeavor and I support you."

She sniffed. "Thank you."

"And I will continue to support you as long as you find joy in what you're doing and screw the money." He thought that would make her happy, and she would see inside his heart and understand how much he cared, but she didn't. Instead, she shrugged him away, brows pinched, mouth pulled into a frown.

"I appreciate the kind words, but let's be honest. You never had to worry about money or paying the utilities. I've hopped jobs, borrowed from my brother in the form of gifts, loans, and everything in between, because I hoped that one day, I could actually support myself. And you know what? That day never came, and now I'm not sure it ever will. What am I supposed to do with that, Law? Keep hoping and praying, waiting for the moment my talents will mesh with what the world believes I'm worth and I can finally support myself?"

I'll support you, he wanted to say. *I'll give you whatever you need to make you happy. Even if the world doesn't understand the value of your art, I do. I understand and believe in the value of you.* But he didn't offer that because it would reveal too much, probably more than she wanted to hear. So, he merely nodded and said in what he hoped sounded like support. "I hope you never give up your dreams and I hope you keep trying because one day, I believe you'll find success." He straightened, held her gaze. "If you follow your passion and never give up, the money *will* follow." Her eyes filled with tears, trickled down her cheeks.

Law swiped at them with the pad of his thumb, whispered, "I believe in you, Ava."

That was the day she began to trust him and shared her art. She taught him about rock painting, where she found the rocks, how she cleaned them, created designs, painted them. Her work was beautiful and touched him deep inside, and when she handed him a rock with his name on it in a vibrant blue with silver swirls and red hearts, he couldn't speak because emotion clogged his words. *I've never known anyone like you,* he wanted to say. *I don't want to let you go. Ever. I love you.* Those words lived in his heart but he couldn't put sound to them. Not yet. But one day soon he would, and then Ava Marie Ventori would understand she owned his heart.

CHAPTER 15

Law had just finished a ham and Swiss on rye and a bowl of beef soup when the young girl walked in. She wore a red parka with fur on the hood and a smile that warmed the whole diner. He guessed she was in her late teens or early twenties and he wondered if this was the young girl Phyllis had told him about: Lily Desantro. It wasn't the fact that she had Down syndrome that clued him in; it was the way the room lit up when she walked through the door. Phyllis said only two people in town could cause such a reaction: Angelo "Pop" Benito and Lily Desantro. She'd also assured Law he'd recognize both when he spotted them. He took in the girl's dark hair, thick glasses, and wide smile. But it was the laughter and nonstop chatter swirling around her that told him this had to be Lily. Law continued to watch her, surprised when she broke from the small crowd and made a beeline toward him.

"You're Law Carlisle, aren't you?" When he nodded, she giggled. "I'm Lily. My brother says your dad lives in the big house with the tennis court, but you live in the woods with the animals." She scrunched her nose and studied him. "Nate says you might be an animal too but he doesn't know what kind yet."

Her voice grew softer as she leaned toward him, whispered in a loud voice, "He said you might be a wolf or a coyote or you might be one of those animals that changes colors. What's it called? A camel? No...chamomile?"

Yup, this was Lily Desantro and she was talking about her brother, good old Nate, the guy with enough sarcasm to fill the Hudson River. "You mean a chameleon?" When the girl smiled, he smiled back, said in a soft voice, "Chameleons don't live anywhere near Magdalena. In fact, they live in a different part of the world, so I can't be one of those."

She giggled again, her blue eyes turning bright. "Sometimes Nate says the silliest things, but he doesn't think they're silly. Mom and I do, though, and Christine, too. Christine's his wife and they have two babies, and my Uncle Harry lives in a big house like your dad." She scratched her chin, slid into the booth opposite him and placed her elbows on the table. "Why do you live in the woods? And why do you have a ponytail?" Her gaze slid to his arm, zeroed in on the dragon's head and swirls of fire wrapping his forearm in bold colors. "That tattoo is way cool. Is the rest of the dragon under your shirt?"

"It is." Law hoped she wouldn't ask to see it, but the girl was pretty inquisitive...

"I heard you had a lot of tattoos. Why do you have so many? Didn't they hurt?" She leaned closer, inspected the flames.

Should he tell her the truth or something that sounded a little more logical? He settled on both. "I was young and wanted to make a statement about who I was, but I think I went a little overboard. I like tattoos, but I probably should have stopped before I covered my forearm."

"I like them," she whispered. "They're cool, especially the flames. I think I'd like to get a tattoo. A rose."

Law was not going to have Nate Desantro accuse him of influencing his sister to get a tattoo. No way. "You have to think really hard about it, Lily, because once you get them, it's not easy to get rid of them."

"Uh-huh. But they look cool." She inched her gaze to his, smiled. "Christine said she thinks they look good on you, but Nate didn't like that. He gave her a big frowny face and said, 'Never mind what looks good on him.' She just laughed. Then Cash said maybe Nate should get a tattoo with…I can't say what it was because it's a bad word." Her eyes grew wide, and she licked her lips. "But I can sort of spell it so you can figure it out. Uncle Harry says it's not the same if you spell it. Okay, the first part of the word is *hard* and the last has three letters. The first one is 'a' and the second two letters are the same." She giggled, made an *s* sound to help him out. "Bet you can figure it out fast, can't you?"

Law could figure out the word *hard-ass* without any help from Desantro's sister. He nodded, slid her a smile. "Yup. I can figure it out, but you better not tell your brother you told me because he wouldn't like it." How had Cash Casherdon gotten away with that comment? "So, Cash didn't say that in front of Nate, did he?"

Another giggle, a big nod that made her ponytail bob up and down. "Yes, he did. Nate gave him a frowny face and that made Cash laugh harder. He's not afraid of Nate, but some people are." She picked at a thread on her sweater, brows pinching together. "It's just how he sounds. He's really soft like a marshmallow, that's what Christine says." *Giggle, giggle.* "Uncle Harry says he's softer than his dog's fur as long as nobody crosses him or his family. Then he can get crusty, like a piece of toast." It was her turn to frown. "How does a person get crusty?"

Lily sure had a lot of questions but he bet she held a lot of answers about the people of Magdalena, too. Maybe she could educate him about what was happening in this town and who knew what. "Lily, your Uncle Harry, who lives in the big house… Is he the same one who owns the restaurant? The man who moved here from Chicago?"

"Uh-huh. That's Uncle Harry."

He'd heard a lot about the guy but hadn't met him yet, or visited the restaurant. He wanted to take Ava, but since she'd avoided stepping out of the house with him, he'd nixed the idea. He didn't like hiding in the cabin with her and very soon they were going to talk about it, because Law had spent enough years feeling he wasn't good enough. His gut told him he'd been a fool to agree to Ava's request, but his heart knew he'd do anything she asked. Still, a person couldn't have a relationship that never ventured outside. Law knew that and Ava should know that, too.

"Law? Why do you have a frowny face like Nate does when he's not happy? Did I say something to make you mad?" She bit her bottom lip, eyes bright, hands clasped together on the table. "I'm sorry if I did. Sometimes Nate says I talk too much about things that aren't my business."

"Some people like their privacy, but I'm sure you weren't trying to be nosy." The frown deepened, the blue eyes misted. "Were you curious? Maybe even concerned?"

Her head dipped in a nod and she said in a quiet voice, "I *am* concerned and I always worry about people. I want them to be happy. I want everyone to be happy, and that's why I ask about boyfriends and girlfriends and people getting married, and that's when Nate gives me a frowny face and tells me not to ask."

What to say to that? *Your brother has a point? Not everyone wants to talk about boyfriends and girlfriends or getting married?* Yeah, she might not understand that one. "You can wonder about it and maybe even poke around, but it's not always a good idea to straight out ask the person too much."

Her expression lit up. "Is it okay to ask if they have a boyfriend or girlfriend but not if they're going to get married?"

"Well…not exactly…"

She rushed on, ignoring his words. "I like to hear about people and what they're doing and I always want to find ways to help them out of their troubles. Pop says I have a good eye to spot when there's a problem and he says *that's* a gift." She tilted her head, studied him. "Does that make sense to you?" When he nodded, her smile spread. "Good, because I wanted to ask you about Ava Ventori. She's so pretty and I like her a lot. Pop says all she needs is a second chance to make her light up like a Christmas tree." *Giggle, giggle.* "He said maybe you just need a second chance, too, and if you had bad luck or a past that took you to jail, that you aren't that person anymore and everybody deserves another chance, right?"

"Right," Law said in a tight voice. This town might believe in second chances, but they sure didn't forget. And what if they didn't have the whole story? Did they make it up to fit what they wanted to hear? A person could only let so much misunderstanding continue, especially in the eyes of a girl like Lily. "Want to know a secret? One most people don't know about, and wouldn't believe?"

"Uh-huh." Those blue eyes turned brighter than the Caribbean ocean. "Is it a secret I can share or do I need to keep it close to my heart? Pop said some secrets are meant to be shared so you can help, and then others are meant to be kept close to your heart and never repeated."

Interesting commentary on the meaning of secrets. Law held Lily's gaze, said in a soft voice just for her, "You can share this secret if you need to or if you think it will help. Okay, here goes. I never spent a minute in jail or anyplace like it. I left Magdalena when I was seventeen and stayed with my aunt and uncle in Pennsylvania. That's where I grew up and learned what it meant to be a good person and an honorable man. I went to college, graduated, and started working with my uncle. But most people don't know that because they can't see past my hair, tattoos, or the stories they've heard about me. Some knew me back when I did things I regret, and many think I'm still that person. I'm not, Lily. I'm not that person at all, and I think your brother could understand that because I'm guessing he's not the person he used to be either."

"No, he sure isn't." She shook her head so hard her ponytail swished against her shoulders. "Nate's not how he used to be before Christine. He was mad all the time with lots of frowny faces and swear words, and he only smiled for me and Mom. Then Christine came and she brought sunshine. Not at first because he wasn't happy she was here, but once he stopped being afraid of sharing me, and worse, of getting hurt, he opened his heart wide and gave her all of his love. That's the Nate who's the best person in the world and the one who protects all of us. He and Christine fell in love and got married and now they have two little girls and maybe someday they'll have another one. Or maybe they'll just have a dog. I don't know, but like Pop says, 'time will tell its own story.'"

Law wondered what Nate Desantro would say if he heard his sister's testimony of love and happily ever after. He guessed the guy would be okay with it. Maybe he'd even crack a smile for his sister.

Lily narrowed her gaze on him, whispered, "Did you say you were never in jail?" She asked that question like it had skipped her radar the first time and now she was circling back for details.

"I did, and I'm telling you people might think I spent time there, but it's not true."

She nodded. "I already knew you didn't do any of those things. Pop said it was all a set-up and he thinks you're a good guy. He said there should be more people like you and if there were, the world wouldn't be getting all turned around with what was real and what wasn't."

"Pop Benito said that?" Law didn't think the guy even knew

who he was, and other than the few times he'd spotted the old man at the grocery store or on the street, Law had no idea who Pop Benito was.

"Sure did. You know he's called the Godfather of Magdalena, right? He makes the best pizzelles in town and he's teaching me the secret. Once he's done being the godfather, he's going to hand over the title to Uncle Harry because Uncle Harry has a way with people that makes them feel comfortable—and he doesn't judge." Her voice dipped. "He had a *colorful* past, as Pop calls it, but he's all settled down now with a wife, three kids, and a dog named Cooper. You should meet him." She tapped a finger against her chin, let out a tiny breath of excitement. "Do you want me to make a reservation for you at Harry's Folly? Uncle Harry doesn't mind if I bring friends." She gave him a bright smile that lit up her eyes. "I like you, Law, and I'd like you to be my friend."

Had he ever had such an open offer, filled with pure innocence and trust? He knew the answer in his heart: never. "I like you too, Lily. I'd be honored to call you my friend." Law reached across the Formica table, held out a hand. She placed her small one in his and they shook. "To friends," he said. "Now how about a slice of pie? I like the coconut cream, but you can have whatever you want. My treat."

CHAPTER 16

Harry Blacksworth was everything the town said he was: good-looking, a class act, a man with a big laugh and a generous smile. When Law entered Harry's Folly, the man himself descended upon him, slapped him on the back and bellowed, "Law Carlisle. Been waiting for you. Don't make me think you're as antisocial as my niece's husband." He raised a brow, let out another laugh that filled the entrance. "Doubtful, because nobody's more antisocial than Nate Desantro. Still, you gotta love the guy for turning into a human being when he met my niece. Now he's a regular family guy like me, and I'm sure nobody ever thought *that* was going to happen."

Law shook the man's hand, nodded. "Nice to meet you, Harry. I've heard a lot about you, all good things. Lily said I had to come here and try the penne pasta with spinach and garbanzo beans."

"Hell, yes. My personal favorite, and the signature dish of this restaurant. Come on in and let me pour you a glass of wine and tell Jeremy to get cooking." He motioned toward the seating area and said, "Follow me and I'll get you set up. You meeting anyone?"

"Nope, just me." He'd thought about inviting Ava but didn't want to suffer the disappointment of her excuses. She didn't want to venture out in public with him, wanted to keep things between them *casual*. Isn't that the word she'd used? Well, casual wasn't okay with him, hadn't been even when he'd agreed to it, but he'd been so damn desperate to be with her that he'd gone along with it. After their first night together, he realized he couldn't do casual *or* short-term with Ava Ventori, and at some point he'd have to tell her and then she'd have to make a choice. Would it be him or would she tell him no thanks, not interested, and find another bed partner? He had no idea, but he couldn't go on with less than half a relationship—he didn't want to—not with her because Ava was worth so much more.

"How about I open a bottle of wine and we'll have a chat? I can fill you in on this town, who's who, what's what, and why, and you can tell me why you're living in a cabin on the outskirts of town instead of lounging in the mini palace on the hill."

Nothing like saying what he thought. Law appreciated Harry Blacksworth's honesty, and that's why he'd tell him. That and something in the man's expression said he knew all about being an outcast. "You got yourself a deal." Law followed Harry to a booth in the back of the restaurant, sank onto leather that felt softer than a couch.

"So, Pop tells me you're the younger Carlisle boy." Harry slid him a smile, and his eyes lit up. "The one with the questionable reputation."

Well, nice to know word had spread through Magdalena and reached strangers Law hadn't even met. "I guess that would be an accurate assessment, but what are reputations anyway other than someone else's opinion of a person, whether it's true or not?"

"You got that right." Harry motioned for the waiter to approach, nodded when the young man held up a bottle of wine, then proceeded to fill two glasses. "Thanks, leave the bottle." He rubbed his jaw, studied Law. "You haven't been back long, so I'll fill you in on bad reputations and such. They don't get any worse than mine and the Blacksworth name in Magdalena was dirt. But people change, so do opinions, and I like to think that's what happened here."

He lifted his glass, saluted Law. "Here's to change and the truth. And let's not forget the good people of Magdalena and their opinions. I might not like some of them, but most are honest, hard-working, decent people." Harry took a healthy gulp of wine, set his glass on the table. "If you ask around, you'll hear my story. I'm the younger brother of the man who divided this town with plenty of heartache. My brother, the one I admired more than anyone, had a secret family and out of that secret family came Lily Desantro. I hear you met Lily." His voice dipped, his expression turned soft. "Now *there's* an angel walking this earth. That girl's got a heart bigger than this whole town. I love that girl… She reminds me what's really important in life, and when I want to feel sorry for myself, Lily's there to make me realize my life's pretty damn good."

Law sipped his wine, considered the man's words. "Lily and I had a nice conversation and shared some pie at the diner."

Harry shook his head. "Don't let that girl talk you into buying her all kinds of treats. She's a con artist, and none of us can say no." He let out a laugh, his cheeks turning ruddy, his blue eyes—Lily's eyes—sparkling. "She and Pop Benito are something else when it comes to food. When they're together, you don't know which way is which and what you've agreed to…especially if it has to do with a pizzelle."

"Thanks for the warning. I've heard a lot about Pop Benito,

and from what Lily's said, he's got a bead on me." According to Lily, Pop had formed several opinions about Law...

"Don't take it personally. Pop's got a bead on everybody in this town, and if he's talking about you to Lily, it's probably good. Or he's figured out whatever he says will get back to you, and that's exactly what he wants." Another laugh, a heavy sigh. "That's our godfather. Cunning, crafty, and calculating, with more wisdom in his pinky than I'll ever have in my whole brain."

Law studied the man, took in the cashmere vest, the silk tie, the starched shirt and gold cufflinks. Harry Blacksworth looked out of place, but when the man talked about the town and the people in it, his words said he belonged here and wouldn't want to be anywhere else. "Thanks for the heads-up. I expect Pop will find me one of these days and request a sit-down." He grinned, added, "Being the Godfather of Magdalena and all."

Harry threw back his head, howled. "You can count on it."

"So, what's going on with you and Ava Ventori?"

Law glanced up from the *Magdalena Press*, forced his expression to remain calm so his brother didn't see his annoyance. He should not have agreed to meet Montrose for breakfast this morning, but Ava had encouraged him to do it, said it was the small steps that made the biggest differences. Sharing a meal with the man hadn't been as bad as he remembered. In fact, it had been borderline pleasant and he'd relaxed enough to ask for another cup of coffee and the *Magdalena Press* after his father left for work. A few extra minutes in the old homestead wasn't going to turn him into a statue. He'd been reading an article about The Bleeding Hearts Society's upcoming homemade ornament contest when Brett strolled in, claimed the chair at the head of the table, and tossed out the question about Law and Ava. Too bad the guy had never learned what "don't want to talk about it" and "mind your own business" meant.

"Law? Don't ignore me. I heard you two were seeing each other." Pause, a snort. "You're sleeping with her, aren't you?"

"Are you spying on me?" He'd be damned if he'd admit to anything with Ava. Whatever was going on between them was nobody's business. What *was* going on between them? Hell if he knew. That wasn't exactly correct; Ava was looking for entertainment and she'd found it with him. Every night, sometimes twice a night: earth-shattering, unforgettable, white-hot. Sex. Too bad it meant a hell of a lot more to him than it did to her. He'd been a fool to think he could ever get her interest for anything other than short-term-feel-good sex. He'd wanted to believe she saw the *real* him, the one who bled and hurt and wanted to be with someone who cared about *him*, not his name, not what he did or didn't do, but the *real* Lawson Carlisle, the one who fought for causes and people worth believing in. But Ava didn't want that, at least not with him, and she'd been pretty clear about it.

Oh, she loved the sex but he'd known it would be good between them; no, not good—great. He'd hung onto the hope that what they shared would carry them past the bedroom, the kitchen, the living room, and the shower. Law wanted her to see him as a real person and a potential partner, not an after-hours sex toy.

"Not answering is answering." His brother's too-white smile pulled at the corners. "Yup, you're sleeping with her." Brett rubbed his smooth-shaven jaw, studied Law with a blend of curiosity and confusion. "Why?"

Stay cool, stay cool. Law held his brother's gaze, clenched and unclenched his fist. "Why what?"

"Why are you sleeping with her? I mean, she's decent to look at and she's got a lot of great curves, but... A grocery store owner's daughter? Even you can do better than that." Brett shook his head, let out a sigh.

Law set down his coffee mug, said in a cool voice, "Talk about her like that again and you'll wish you hadn't." That was the problem with his family; they always thought they were better than everyone else and never understood they were worse.

Brett paused, coffee cup midair. "Hey, I didn't know you had a thing for the woman. Like I could care. You can bang anybody you want but I didn't know you were working the blue-collar market."

Law thrust back his chair, lunged at his brother, and yanked him to his feet by his necktie. "Apologize, you sonofabitch." Brett gasped, tried to get away, but Law tightened his grip. "I said apologize. Now."

"Okay, okay." More gasping and a strangled "I apologize. Damn it, let me go."

Law pushed him away, fisted his hands on his hips, and growled, "You know the problem with you, Brett? You think you can say whatever you want and get away with it. Well, you can't, and you've never understood that. One of these days it's going to catch up with you." All his brother had to do was keep his mouth shut and offer a simple *I'm sorry*. But Brett Carlisle couldn't do that because he'd been raised to believe rules didn't apply to him, and whatever he did could be forgiven or gotten out of, no matter what.

Brett straightened his tie, shook his head. "You stayed in the boonies too long living with that hick uncle of ours that nobody ever talks about. Why don't you go back there and clean out a few stalls? Take that Ventori bitch with you."

The first punch landed on Brett's perfect nose with a crack and a thud. The second connected with his jaw as he staggered back, fell to the ground in a whimper and a moan. Law stood over him, tossed a linen napkin at his back. "Stay the hell out of my way and if I hear you talking about Ava again, I'll be back for round two."

CHAPTER 17

Ava spent most of the day thinking about tonight and what she had to say to Law. She'd heard he'd chatted with Lily Desantro at Lina's Café and word had it, he'd even bought her a slice of pie. What a kind man. She'd misjudged him and while she might pretend she didn't want long-term or serious with Lawson Carlisle, that was just a way to protect her heart—a heart that already belonged to Law. What would he say when she told him casual wouldn't work, that she wanted more? He seemed to want that, too, but she'd been so adamant about not getting in too deep that maybe he'd changed his mind. Maybe he was content with sharing a bed, dinner, and conversation. Her chest ached as she considered this, but the other possibility scared her more. If he admitted to wanting something deeper with her, she'd have to open up to him and that meant risk getting hurt again.

Could she do it?

They hadn't talked about seeing each other tonight, though they'd spent almost every night together. But it usually started with an invitation from Law. There'd been none today. No mention of dinner or after.

The absence of an invitation had prompted her to share spaghetti and meatballs with her parents and while there'd been no questions about why she was gracing them with her presence tonight, the eagle-eyed stares and pointed looks said they'd formulated their own opinions.

No plans tonight? her mother asked.

No dinner date with the mystery man? her father added.

Ava's response had been vague: a shake of her head and a quiet *none*. After dishes, she kissed her parents and shrugged into her jacket. *I'm heading out for a while.*

When her mother hugged her, she whispered, *Good luck*, as if she sensed Ava's quietness had to do with a man. What would Lorraine Ventori do if she knew the man were Magdalena's very own rich-kid-turned-rebel, Lawson Carlisle. Instinct told her that her mother would not be happy. Ava pushed aside thoughts of her mother's opinion and drove to the cabin, pulled into the driveway, and parked behind Law's old truck. She usually carried an overnight bag with her, but she left it on the passenger seat and grabbed her handbag. The lack of an invitation said she should not assume anything, least of all an overnight stay.

Ava made her way up the front steps, knocked on the door, and scanned the porch as she waited. A section of railing stood out, crisp and new, a sign that Law had been busy yesterday. Is that why he hadn't called her? He'd been so caught up with repairs that he'd fallen asleep on the couch and slept through the night? The idea was ridiculous.

"Ava?"

Law stood in the doorway, staring at her. He didn't look surprised to see her—or happy. "Hi. Can I come in?" She worked up a smile, held it in place as those green eyes sparked with something that looked a lot like anger. Or distrust.

"I've got a killer headache," he said, rubbing his left temple. "I'd be terrible company tonight."

"Oh." She clutched the strap on her handbag, sucked in a breath. She hadn't planned on not having an opportunity to talk to him. "I...it's kind of important." Ava licked her lips, pushed out more truths. "It's about us."

He narrowed his gaze on her, rubbed his other temple. "I see. Guess I didn't realize there was an *us*."

There is, if you want there to be. "That's what I came to discuss. That, and to tell you how sweet you were to spend time with Lily Desantro."

Red crept from his neck to his hollowed-out cheeks. "She had a few questions and I guess I had the answers. No big deal."

"But it *is* a big deal, Law. I should have seen it before." How had she missed the kindness, the gestures that said he was so much more than a former bad-boy-rich-kid with tattoos and a history? "I'm sorry for not trusting you more, and for not giving you a chance. You didn't deserve that from me or anyone else."

He nodded, looked away. "Okay."

"Okay? Okay, we're good, or okay, I don't care if you're sorry?" She'd hurt him and he didn't deserve that, but she was trying to make things right between them—trying to show him she wanted so much more than casual.

He moved toward her, stopped. "Both. Look, you were honest about what you wanted from the beginning. No strings, nothing permanent. Casual. Fun." His eyes sparked with emotion, turned dark. "*For now*, is what you said. I memorized those words so I wouldn't forget." Law reached out, fingered a lock of her hair. "Because I was looking for more than that, even though I didn't know it. Once I was around you, long before we slept together, I knew I wanted more with you." His voice dipped, turned soft, "And I knew I was never going to get it. Ava Marie Ventori has standards, right? And while she might sleep with me, she sure as hell wasn't about to parade me around town as her guy." His lips pulled into a tight smile. "You thought I didn't mind that you always wanted to meet at my place, keep our *relationship* between these four walls?" He slashed a hand toward the back of the house. "Or in the lounge chair on the deck. And when I visited at the grocery store, I had to pretend we were casual acquaintances and stick to the no-contact policy? Did you think I wouldn't mind, Ava? Did you really not think at some point it might be an issue?"

"I didn't mean to...I wasn't ashamed of you." She held his gaze, whispered, "Or of us." There. She'd said what her heart had known long before her brain did. She cared about Law Carlisle—a lot—and wanted to be with him, in *and* out of bed. The caring was real and petrifying but she didn't want to fight it or pretend around it any longer.

"Us?" he spat out. "There *is* no us, Ava. How can there be when all we've got is what happens in this house?" He pointed toward the living room and bedroom. "Your parents don't even know I exist. Don't you ever get tired of lying to them?"

"They...they don't ask." But that wasn't quite true. Ava had created a storyline that included friends who had someone they wanted her to meet. The notion of a potential mate for their thirty-three-year-old daughter made them ecstatic, and all further questions were geared toward guessing the mystery man's name. Of course, she couldn't tell Law *that*.

"And I'm sure you don't offer." He shrugged, a gesture she recognized as his attempt to act as if he didn't care. "I tried to convince myself it would be enough, but it's not. I'm done playing games."

She stared at him. "But I..."

He shook his head. "Don't. I think you should leave."

Ava stood in the entranceway, clutching the shoulder strap of her handbag as the man who'd snuck into her heart turned her away. She never thought she'd care about a man again and certainly not Law Carlisle, whom she assumed had grown into an adult version of his younger self. But he wasn't that person anymore, if he ever had been. Law was one of the good guys, a man of honor and integrity, like Nate Desantro and Cash Casherdon.

Had his past or his appearance made her believe he could never pledge his heart or honor his word? She'd called her father judgmental and prejudiced, but she was no better... No, she was worse because Law had tried to show her who he was, and she'd shut him down. "I'm so sorry." She moved toward him, swiped at her cheeks. "Please, can you give me another chance?"

He closed his eyes, dragged both hands over his face. "Ava." One long sigh before his eyes inched open, bright, glittering.

"Please, Law?" She let the tears fall, let him see how much she wanted another chance with him. "I was wrong about so many things, especially you."

"I can't do casual with you, Ava." His lips flattened, his voice turned rough. "I just can't."

"I know." She nodded as a glimmer of hope filled her. "I wanted to, and I tried...but I can't. Not with you."

"Ava," he murmured, framing her face with strong hands. "I never planned for any of this to happen..."

"I know. Me neither."

"...but now that it has, I don't want to give it up."

How had she ever thought he could be a casual pastime? She leaned on tiptoe, eased her fingers through his hair. "Then don't. Please?"

There was no talking after that as he scooped her into his arms, carried her to the bedroom, and showed her just how much he did not want to give her up.

CHAPTER 18

There were times when questions required a face-to-face conversation with the person holding the answers, and now was one of those times. Law didn't want to leave Ava and head back to his uncle's in Pennsylvania, but Cal might be able to provide insight into what was going on with Brett. It wasn't that the man particularly liked Law's brother, but Cal had a way of keeping tabs on people and situations so there were no surprises.

Law made the four-hour drive to his uncle's and after a working lunch that included updates on current projects and potential clients, he figured it was time to tell Cal the real reason he'd made the trip. Cal Beaumont appreciated straight-out questions, minus the fancy footwork and bouquets of BS some people thought smoothed the way for straight talking and that's exactly what Law gave him.

"Do you think Brett could be stealing from our father's company?"

"Stealing from Montrose?" Cal raised a brow. "I did not see that one coming. I figured you'd have a few questions, but I expected they'd have to do with your father." He rubbed his jaw, eased back in his worn leather chair. "Brett, huh? I never did like that boy's smile. Didn't turn up at the corners or reach his eyes." Cal made a sound that fell just short of a snort. "Can't trust a person who doesn't know how to smile."

"So...Brett's smile says 'I can't be trusted'?" His uncle had a lot of interesting ways to dissect a person's trustworthiness, but this was a new one and Law had thought he'd heard them all.

Cal shot him a look. "What? Facial expressions, especially smiles or their absence, tell their own story. Besides, you wouldn't have driven all this way to ask that question."

Law fought the heat slithering to his cheeks. "I told you I wanted to talk about the Reynolds project and the Harris deal."

His uncle laughed. "Uh-huh. And I want to talk about learning how to tango. Give it up, boy. Let's talk about your brother."

The brother he'd once idolized until he discovered most of what he'd believed was a lie. "Let's just say we have issues that go way beyond what he does with his lips."

"Uh-huh. Such as?"

"He's got a mean streak running through him, and he's arrogant. Entitled, too." Law thought of the car Brett wanted detailed even though he didn't drive it in until twenty minutes before closing. "Inconsiderate" slid out of his mouth. "Rude." Since when was it okay to ignore other people sitting next to you, especially if they were family? "I can't see the books, but I want to..." He thought of the way Brett tore into him when he'd asked a few business-related financial questions, concerns their father had voiced. "Something's off."

"Like I said, that boy's got a smile you can't trust, and if you can't trust the smile, you can't trust the person."

"What do you suggest I do? Sneak into his office and steal the financial reports?"

Cal shook his head. "Nah, but you're going to have to find a way to get those books and poke around. If there are inconsistencies, you'll find them, no doubt about it."

Law would have to think on this and maybe dig around a bit into his brother's personal situation. Lifestyle and spending habits said a lot about a person and if both were extravagant and the opportunity to sneak a bit here and there presented itself, maybe Brett had taken advantage of it. Who knew what the guy did or why? Certainly not Law, who understood more about what went on in Lina's Café than what happened with his own family. "What about Cynthia? Nobody talks much about her. Is she on your spoiled-and-in-need-of-life-skills-lessons, too?"

That made the man laugh. "Cynthia? That girl doesn't know the meaning of life or skill, but she does know spoiled rotten." Another laugh, a shake of his head. "Your mother used to say if Cynthia could add *sit, stay, wait*, and *leave it* into her own life instead of her dogs', she'd be on her way to finding happiness."

He'd wondered about his sister and her canine infatuation that, according to a few of the townspeople, had her dressing up her dogs like babies, carting them around in bonnets and high-end strollers, and taking them for weekly grooming. Some said it was her attempt to compensate for the lack of male companionship, while others said it was because she wanted babies. Who knew if they were close to the truth or way off base? Who cared? He hadn't seen Cynthia in four years and now she was off traipsing the West Coast with her dogs and some girlfriend who sounded like a sidekick and a real pain-in-the-butt. Law slid a glance at his uncle, locked gazes. "You know, I think I'll take my shady past over my brother and sister's issues. Actually, I feel almost normal compared to them."

"You're about as normal as they come, Law, and I'm glad you're finally realizing it."

"I don't think the residents of Magdalena would agree." He thought of the long stares and cautious looks that still followed him around. And then he pictured Ava's bright smile and gray eyes welcoming him into her arms and adjusted his thoughts. "At least most of them wouldn't."

"Ah. You're talking about a woman."

It wasn't even a question. Law fiddled with the paperweight on his uncle's desk. "I'm kind of seeing someone." *Kind of?* Is that what he called inviting her to share his closet, meals, conversations, his bed? Thinking about Ava when she wasn't with him? Missing her before she even left?

"Well, admitting an attachment to a woman even in a 'kind of' situation is a big step for you, Law. I'd hoped for the day, but I'd started to wonder if it would ever happen." A smile spread across Cal's weather-beaten face. "And I sure am glad, son. Indeed I am."

"A PONYTAIL. HUH." Salvatore Ventori leaned toward Law, squinted. "What's with all the tattoos? Were you in the service?"

Law cleared his throat, turned his arm so the details of the tattoo weren't as obvious. "No, sir."

"Huh." Ava's father adjusted his black-framed glasses, rubbed his jaw. "Interesting."

"Papa, please." Ava touched her father's shoulder. "You promised. No interrogations."

Sal turned to his daughter, grumbled, "Since when is asking a few questions considered an interrogation? Can't a father want to know about the man who's spending time with his daughter?" He cut an eye toward Law, raised a brow. "A *lot* of time, judging by the early morning hours you've been keeping."

Ava's cheeks burst with pink. "Papa!"

The man didn't have to spell out his meaning; he'd guessed Law and Ave were sleeping together. There'd been a lot of women in Law's past, but he'd never stood in their parents' living room and been questioned about what he was doing with their daughter.

Ava was different. *She* was worth it. For a chance with her, he'd suffer ten interrogations.

"Well, sit down, young man." Sal Ventori pointed a stubby finger at a couch that had to be as old as Ava. "It hurts my neck to look up at you. You sure are a tall one; probably as tall as my son." He leaned back in his chair, clutched the armrests. "Do you remember my son, Roman?"

"I do." Who didn't remember the super-hero who got screwed over by a pregnancy accusation? Hard to forget that story.

Ava slid next to Law on the couch and laced her fingers through his. "Of course, he remembers him, Papa. Why are you asking about Roman?"

The old man's face turned red, his breathing harsh. "Because if he remembers your brother, then he also remembers he got framed for something he didn't do."

"That was a bad deal." Law squeezed Ava's hand. "I always thought he got caught up in someone else's dirt and paid for it." He shrugged, said in a quiet voice, "He was too nice and some-body took advantage of that." Sal Ventori zeroed in on Law as though he planned to lunge at him, which would be a feat and an interesting visual since the man was a solid fifty pounds over-weight and not much taller than Ava.

"*Somebody* did take advantage of him." The old man leaned forward, spat out, "Tried to ruin his life, turned the whole town against him." His voice cracked. "Even me."

There was a lot of emotion floating in the room, but what did it have to do with Law? He didn't even really know Roman Ventori, and the whole deal with the pregnancy accusation happened too many years ago, at a time when Law had his own issues. "Ava said he's doing well. Living in Chicago with his wife and son."

"They're pregnant again," Ava added. "And don't forget the dog, Papa."

Her words fell out fast and cheery, like she was trying to get her old man on a different track, one that did not include Roman's past or the raw deal. But Salvatore Ventori was a tough one who would not be sidelined or distracted—unless his wife stepped in.

Lorraine Ventori was petite, dark-eyed, dark-haired with streaks of gray, and a no-nonsense style. It was the no-nonsense style she used on her husband. "Salvatore Ventori, what do you think you're doing?" She fisted her hands on her hips, let out a huff. "Is this any way to treat our guest?" *Tsk-tsk.* "It's been years since Ava's brought a young man home, and you're going to scare him off before he has a chance to taste the lasagna?"

Ava's father might be the bluster in the family, but his wife carried the clout. No doubt about it. Law liked her already. He stood, moved toward Lorraine Ventori, hand outstretched. "Hello, Mrs. Ventori. Nice to meet you."

She nodded, studied him, then offered a smile and a hand-shake. "Hello, Lawson. I remember you."

The tone said it all. He fought the heat snaking up his neck, cleared his throat. "Thankfully, that was a long time ago and I've grown up."

"I should hope so." She shook her head, said in a no-nonsense voice, "After the incident with the car, Harriet Schuster made sure she told everyone the dangers of leaving a car door unlocked. She made it her mission to check random cars and heaven forbid if one of them was unlocked. Do you know what she did then? She jotted down license numbers and turned them into the police station." A sigh, followed by a raised brow. "You certainly unsettled her."

Back then, Law hadn't considered how his actions might affect others. He'd only wanted to lash out against a father who couldn't accept him for not fitting in with the Carlisle perfection. His uncle taught him that blame is a coward's way and destiny rests in the hands of the individual, not society, family, or circumstance. "Does she still live in Magdalena?" Maybe the woman was dead. She'd been old sixteen years ago with frizzy gray hair and a shriveled face...

"She's alive, but her driving days are over. Now she walks five miles a day, no matter if there's six inches of snow or pouring rain. And she lets everyone know how fit she is and how refreshing a walk in nature can be." Lorraine rolled her eyes. "It's downright annoying."

So, Harriet Schuster wasn't Lorraine Ventori's favorite person. "Maybe I could pay her a visit, apologize for what I did."

"Apologize to that woman?" Ava's mother half-snarled. "Absolutely not."

Salvatore Ventori let out a howl, slapped a hand on his knee. "Just wait until old sourpuss finds out the Carlisle boy who stole her car is dating our Ava." More laughter, rolling over them until it filled the room. "She'll blast you right out of the grocery store. I can hear her now."

Lorraine sniffed, straightened her shoulders. "I can handle myself, Sal. Let that old biddy say one word against Ava or Lawson, and she'll wish she hadn't."

The woman was going to defend him? His own family hadn't been willing to do that. He glanced at Ava, caught her watching him, gray eyes bright. The Ventoris believed in family, doing right, and protecting those they cared about. Aside from his aunt and uncle, no one had stepped up for him in a long time, and it felt damn good.

What Law didn't understand, but would learn before he'd finished his first helping of lasagna, was that close-knit families didn't hesitate to offer opinions, observations, or commentary—even the negative kind. Law had a forkful of lasagna in his mouth when Salvatore Ventori raised his glass of Chianti, leaned toward Law, and said, "To you and Ava. May you live a long, happy life together and make beautiful dark-haired babies."

CHAPTER 19

Contentment was not a familiar word to Law, but that's what he'd felt these past few weeks and he'd be a fool to pretend Ava wasn't the reason for it. Being with her was about a lot more than passion, excitement, and good sex. Being with Ava brought him contentment and he'd never known that before, not even as a kid growing up in the mansion on the hill.

How was it that she could anticipate his mood a second after he walked in the door? And if the mood wasn't a good one, she knew what to do about that, too, and the answer wasn't sex. Well, it might end up with sex, but not until she'd gotten to the bottom of whatever situation had put him in a foul mood—usually involving his family—Brett, in particular. The guy he'd once envied as the favorite child had turned into a jerk with money, power, and an arrogance that disregarded anything but his own interests.

Law avoided his brother, but he'd have to start spending more time with his old man if he were going to honor his deal with Cal. It wasn't a situation he looked forward to, but he wasn't about to renege on the promise he'd made his uncle. He didn't have to like his old man; he just had to look him in the eye and not want to punch him in the face. He'd get there eventually, but not today. Being with Ava would help. Working on the cabin helped, too. It provided a challenge and a purpose, and he hadn't been this excited about a project since Cal brought him into the business. He hadn't given much thought to taking over the business lately. Not that he didn't want to earn the right to do it, because he did—hell, yes, he did—but the urgency had dulled a bit, the desire had lost its sparkle.

How could anything shine next to Ava? She was the reason he'd been distracted and not salivating for the company; that and knowing he had to "make nice" to his father. But he never considered there might be a bigger reason he was avoiding his father, one that had nothing to do with past wrongs, bad choices, or grudges. It had to do with Ava Marie Ventori: keeping her happy, keeping her with him...*keeping her*.

Ava was on his mind when he ran into town, picked up a box of screws at the hardware store, and grabbed a chocolate éclair at Barbara's Boutique and Bakery. He stopped at Sal's to deliver the éclair, which earned him a bright smile and a kiss from Ava, along with a promise to thank him better in private. Twenty-eight minutes later, he was back at the cabin, and it looked like he had company. Law pulled into the driveway behind the late-model sedan and hopped out of his truck. The car door opened and a woman stepped out, one he recognized as his sister-in-law.

"Katrina? What are you doing here?" Law had spoken less than fifteen sentences to her the entire time she'd been married to Brett. Most included, *Hey, how's it going?* Or *Good to see you.* Always surrounded by other people, usually her husband.

"I need to speak with you. I can't stand by and watch your life unravel again. You don't deserve it and if I don't warn you, you're going to lose Ava."

Ava? A slow panic swirled from his belly to his chest. "Come inside so we can talk." He motioned for Katrina to follow and didn't speak again until she was settled on the couch, looking out of place and nervous in her coat and designer handbag. And diamonds. Lots of diamonds. Law slid into the chair next to her, kept his voice even. "Does this have to do with my brother?" Since the brawl, Law and Brett avoided each other, but when you live in a small town and your family has a business *and* money, and the oldest is obsessed with his importance, everybody knows who you are...and who the oldest is...

"May I have something to drink?" Katrina tucked a strand of pale blonde hair behind her ear. "I've been struggling over what to do for a week now and I need something to steady my nerves."

Brett's wife had always reminded him of a sparrow, timid, fragile, vulnerable to the harsh conditions, namely, a controlling husband. He hadn't known her before she married Brett and had only seen her a few times, the last was at his mother's funeral. She unbuttoned her coat, shrugged out of it, her thin frame wrapped in layers of wool: sweater, slacks, scarf. A cocoon of sorts, protecting her from outside threats. Was Brett one of those threats? "What would you like to drink? I don't have any wine, but I've got whiskey, bourbon, maybe a little vodka."

The woman sniffed, darted a glance at him. "Bourbon please." Pause, another sniff. "Neat."

Law fixed her drink, grabbed a water for himself, and made his way to the living room where he handed her the drink and sat next to her. He didn't miss the big gulp she took that drained half the glass or the way she licked her lips, savoring the taste. "Okay, what's this about Ava?"

One more drink, this one not quite a gulp, but certainly not a sip. "Brett wants to destroy you and Ava, and he's going to do it by discrediting you."

"Discrediting me?" Now that was interesting. And ridiculous. He shook his head, let out a quiet laugh. "He might find that hard to do when most of the town already thinks I'm pond scum. As for Ava, she's no fool. She won't fall for Brett's lies."

Those pale blue eyes burned with fear and anger. "That's what we all say, because we think we'll never fall prey to liars. We believe we'll know how to pick them out, pluck the truth from the lies, because we're smart, not gullible. But do you know what happens when the liar is so good he makes you question yourself and your own reality, even when the evidence is sitting right in front of you? The perfume on the suit jacket, the hotel receipt, the unexplained absences ... Even when your brain tries to register this information for what it is, you smother it, tell yourself it can't be true because he would *never* do this. He has a family, children, a role in the community, and you are his wife, the woman he's pledged his heart to, the woman he loves. But then one day you're walking down the street and you see the evidence staring back at you." She blinked, clutched the glass with both hands. "And you can't ignore the truth any longer."

Law reached out, patted her cold hand, gave it a squeeze. "I'm sorry, Katrina; nobody should have to live like that."

She swiped at her cheek, bit her bottom lip. "No, they shouldn't, but you'd be surprised how many of us do. We tell ourselves stories to get through it. Pretend, that's what we do, until one day we wake up and find ourselves trapped in the hell we've created."

So, Brett had cheated on her, probably more than once. Somehow, that didn't surprise him. Back in the day, when Law had been a jerk teenager, he'd thought his brother was perfect, something Law would never be. But a cheating husband? A man who disregarded his family? That was disgusting and inexcusable. "Did you ever think about divorce?"

She let out a sound that was a mix of pain and hopelessness. "Of course I have. I've even consulted an attorney, but Brett found out and threatened to take the children from me. He said he didn't care how much money it took, he'd make sure he got custody." She lowered her head, pinched the bridge of her nose. "Your family's too powerful. Brett would do what he said, even if he didn't want them. I can't risk that. Those children are my life." Her voice cracked, split open. "I can't lose them, no matter what I have to put up with to keep them."

What the hell was really going on? "Katrina, it sounds like he's been unfaithful, maybe more than once." He gentled his voice. "You don't have to put up with that. Just because he says he's going to do something doesn't mean he can. You know that, don't you?"

"He says I'll never see them… Said he'll tie it up in court and he won't have to pay me money and he'll blackball me in this town so I'll never get a job even though I have a teaching degree and a master's. You've been gone a long time, Law. You don't know your brother. He's nothing like you." She squeezed his hand, pulled hers away, and swiped at both cheeks. "He always told me about all the horrible things you did and how you disrespected your family and wanted nothing to do with anybody. But when you came home for the funeral, you didn't seem cruel at all. Brett was the one who made sure you knew you weren't welcome. And I think he convinced Cynthia to ignore you as well. She's not so bad, just confused about what's important in life. I have nothing against people who love their animals more than humans, but that doesn't give them the right to demean or ignore those who aren't as fortunate as they are. She'll learn one day. And your father? He's been lost since your mother died. He just wants to make things right with you because he knows that's what your mother would have wanted."

How did Katrina know anything about what his father wanted? "Did my father tell you this?"

"Yes. Several times. We used to have Sunday dinner and

somewhere between the first and second course, Montrose would mention your name. His voice would turn sad and he'd say how much he wanted to see you again and how he wanted all of you to be a family. Brett didn't like that. He'd say there was no room in the Carlisle home for cheaters or swindlers, and he'd say it with such sincerity, as though *he* weren't cheating on me, or swindling your father." Her eyes grew bright, her voice steady. "I can't prove it but he must be stealing from Montrose."

"Why do you say that?" Law took in the diamond studs, easily a carat, the diamond pendant, probably two carats...and the rings. How many carats in those two rings?

She caught him assessing her jewelry. "You think I care about these?" Katrina pointed to the diamond studs, the necklace and rings. "This is insurance, Law. I'd never get what they're worth, but at least they convert to cash." Pause, a long sigh. "Just in case."

Just in case? *Just in case what?*

"I don't care about the fancy lifestyle: the house, the cars, the maids. All I ever wanted was Brett, and now I can't stand the sight of him. He's cheating your father, and Montrose is going to get blindsided and robbed unless you expose him." She must have seen the doubt on his face because she added the missing piece that made her words take shape and gain credibility. "There's no way Brett can support two households without stealing."

"Two households?"

A hint of a smile crept over her face. "Two households, Law. Ours and his lover's. You can find her in Renova with their two children: a boy and a girl. I even know her name, and so do you."

Brett had children with another woman? What a bastard. "Who's the woman?"

"Paula Morrisen, the woman Roman was accused of getting

pregnant. You see where the problem is, Law? I doubt many people know Brett's the father, but that lie Paula told almost destroyed the Ventori family, and it certainly destroyed Roman for a long time. I heard all about it. Brett can't stand Roman, and he's jealous of your father's affection toward you. That's why I'm afraid he'll try and do something to hurt you and Ava." Her next words snuffed the oxygen from his lungs. "Don't let that happen. Please tell her before it's too late."

CHAPTER 20

Being intimate with Lawson Carlisle was all-consuming and surpassed her best fantasy—on so many different levels. The man knew how to please a woman with a touch, a kiss, a whispered word that made her believe she was the only woman in his world.

Law made her believe she *was* his world, but there came a time when she had to understand the rest of his world, starting with his family.

Ava knew all about the Carlisle mansion but she'd never been inside the place, never even ventured toward the circular driveway. That was for privileged visitors, not the daughter of a grocery store owner. But as she sat in the Carlisle library, Law didn't act like she was out of place. He smiled at her, held her hand, made her feel like she belonged—*with him*. Despite his questionable reputation and refusal to accept his family's lifestyle, he was still a member of one of the wealthiest families in Magdalena. He might not think that mattered, but it did. A lot.

"Relax," he said in a gentle voice, brushing a kiss on her temple. "There's no need to be worried."

Easy for him to say. He didn't know about the uncertain and

insecure parts she kept locked away deep inside, the ones that said maybe they really shouldn't be together and maybe it was about a lot more than the fact that he'd been a rich-kid-trouble-maker who was sent away by his own family. Maybe money and social class would always separate them. The faded jeans and navy sweater might be old, but they were high-end. Ava tried for a smile and a lighthearted comment. "Chandeliers? A double staircase? The marble foyer?" She forced the quiver from her voice, pushed out more truths. "Showcasing valuables under lights and glass might seem ordinary to you—" she pointed to the cabinet at the far end of the library that housed a collection of fancy crystal figurines "—but it's intimidating to someone who's only seen displays like that in magazines and museums."

He frowned, his expression filling with concern. "Don't do that to yourself, Ava. You're worth more than fifteen of those damned showpieces. I'm not asking for my father's approval, but I wanted you to meet him."

Their relationship was moving fast, filled with so much emotion, heat, and passion that she couldn't always think straight or in a logical sequence. Hadn't she told Law she wanted a no-strings thing with him? And then, hadn't she changed her mind when he told her that wasn't enough? They'd never talked about what that meant or where it would lead. But they should, shouldn't they? What if he meant long-term, as in building a life together? *Could* such a thing exist between them? They weren't like her brother and sister-in-law, or the Desantros, or the Cash-erdons who had rock-solid relationships. But maybe in time they could be if they trusted each other enough...loved each other enough... The truth behind her feelings for Law Carlisle burst through her, sucked the air from her lungs and made her dizzy. *She loved him* and a year or fifty years together wouldn't be enough.

"Take a sip of wine," Law whispered. "It will help your nerves."

She cast him a glance, still shaken from her sudden epiphany. "I'm not nervous." The raised brow and twitch of his lips said he didn't believe her. If he only knew...

The library door opened, stealing his next words that were no doubt more reassurances about his father as a man not to be feared. But when Ava turned and Montrose Carlisle approached —silver-haired, tall, in command—she doubted Law's assurances.

"Ava, my dear. What a delight to meet you." She stood and he clasped her hand in both of his, offered a smile that reached his eyes and made her relax a bit. "My son certainly has good taste."

Law snaked an arm around her waist, pulled her close, and shook his father's hand. "She's as beautiful inside as out."

The older man's smile spread over his elegant features. "Indeed. True love lasts long after the outward beauty fades." His voice dipped, filled with a sadness that smothered the room. "I regret Law's mother and I didn't have enough years together for her beauty to fade, though in my eyes, I know it never would have."

There'd been so many stories about Montrose Carlisle's controlling ways, his manipulative efforts, his swindling deals. But the man who stood before her was sad, perhaps heartbroken with grief for a wife who was no longer with him. The confession made her look at him without the stories, without the rumors or the judgment. Law seemed to appreciate his father's words because he pulled her closer, said in a gentle voice, "That sounds about right."

Ava glanced up to find him studying her, eyes bright, expression serious, as though she really *were* special, really *were* beautiful inside and out minus the insecurities, doubts, and occasional pettiness that sometimes plagued her. "I never met your wife but Law said she was a very special woman." He'd not been so kind in regard to his father, but how could a child forgive a parent who sent him away and gave up on him? Still, compassion filled her for the loss of his wife.

"She was an angel," Montrose Carlisle said. "A beautiful angel sent to me, though I didn't deserve her and—"

"Can I get you a drink?" Law cut his father off, his tone changing to what sounded an awful lot like anger mixed with annoyance.

Was it because of Montrose's last comment about Law's mother being an angel? Or because he said he didn't deserve her? Ava didn't miss the tenseness in Law's stance: stiff, unbending. Unforgiving?

"Whiskey?" Law bit out.

His father nodded. "Thank you. On the rocks."

Law released his hold on Ava and moved toward the liquor cabinet. She'd spent enough time with him to know when he wanted to change the subject, and his father must have sensed it too as he sank into his chair, let out a quiet breath. Ava slid onto the couch while Law fixed two drinks, crossed the room and handed one to his father. Could he not be a bit...kinder to the man, or at least not so obvious in his distaste?

His next words said apparently not. "Ava's never been here, and I wanted to show her that this place is just a structure, filled with the same stories as any other place where families grow up." *It's a damn mausoleum... No laughter, no joy, nothing without my mother...* He'd confessed this days ago, made her curious to see the house where he'd lived but never quite fit in. She knew all about not belonging, even though her postage-size house was a lot less significant than this one.

Law's father sipped his drink, nodded. "I could never say no to Law's mother. Evelyn was the queen of my universe, and when I lost her, I lost a part of myself." His eyes filled with tears, his voice cracked. "The other tragedy was watching my son leave."

Law downed his whiskey, blew out a long breath. "Past is past and there's no way to rewrite it."

Ava couldn't stand the pain on the older man's face and offered a gentle, "No, we can't rewrite it, but we don't have to live in it or be punished by it. It's our choice to move on and change."

"You're not only beautiful, but kind and compassionate. I wonder if you have forgiveness in your heart as well?"

Was he asking forgiveness from *her*? Or was this a general question? Ava glanced at Law, noted the clenched jaw, the pinched lips... As though he wanted to get as far away from this conversation as possible. She couldn't ignore Law's father, not when he might need the forgiveness she could offer. "Excuse me? Do you speak of forgiveness in general terms, or is there something more specific you're asking?"

Law jumped in before his father could respond. "My father speaks in generalities, Ava. That's one thing you'll learn about him. He doesn't admit to anything *or* commit to anyone unless he knows he's got the upper hand, especially if it means protecting the family."

"Lawson—"

"Sorry, I guess I still haven't mastered the finer points of subterfuge." He glanced at his watch, set his glass on the coffee table, and stood. "We've got somewhere to be. Thanks for the drink."

His father nodded, eased out of his chair, and clasped Ava's hands. "It's been a pleasure to meet you, my dear. I hope we'll see each other again soon."

"Thank you. I'd like that." Law might have issues with his

father, but there was still such a thing as common courtesy, and if he couldn't show it, she would.

He didn't speak to her until they were in his truck, heading back to the cabin. "My father wants forgiveness from everyone, even when it hasn't been earned."

His tone, the closed expression, the way he gripped the wheel, said he wasn't just upset; he was furious. But why? "I think he wanted to tell me something and I don't know why you shut him down."

"The man might seem innocent and bent on seeking absolution, but he still destroyed a lot of people in this town, and whether or not he's sorry now is really not the issue."

Why the sudden, intense anger? "Haven't we talked about forgiveness and not judging and accepting people for who they are? Was that all just talk? Did you not mean any of it?" The thought that he'd played her and told her what she wanted to hear made her queasy. What if the person she'd fallen in love with wasn't the real Lawson Carlisle? What if the real Law was the cold, unforgiving one sitting next to her?

Could she accept that?

He kept his eyes on the road, jaw clenching and unclenching as though he had a lot to say and none of it good. "Don't be naïve, Ava. There's always more to the story than just the story."

"Meaning? People aren't who they say they are? They're hiding behind a facade of who they want us to think they are?" The queasiness jumped from her stomach to her throat, spilled out in accusation. "What about you? Is there a story behind *your* story? Are you the person I've seen these past weeks, or are you someone else altogether? Someone you don't want me to know about?"

More jaw clenching followed by a clipped "You know who I am."

"Do I? Maybe I'm only seeing what I want to see, not what's

really there." He opened his mouth to respond, closed it. "Please, don't shut me out. Tell me what you don't want me to know; it's the only way this thing between us can go anywhere."

Another sigh, a muttered curse under his breath. "I know that, trust me, it's all I think about."

What was he hiding? Fear gripped her, squeezed hard, but she pushed on. "Please don't lie to me. Please just tell me the truth."

"I will. Soon."

CHAPTER 21

Magdalena fell in love with the river rocks that appeared in the checkout counter of Sal's Market. Soon the counter wasn't enough to carry the requested stock, so Lorraine Ventori suggested setting up a separate display and decided to call it River Rock Christmas. Since Ava had the connections to the anonymous artist, her mother asked if she could get more Christmas-themed designs, and also some of those love, hope and inspiration ones. *Seasonal are great, too*, Lorraine said. *I love them all.*

Soon, people stopped in the grocery store to ask Ava if the mystery artist took special orders.

Could we commission her, do you think?

I love the Gerbera daisies. Do you think she would paint a set of six for me?

Even Mimi Pendergrass, an artist in her own right, wanted a river rock display. *I'm thinking something for the entryway, maybe a bakery theme: cupcakes, breads, cookies...*

Pop Benito approached her one morning, raised a bushy brow and said in a conspiratorial voice, *Pizzelles would sure look good on one of those rocks, now, wouldn't they?* There was something in that look that said he knew more than he was letting on.

Ava spent most nights creating and painting the rocks while Law worked on the finish trim in the bathroom, cooked the meals, and made sure she got her rest. When her shoulders grew stiff and uncomfortable from too much crouching, he massaged them, and if she really looked worn out, he drew her a bath, poured two glasses of wine, and sat next to the tub while she soaked in the warm, scented water. Sometimes he even joined her.

This was what happiness felt like and it was all because of Law. He accepted her for who she was and she didn't need to pretend, didn't need to posture and pose or toss out big words or make up stories about what she wanted to do with her life. He didn't care that she was a bad cook, couldn't tell the difference between endive and escarole, or wasn't in a high-profile profession. He didn't even care that she spent her free time in sweatpants and his ratty old flannel shirts.

When would he realize that she didn't care about his past, his lack of financial means, or anything other than the moment he walked back into her life? They were good together and she wanted to be there for him because that's what real love did, but he had to open up for that to happen. What could be so horrible that he didn't want to tell her? She'd be patient a little while longer, but then the man was going to talk.

THANKSGIVING at the Ventoris was always about more than just food. Of course, there was the traditional feast: turkey, stuffing, mashed potatoes, candied yams, green bean casserole, homemade rolls, cranberry sauce, and pumpkin pie. But in the Ventori household, Sal and Lorraine believed in honoring their

Italian heritage with a side of cavatelli, braised short ribs, and cannoli. And would Thanksgiving be complete without the stories, old and new, most embellished and all enjoyed with a glass of Sal's homemade Chianti? And there was Lorraine Ventori's gift-giving, too: an ornament, a specialty coffee, a box of chocolates. But this year was different from the others because this year Law sat beside Ava, sipping wine, devouring turkey, potatoes, cavatelli, and smiling. Lots of smiling. Laughter, too. There was another difference with this year's Thanksgiving and it had to do with Sal. *He* was the one doing the gift giving.

Sal waited until coffee and pumpkin pie sat on the table, along with a platter of cannoli. Law patted his belly but didn't turn down pumpkin pie with whipped cream *or* a cannoli. Ava's father asked for the same serving and received a smaller portion along with a frown from his wife.

"Okay, okay, I know I have to watch my sweets." It was his turn to pat his belly, chuckle. "Pop says I'll be a fill-in for St. Nick if I keep going, but why is it that man can eat servings of everything and still look like a string bean?"

Ava's mother shot her husband a look. "It's called portion control, Sal."

"Bah. It's genetics, no doubt about it."

It was Lorraine's turn to chuckle. "Genetics might be part of it, but the extra donuts and heaping plates of pasta are the bigger part. Why don't you ask Pop how often he has seconds or if he's eating half a pound of spaghetti in one sitting? Maybe you should follow him for a day and match *his* food intake. I bet you'll triple it by dinner time."

Sal knew all about scowls, and the one he tossed his wife said too much information had been offered at the table. "Maybe. Maybe not. But isn't Thanksgiving a time to enjoy *and* overindulge? That's what I tell my customers, and if everyone starts counting calories and pushing food away, there won't be a business to sell."

Lorraine poured his coffee, dropped a hint of cream in the cup, and stirred. When he reached for the sugar, she shook her head. "Choices, Sal. It's all about choices."

He rubbed his jaw, darted a gaze to Ava and Law. "You know another name for nagging? It's called Lorraine Ventori."

"Papa!" Talk about embarrassment. Law must think her parents couldn't stand each other. He wouldn't know it was just their way and the sniping was a show of affection. *Show me a man who doesn't tell his wife the manicotti isn't creamy enough and I'll show you one who doesn't care about her.* Well. Still, was it necessary to be so darn honest? Apparently, her parents believed it was. She glanced at Law, caught his smile as he reached for her hand under the table, squeezed.

Sal patted his wife's hand, grinned. "That was a good one, wasn't it?"

Lorraine slid him a smile, her eyes bright. "Indeed it was, Sal. One of your best. I'll remember that one in case I want to use it on you." A pause, a raised brow. "Have you and Pop been practicing jabs with each other? Making sure neither of you has lost your touch?"

The red that inched from his thick neck to his round cheeks said he'd been found out. "A few."

"I appreciate the humor, Sal, but poor Law might not." Lorraine turned to Law, offered a sympathetic, "Our family has a strange way of showing we care about each other. Please don't be offended."

Law's expression lit up. "I'm not offended, Mrs. Ventori. I'm honored to be sharing this meal with you. Anyone can see how much you all care about one another and that's special." He paused, his voice dipping, "And rare."

He was talking about his own family and their lack of closeness. Ava squeezed his hand, wanted to tell him she'd make sure he never felt alone again.

Her father laughed, saluting Law with a cannoli. "We're a rare breed, that's for sure." His dark eyes landed on Ava and his expression softened. "And this old dog is finally learning that different isn't all bad. In fact, it can be very good." He set his cannoli on his plate, reached into the grocery bag resting beside him and withdrew three small boxes tied with string. "One for each of you," he said as he handed out the boxes. "I wrote your name on the lid so I wouldn't get them mixed up, but I suppose you could trade if you don't like the one you got."

His cheeks turned red, his voice gruff as he blustered through an explanation. "Pop said these are up and coming and they're a way to express emotions without saying the words." He cleared his throat, once, twice, three times. "At first I thought they were a lot of nonsense, but then I got to thinking about Angelo's words and how people are so busy with the cell phones and the computers they don't talk anymore." Sal pointed to the boxes. "What's inside there reminds us to talk and share." One more throat clearing. "Enough blabbering. Open your boxes."

Ava untied the string that looked like the kind her father used to make braciole. Had her father ever selected a gift for her on his own? That usually fell into the "Lorraine Ventori" category unless food was involved. Then, Sal made the recommendations and the only wrapping he used was the product packaging: prosciutto, hard salami, Buffalo mozzarella, Jordan almonds. She fingered the edges of the small box. It didn't seem like a food item unless it was some fancy chocolate. Unable to stifle her curiosity, Ava lifted the lid. And stared. A shiny white river rock with the words "Find your happiness" rested on a bed of pressed cotton, its bold red lettering staring back at her. She'd painted this a few days after she first ran into Law at Boone's Peak.

Law squeezed her hand, leaned close and whispered, "It's beautiful, and perfect."

"It's one of those river rocks we've started selling at the store, isn't it?" Her mother peered at the river rock in Ava's box, her face bright with excitement. "I'm so glad you came up with this idea." Her words shimmered with admiration. "They're simple and yet the meaning is so powerful."

"Open yours," Sal said, inching the box closer. Lorraine untied the string and seconds later let out a soft "Oh my." She lifted the vibrant blue rock, held it in her hands. "Heart. Home. Family."

"I thought you might like that one since you're always talking about your heart being with Roman or Ava or one of the grandkids." Sal placed a hand on his wife's shoulder, said in a gentle voice, "You're what made this place a home, Lorraine, and you're what keeps it that way."

She sniffed again, swiped at the tear. "Sal, I think that's one of the sweetest things you've ever said to me."

He scratched his chin, shrugged. "I'd say this rock painter knows how to make a person cry."

Lorraine nodded, laughed. "I'd say so." She hugged the rock to her heart, smiled through tears. "Thank you, Sal." She turned to Ava. "And thank you, dear, for bringing the river rocks into our lives."

If they only knew... What would they say if she told them *she* was the one who'd painted the river rocks, had been painting them for two years? She couldn't tell them about it yet, maybe not ever, but she could enjoy their excitement. "Law? Open yours." What would her father choose for him? Seconds later, Ava found out—and wished she hadn't. The rock was a shiny black with a bold silver scrawl that read *The answer is yes*!

"Huh." Law held up the rock, careful to avoid Ava's gaze and showed her parents. "Interesting."

"Isn't it?" Sal rubbed his jaw, nodded. "You can take that a lot of different ways, if you care to consider it."

"Yeah, guess you can." Law set the rock back in the box, closed the lid over it. "Thanks, Sal. I appreciate the thought."

Her father nodded, his dark eyes studying Law like he did when someone tried to tell him you could substitute Swiss chard for endive in wedding soup. "Happy to help, and if you ever feel the need to debate the meaning of that statement, my friend Angelo Benito is a top debater."

Law cleared his throat, shifted in his chair. "Good to know."

Could life get any more embarrassing? Why didn't her father just say, "When are you going to propose to my daughter?"

CHAPTER 22

Harriet Schuster was the reason Law got booted out of Magdalena and maybe she would be his redemption. Either way, he owed her an apology for the BS he'd pulled as the smartass kid who wrecked her car sixteen years ago. He'd never realized how much harm he'd done or the scars he'd left through his reckless behavior, but word had it, she was old and her time was short. She lived in a little bungalow on the far side of town, tucked away from onlookers and the curious, a place that needed a good coat of paint and some serious yard work. The house might have once been gray but had faded to dirty white, the paint on the shutters peeling in long strips, the trim gouged with rot. Overgrown hedges snuffed out the bottom of the windows, and the tiny beds on either side of the walkway sprouted weeds.

Were there no relatives or friends to help with the upkeep? There must have been a husband at one time since people referred to her as *Mrs.* Schuster, but he'd never heard about children, or even a cat living with her. The woman had been old sixteen years ago, and he figured she must be ancient now. When she opened the door, he realized ancient was a kind term.

"Hello?" Dark eyes narrowed to slits, multiplying the wrinkles crisscrossing her face. She leaned closer, turned her head to the right to reveal a hearing aid. "Who are you?" The voice rose, turned shrill. "Are you one of those boys peddling Internet services? I don't need any of that."

Law moved closer, spoke to her right ear. "No, Mrs. Schuster, I'm not selling anything. My name is Lawson Carlisle and I've come to apologize for the time I stole your car." If shock had a face, it would be Harriet Schuster's. The thin lips pinched, the squinty eyes widened, the pale face turned white.

"Lawson Carlisle?" She stepped back, positioned her cane to support herself, and repeated, "*Lawson Carlisle?*"

"Yes, ma'am. May I come in?"

"What do you want? Please, have you come to hurt me?" She backed up further, her thin legs shaking, real horror slithering through her voice. "Please, just leave me be. Please… Don't hurt me. I'm sorry. So sorry."

Law stepped inside, closed the door, and extended his hands palm upward. The woman was petrified of him, but why? "I'm the one who's sorry, Mrs. Schuster. I never should have taken your car and I definitely should not have blamed you for what happened to me because of it." The woman continued to back up until she reached a couch and collapsed into it.

"No, no, no…" She dipped a hand into her pocket, pulled out a handkerchief and wiped her nose. "What do you want?"

Law eased into the rocker beside her, careful to keep his movements slow, his voice calm. "I want to apologize for my behavior when I was a teenager. It took me years to admit I was the one in the wrong and you were only protecting what was yours."

The woman crumpled right in front of him. "I'm sorry. I didn't want to do it." She clutched the handkerchief between her gnarled fingers, shook her head until the frizzies bounced. "It was only a car and I didn't want to do it, but... I just wanted your parents to scold you, ground you, maybe, but never to send you away." More handwringing and head shaking, accompanied by a sorrowful, "I never wanted to do it, but I had no choice. I was forced."

Forced? "Mrs. Schuster, I don't blame you. I'm very sorry for what I did, and I'd like to understand what you were forced to do." He held her gaze, offered a smile. "Would you tell me what happened?"

She leaned toward him, her face scrunched into a thousand tiny wrinkles, and whispered, "I had to do it because if I didn't, my nephew would lose his job on account of the drinking and all. I couldn't have Johnny lose that job. What would happen to the children? How would he support them? His wife was sick so much of the time and the babies were so young. Johnny never missed work... Never. He just fell off the wagon on the week-ends, but by Monday morning he was ready to go. Didn't matter, though...all that mattered was making me say something I didn't want to... Something I knew would ruin your life, but I couldn't help it." Her voice turned desperate. "I had to save my nephew, and I am so sorry for what I did to you. Can you ever forgive me? God won't, I know that, and that's why the town ignores me and I've been riddled with ailments. It's punishment for what I did to an innocent boy."

How could his father do this? Bad enough he'd sent Law away, but to blackmail a poor woman so that the reason Law left town would appear necessary? *What kind of person did that?* Not one with a soul, that was for sure. "Mrs. Schuster, most people in your position would have done the same thing. I don't blame you, and if there's any forgiveness to be asked, it's me doing the asking. I'm so sorry for my father's actions."

"Montrose? Your father wasn't behind this. He didn't even know about it." A tear slipped along her wrinkled cheek. "He begged me to change my mind, said he'd do anything, pay anything, but I couldn't." Another tear fell, then another. "That poor man never knew he'd been betrayed by his own family."

The woman's words ricocheted from his brain to his heart, skidded to a halt somewhere between logic and disbelief. *Betrayed by his own family?* "I don't understand."

Harriet Schuster's lips flattened, her shoulders slumped. "I promised I'd never speak of it because I feared for my nephew's livelihood if I ever did. But now you're here and I can't keep it inside any longer, not with you thinking you've done wrong. *It was never you, Lawson.* I was angry and wanted you punished, but more to teach you a lesson in hopes also that your family would learn about discipline. But what they did to you, and what I was forced to do, ruined both of our lives."

"Mrs. Schuster, tell me the man's name."

"Man?" Her eyes grew wide, the thin lips opened to reveal a secret Law never saw coming. "There was no man, Lawson. It was your mother. She's the one who threatened to destroy my nephew if I didn't do exactly as she said."

"Did you know my mother blackmailed Harriet Schuster to get me out of town?" Law stood in his uncle's living room, hands fisted on hips, staring at the man who'd taught him about honor, integrity, and doing right, no matter the cost. Was it all a lie? Had the man brainwashed Law with ideals he didn't believe? Strung him along as part of some grand scheme to get him to do what? Become a Beaumont? Despise his father? Reject his siblings?

Well, if that were the goal, then he'd succeeded. Law was more Beaumont than Carlisle, and he *did* despise his old man. As for his brother and sister? He had as much feeling for them as he did for the seltzer water at the grocery store. None. Law sucked in air, waited for his uncle to make a great revelation. Or just admit what Law had already figured out.

The paleness around the man's lips and the shock etched across his weather-beaten face said he hadn't expected this kind of reunion. No, he probably hadn't. Neither had Law. He'd wanted a quiet night with a thick steak on the grill, a scotch or two, and easy conversation, but the meeting with Harriet Schuster ended all of that. *It was only a car and I didn't want to do it, but... I just wanted your parents to scold you, ground you, maybe, but never to send you away... I never wanted to do it, but I had no choice. I was forced.*

"Cal? Tell me what really happened. Did you convince my mother to blackmail Harriet Schuster and demand my punishment so I'd get booted to your place?" He paused, let his disgust trickle through his next words. "Did you script it all out for her, including the part about the nephew? You know, the one with the drinking problem and the kids?" The man took so long to respond Law thought maybe he wouldn't. The Calvin Beaumont he thought he knew would never attempt to conjure up a lie. Nope, he'd shoot straight and let honesty rule. But the one who manipulated lives and threatened little old ladies and their families? That man he didn't know.

Cal closed his eyes, dragged a hand over his face. "I swear I didn't have anything to do with it. Your mother would call and tell us how worried she was about you, how she thought you'd end up destroying yourself one day." He blinked his eyes open, swiped at the corners. "She'd beg us to do something before it ended with a funeral, but short of straight-out kidnapping you, there wasn't much we could do. Then one day your mother's tears stopped and she asked if you could stay with us, said something about divine intervention and the Lord providing. Made no sense to me or your aunt, but we listened and agreed." His concerned gaze burned into Law's. "Five weeks later you landed here."

Law stared at him, tried to comprehend what he'd just said. "Are you saying my mother devised the plan against Harriet Schuster?"

A nod, a sigh, and then "I hate thinking that, but there were too many coincidences. Maddie thought so too, and your aunt was never wrong about people. I should have confronted your mother, but I couldn't do it. I guess a part of me didn't want to know." Cal straightened, his expression shifting to one of sadness and regret. "You want to know the truth?" The man whose opinion and guidance Law valued more than anyone else's let out a bone-tired sigh. "Your mother was my baby sister and I loved her; we all did. None of us ever wanted to see Evelyn go without, and that included giving her things she shouldn't have. I'm not talking about an extra dollop of chocolate sauce on a sundae." A pause, another weary sigh. "I'm talking about your father."

"No surprise there. They never fit together and it didn't take long to figure that out." Law was no relationship expert, but shouldn't the parties involved at least share in a 50-50 relationship? The give-and take-stuff, the doing for the other even when you didn't want to do it? In the minimal time he thought about his parents' marriage, even a pain-in-the-butt teenager could see it was a mismatch with his father bent on pleasing his mother, no matter what the request. And his mother, so beautiful and refined, always having one more request...

"Your mother realized early on in her marriage that your father had deficiencies." Cal squinted, rubbed a stubbled jaw. "I'm not talking about a physical or mental issue because that would have been easier to fix. She was too good for him, and damn if we didn't all see it. But you can't do anything about a problem if you don't know one exists, now, can you? None of the family knew Montrose Carlisle existed until the day Evelyn brought him home and announced the pregnancy."

"Pregnancy?" *Pregnancy?*

"Yeah, Brett. Our father paid a lot of money to have the marriage certificate backdated, and when Brett was born, they'd already moved to Magdalena, so who would guess? I'll tell you who...nobody. Nice and neat, with no tarnish on Evelyn or the new baby boy."

"I did not expect that." They'd seemed happy as far as he could tell, but how much did a teenager pay attention to his parents' marriage?

"Right." Cal's lips pulled into a scowl, his gaze narrowed. "Montrose stood in the living room with his arm around Evelyn's waist and announced she was going to have his baby, but he intended to do right by her." The scowl deepened, the eyes burned. "Ha! The only *right* we were interested in was getting him out of her life."

"Looks like that didn't work." A pinch of what almost felt like sympathy inched through him but he smothered it.

"No, it didn't." Cal sucked in a deep breath, held Law's gaze. "And I've spent too many years trying to rewrite that story." His voice wobbled, cracked. "If I'm honest with myself, I have to admit Evelyn got the better end of that marriage, in every aspect. Your father worshipped her, gave her everything, no matter the cost to himself. She only had to show a hint of concern or displeasure, and Montrose would make it right for her...or try to... I know because she did the same to me." He cleared his throat, his eyes wet. "When she came to me about you, I thought it was the right thing to do, so I agreed that if the time and opportunity presented itself, Maddie and I would take you in. We never thought she'd *make* an opportunity for you, especially by way of threats and potential blackmail."

"All this time..." Law had spent years despising his father for booting him out of town when his mother had been behind it. *Because she'd wanted to protect him? Because she didn't want him to be a Carlisle? Why, damn it, why?*

"Was this about power or control? Did you agree to take me in to show my father how insignificant he was?" Despite his feelings for Montrose, this was just plain wrong. Nobody should control another person like that, no matter how much they loved them.

"It was about love and an inability to say no. Our family never learned what tough love was, and neither did your mother. She couldn't stand to see one of you kids hurting or in jeopardy, even if it was of your own making. There's more that you don't know about, but—"

"You mean how they saved Brett by pinning Paula Morrisen's pregnancy on Roman Ventori?" A small dip of his uncle's head said that was exactly what he meant. "Was my mother behind that, too?" When his uncle looked away, Law knew that meant she was. "How could you let her do it?"

"It was wrong, and if there was a way to make it right, believe me, I would."

CHAPTER 23

I f Ava had been given another chance, she would not have pushed Law to tell her what he'd been hiding. She would have waited and let the truth seep into their lives slowly, after they trusted each other more. But she didn't. No, she stood in his kitchen while he chopped green peppers for the chili he planned to make that evening and demanded he share. "Whatever you're hiding is going to tear us apart, you know that, don't you? One piece at a time, until we only tell what we think the other wants to hear, or what causes the least amount of grief." Frustration made her desperate. "Don't you want us to work? Law, just tell me now, because from my position, you're not all in."

Law set down the knife, wiped his hands on a dishcloth and met her gaze. "You think I don't want us to work? Maybe what I'm doing is *because* I want us to work. Ever think of that?" He shook his head, frowned. "One thing I learned pretty quick when I got back here is that you can't get away from your family. Guilty by name, associated by blood. Whatever they've done, you've done, whatever they've said, you've said." His gaze turned dark, the frown deepening. "Doesn't matter if the thought of what they've done or said repulses you. Nothing matters but the damn bloodline. If I'm a Carlisle, then I must be a self-serving, egotistical jerk—like my brother. Right?"

"No, that's not what I meant. I'd never judge you and you know that, but you're keeping something from me; I saw it on your face the night we visited your father." Ava moved toward him, touched his arm. "Tell me, Law. Trust me enough to tell me."

"I've never been in jail."

That's what he'd been hiding? "Oh. I wondered about that."

His brows pinched together. "Or juvenile detention."

"Okay."

"Or anyplace with bars." His jaw twitched, his nostrils flared.

"Even though rumors had you in both places?" He nodded, looked away. "So, where were you?"

"My aunt and uncle's farm in Pennsylvania." He slid his gaze to hers. "It's where I learned how to be a decent human being. It's as far away from life in the mansion as living in this cabin is."

"So, why do you let everyone, including me, believe otherwise?" That's what she really wanted to know. Was it to prove a point, show the town how much he didn't care what they thought, or was it a way to keep the real Lawson Carlisle hidden?

He shrugged. "It seemed easier at the time."

"Easier?"

A hint of a smile crept over his lips. "I didn't say it was smart. I said it was easier."

Ava crossed her arms over her chest, sighed. "Uh-huh. Just so you know, that's a ridiculous reason to trash your reputation." But it wasn't horrible, and if that's what he'd been hiding, she could absolutely live with it. "So, that's what's been bothering you? You didn't tell me you weren't in jail or juvenile detention?" She'd hoped he'd laugh and the whole situation would seem funny, but the look on his face said there was more. A lot more.

"Not exactly."

"Okay then.

He cleared his throat, fiddled with a piece of green pepper. "Do we really have to have this conversation right now? I thought you were hungry. Can't it wait until after dinner, or maybe tomorrow?"

She eyed him, not happy with the avoidance tactic. "No, it can't. You had days to tell me, and you didn't. If you care about me and think we have a future together that isn't going to explode in the next two seconds, then you better tell me now."

"I'm not just a nobody and the youngest Carlisle with a broken-down truck and nothing to his name. I'm a businessman who works *with* my uncle, not for him, and he's a lot more than a farmhand. Calvin Beaumont owns tracks of land and real estate investments worth millions. He's got more money and clout than any of the Carlisles, and I guess you could say that since he considers me family, so do I."

"You let me believe you had nothing? Why would you do that?"

Those green eyes turned bright, his voice soft. "I could say it was because I wanted you to love me for myself and not because I had money, but that would be a lie. I knew from the minute I saw you at Boone's Peak that you didn't care about money or status. This was always about my family and it was easier to keep the story straight if you thought I was broke. That truck I've been driving is my uncle's beat-around. I've got three cars: an Aston Martin, a Mercedes, and a Cadillac SUV, but I wasn't going to drive one of them into Magdalena for everyone to see and start asking questions. My plan was to get in and out of this town without anyone getting to know the real me." His voice turned rough. "And then I met you."

His confession pierced her soul because she'd believed he wouldn't lie to her and maybe technically he hadn't. No, but he'd withheld a heck of a lot of truth and let her form her own opinions from the skewed information he fed her. Was that honest? Was that a relationship? Was that who the real Lawson Carlisle was? "Is that everything? And if there's more, this is the only time you get to own up to it." She squared her shoulders, forced out the next words. "I'm serious, Law. Tell me the truth, all of it."

He dragged a hand over his face and said, "Okay, but... It's about Roman and Paula Morrisen." His voice cracked. "I'm so damn sorry."

Roman and Paula Morrisen? The nightmare that suffocated her family and split them apart for years? The disaster that drove her brother out of town and kept him away, leaving Ava to fix her parents' heartache—one that could never be fixed? "What about Paula Morrisen? Tell me, Law. What did your family have to do with that?"

"Brett's the father; Roman was just the fall guy."

CHAPTER 24

"**B**rett? He and Paula Morrisen? How can that be? He had a girlfriend and I never saw him and Paula together. Ever." It made no sense. Yet in some way it did, especially after Paula started with the accusations that landed straight at Roman's feet. And then there was the family's sudden departure from town. It was almost too easy, too smooth, and what about the attempts to discredit those who maintained Roman's innocence? It didn't seem to matter whether he was innocent or guilty. All that mattered was pinning the deed on her too-kind brother. "Does Roman know? And what about my parents? Do they have any idea what really happened and who was behind it?"

The agony on his face spread through his words. "I have no idea, but if they don't, do I tell them? Do I dredge up the past and uncover old wounds?" He clasped her hand, brought it to his chest. "Do I risk losing us? I feel like your father is finally giving me a chance, and I don't want to lose that... I'll do anything *not* to lose it." He moved toward her. "Anything."

Ava believed him, but the question was, would *she* do anything not to lose what they had, even if it meant deceiving those she loved? "How could they? Didn't your family care if they ruined a person's life? Was it all about saving one of their own, no matter what?" Roman had been so devastated by the accusation and worse, that his own father questioned his innocence, that he'd turned bitter and distrustful. Maybe that's what had driven him to make a bad first marriage. The fallout from Brett Carlisle's lies had affected all of them and it had taken *years* to recover.

She'd just begun to believe life could be good, she could have a chance at real happiness, and now? The family of the man she loved had almost destroyed hers? Lies, cheating, deceit—*this* was what she'd always believed the Carlisles were about. But there was so much more to uncover before she decided whether to tell Roman and her parents the truth or bury it. "How did you find out?"

"Katrina paid me a visit; told me the whole sad story." He shook his head, said in a disgusted voice, "There's a lot more, too. Seems my brother never stopped seeing Paula and now they've got two children in a fancy house in Renova. Katrina knows about it and hates him for it, but she's trapped. She says she wants to leave but he's threatened to get custody of the children, no matter what he has to do to get it." More disgust filtered his words. "And of course, he'll blackball her so she'll never find a job anywhere near Magdalena."

This. This was one of the many reasons Ava avoided relationships. People you trusted lied to you. People you loved didn't love you back or they didn't love you enough to be honest or keep their promises. Brett Carlisle had a wife and two children, money, and a fancy lifestyle, but it wasn't enough for him. He needed the mistress and the other children too, the secret family who treated him like a king and expected nothing but an occasional visit and a comfortable house. Or did they? Were they his *real* family? Were Katrina and her children merely possessions he no longer cared about but wouldn't give up? Surely Brett had once loved Katrina; maybe in some way he still loved her.

But look what he'd done. Were all relationships doomed to end in disaster and heartbreak?

Was it only a matter of time before Roman knew that kind of heartache with Angie? No, she couldn't believe that would happen to them. Or Nate and Christine Desantro. Not Tess and Daniel Casherdon either. *But what about Ava and Law?* He was from a different class, ones who knew power and money and getting their own way, and while he might shun his family and their lifestyle, he *still* belonged to a family that had power and money. He must have sensed what she was feeling because he pulled her to him, cupped her chin, and said, "I'm *not* my brother, Ava. I'm not like him or the rest of the Carlisles. I'm just me. You know that, don't you?"

But she didn't know that, not really.

"Ava? Please, don't shut me out." Law leaned in, kissed her softly on the mouth. "I need you." And then the words she'd waited forever to hear slipped out. "I love you."

Lawson Carlisle loved her. Would that love be enough to carry them through the hardships all couples faced at one time or another? Did she want it to be? Was she willing to stand by him when he told her family what his had done? She didn't know if she could do it. Ava fixed her gaze on his chin, forced out the truth. "I'm going home now. I need to think. I'm sorry, but I need some time alone to figure this out."

"Sure." He moved away, said in a quiet voice, "I love you, Ava, and I want us to work. *I'm not my brother.* I'll tell Roman and your parents, whatever you want, just don't shut me out."

Loving Law Carlisle was never going to be easy, but Ava hadn't thought it would be impossible. She needed to talk to someone, but who could help? She spent the next two days considering life without Law. She would be back to her old self:

alone, empty, miserable. There would be no expectations or anticipation... No sheer happiness at seeing another person, hearing his voice, enjoying his touch. The days would stretch long and lonely and the nights would be unbearable. If they told her family about Brett and Paula, then they'd have to face the wrath that entailed, and nobody wanted to be on the other end of Ventori anger.

Would they refuse to accept Law? Call him no-good and lump him with his untrustworthy relatives? They couldn't actually *demand* Ava break it off with him, but they could put on the pressure and for a tight-knit family like hers, that was as good as giving him the boot. The relationship would be doomed before it had a chance to fully blossom. Ava needed guidance and someone with a clear head who could point out a path through the landmines in this situation. There was only one person in this whole town who could give her both: Angelo "Pop" Benito. When she called him after work one afternoon, he didn't seem surprised by her request to visit him. In fact, the tone of his voice said he'd been expecting her call. When she arrived, Pop invited her in with a hug and an invitation to dinner.

"My daughter-in-law sent me a loaf of fresh-baked bread and a batch of minestrone soup. Good stuff, loaded with the healthy greens and just the right amount of salami. Ramona knows how I like my salami, but she sure is stingy with it. If you haven't tasted her bread, then you haven't tasted Heaven. Your father's a big fan of it, but we don't tell your mother about it." He raised a bushy brow, his dark eyes lighting up behind his glasses. "You can't tell her either. It will be our secret."

Ava nodded and repeated in a soft voice, "Our secret." What would Pop say when she told him *her* secret? *Brett Carlisle is the father of Paula Morrisen's child, and rumor has it they share another one, and he's keeping a secret family in Renova.*

Pop asked about the grocery store, whether her father was

obeying the rules, and if her mother had caught him eating the donuts. They shared a glass of Chianti, two bowls of minestrone soup, and the best homemade bread Ava had ever tasted. She'd heard the stories about Ramona, Cash's aunt, and how she'd married Pop's son, Anthony. They were the most unlikely couple ever, and yet Ava had seen them together and they seemed perfect for each other. Maybe love could conquer differences.

But lies and the betrayal of a family? Could love conquer that?

"Okay, young lady, why don't you tell me what's on your mind because the anticipation's gonna give me indigestion—" he slid her a smile, placed his hands over his belly "—and then I'll have to blame it on the minestrone and Ramona won't be happy about it." *Tsk-tsk* and a shake of his head. "That woman takes her cooking seriously and a person does not want to cross her, especially when the meals are as good as any fancy restaurant." He chuckled. "And free."

Word had it nobody dared cross Pop's daughter-in-law or her no-nonsense attitude. Ava hadn't ever actually spoken to the woman, but she'd heard the tales about the *witch in black who never smiled.* But Sal had a different recollection of Ramona, one that included words like *down-to-earth, practical,* and *no-nonsense.* He said anybody who gave up her own plans to raise a child that wasn't hers and then fought like the devil to protect that child, no matter his age was truly special.

Of course, the child he meant was Cash Casherdon—the former bad-boy troublemaker who reminded her a lot of Law. Ava cleared her throat, searched for the right way to broach the subject, ended with the short version. "I was made aware of a wrong committed against my family, and I don't know if I should tell them or not." She turned toward Pop, her gaze inching past the large portrait of his dead wife, Lucy. People said he talked to her and they said he swore she answered...

"Well then, that's a problem, isn't it?" Pop shifted in his chair, gave a double nod. "You ready for a pizzelle yet?"

Ava shook her head. "Not yet." She hadn't eaten much these past few days, but spending time with Pop Benito made her forget her heartache and she'd finished two bowls of minestrone and three slices of bread *with* butter. Way more than she needed to eat.

"Just let me know when you want me to fix a plate because dinner's not complete without a pizzelle. Now, let's think on your situation. Are you friends with the person or persons who 'made you aware' of the wrong?" When she nodded, he continued. "Then it gets tricky. I'm guessing the wrong is a doozy or you wouldn't have looked so pale when I opened the door. Of course, if you have a close connection to the person who told you—" he shot her a look, raised a brow "—and if that person's related to the wrongdoers, well then, that's what I call an inch short of disaster."

The expression on Pop's face said he knew more than he was letting on. But what exactly did he know? Had he figured out Law was the one who'd told her, or was that just a calculated guess? Maybe that's why he'd asked about the close connection part, so he could confirm his suspicions. The man was tricky and if a person weren't careful, they'd fall right into his trap of fancy footwork and information sharing. Still, if she weren't honest with him, how could he help? Ava sucked in a breath and offered the whole truth. "I suspect you've already got a good idea what I'm going to tell you, but I'll say it anyway. Law Carlisle told me. It's about what happened between his family...and mine." She had to keep going before she lost her nerve. "Do you know anything about Paula Morrisen's accusation against my brother? The real story, not the manufactured one?"

"I heard things. Always suspected there was more to that story than what came out of that girl's mouth, but those were difficult times and there was a hard sell going on around here. Nobody wanted to stop and think it through. All they wanted was a name, didn't even matter if it was true or not. That's what happens when emotion takes over and crowds out common sense." He shook his head, glanced at the portrait of his wife. "Those were some dark days for a lot of us."

"My father thought Roman was guilty, and that accusation tore our family apart for a lot of years." Memories of those days and the pain that came with them shot through her, singed her soul. It was that pain that had forced her to try and be the perfect daughter, find the perfect life, ultimately choose the wrong man. "I tried to do things that would make up for what happened to Roman, especially later when he never came home and I felt like an only child. There's so much pressure to keep parents happy when you see their despair and sadness. I couldn't do it." She blinked hard, fought the tears. "I just couldn't. I wasn't strong enough, or mature enough, or maybe *I* just wasn't enough. Maybe I'd never have been enough, even if I did everything exactly as they wanted…because I wasn't Roman."

Pop reached for her hand, gave it a gentle squeeze. "Ava Marie, your parents have always been proud of you."

"Thank you, but that's not exactly true. Who has an almost fiancé who cheats on them and who decides to drop out of a nursing curriculum to pursue art? And who can't tell escarole from endive? They didn't understand that *I* wasn't Roman, that I couldn't be perfect or even half perfect, and that I was going to mess up. But what they didn't understand was that I'd never give up trying to find my own way, whatever that meant or wherever it took me. Shouldn't that have counted for something?" Her voice drifted, her throat clogged with tears. "They gave up on me and then they settled. By the time I hit thirty, they just hoped I wouldn't end up alone. I think my father wanted a grandchild, even if there wasn't a husband."

"Sal has some strange ideas and it doesn't make them right. He's opened his eyes since Roman and Angie got together and the heart attack shook him up. Nowadays he's more bluster than anything else and he just wants you to be happy, even if it's with that Carlisle boy."

"Did he say that?"

Pop shrugged. "He implied it, and I can read between the lines."

"But what would he say if he knew it was Law's family who set up Roman and Brett was the one who got Paula pregnant?" Ava hadn't been sure Pop knew about the Carlisle's manipulative tactics to destroy her family, but when his expression went from sad to sadder, it was obvious her words were no surprise.

"Did something happen with you and Lawson? Did you have a falling-out over this mess? Maybe he even offered to make it right and you can't get past what his family did to yours so you're thinking about giving him up?" He squeezed her hand again. "Don't do it, Ava. Lawson Carlisle is a good boy and he cares about you. You care about him, too, if that look on your face says your heart is aching. That boy's never had a person accept him for who he was... It was all about Brett and keeping the mother happy. Don't know about the uncle and aunt who took him in, so I can't say." His expression softened. "Love him for himself. And don't worry about your parents or Roman or what they'll say when they find out who's behind the pregnancy mess." Another squeeze of her hand and then a gentle "Because they already know and they've known for a long time."

CHAPTER 25

Ava debated confronting her parents with Pop's assertion that they knew the truth behind Paula Morrisen's pregnancy. If she did, they might offer up details Pop hadn't, but they might also inquire about Law and why she wasn't spending time with him. That was something she didn't wish to discuss, not when she hadn't spoken to him in four days.

It was time to have the conversation she'd been thinking about since the night she learned the truth about Brett and Paula. Better to do it in person, but easier to handle over the phone. Ava sighed, knowing she'd choose right over easy when it came to Law. She grabbed her cell, punched out his number, and waited. She did not expect his voicemail to kick in, but when it did a swirl of panic crept through her. Was he avoiding her? Had he grown tired of waiting for her to figure out how and *if* he fit in her life?

He wouldn't just quit on her.

Would he?

More panic shot through her, squeezed her belly and made

her nauseous. Had he decided she wasn't worth the effort or the hassle?

Ava had never been known for rational behavior, especially when emotions took over and choked out logic and common sense. Fifteen minutes after the phone call that landed in Law's voicemail, she made a flimsy excuse to her parents about running an errand, grabbed her jacket, and headed toward the cabin. Another three inches of snow had fallen since noon and while the main roads were clear, the back one leading to the cabin hadn't been plowed. That meant snow and possible ice. Ava crept along, sliding her way toward the cabin amidst a string of intermittent prayers and curses. When she pulled into the unplowed driveway, Law's truck wasn't there.

Now what?

The lack of tire tracks said he hadn't been home all day. So, where was he and why hadn't he answered her call? Magdalena was small but they had decent cellular service—unless a person wanted to pretend they didn't. She'd done that a time or two herself when her parents asked why she hadn't answered her phone. It wasn't like she could tell them she and Law were preoccupied, as in naked and in bed. White lies served their purpose, especially if they were told to protect parents from too much information regarding their adult children.

Ava turned off the car, opened the door, and stepped into the cold night air and six inches of white stuff. When Law got back, they were going to have a conversation about travel and phone etiquette: let the other person know when you plan to be gone, and don't ignore phone calls unless you're driving and the roads are treacherous—like tonight. She didn't bother to acknowledge that she'd told him she needed time and space to think about their situation, or that she'd blown him off for four days. None of that mattered because Ava was worried about Law, and once she saw his face and knew he was okay, she planned to let the worry turn to real anger.

She crunched toward the front steps, banged on the door despite shreds of common sense that told her he wasn't home. A muttered curse later, Ava tried the door and found it unlocked. "What the..." Of course, she knew better than to enter a dark cabin that had been left unlocked and unattended for several hours, especially if said location didn't belong to her. *None of your business* shouted back at her but she ignored the warning, stomped her feet on the rubber mat and stepped inside. The scent of pine and cedar reached her, made her think of Law and outdoors. Ava flipped on the foyer light, squinted into the darkened living room.

Well, he certainly had made a mess of the place, despite his comments that he liked order and neatness. Magazines were strewn on the coffee table, his laptop perched on the couch, two coffee mugs and an empty beer bottle sat on the end table. And were those peanut shells in a bowl? On the floor? So much for order and neatness. Ava kicked off her boots, shrugged out of her jacket, and looked around. Three flannel shirts had been balled up on the seat of a chair, one tossed on top of the other, as though cast aside in a rush.

What the heck had he been doing?

The place was a disaster. She worked her way to the kitchen to find an equally trashed area: dirty dishes stacked in the sink, a frying pan on the stove with remnants of egg in it... Ava grabbed her cell phone from her back pocket, tried Law's number again. Still no answer. This time, she didn't leave a message. Who knew when he'd be home? Would it be tonight, tomorrow, next week? If there was a chance it might be tonight, then she was going to wait for him because they needed to talk. She scanned the kitchen and the living room, rolled up her sleeves and got to work, practicing what she'd say when and if Law returned tonight.

An hour and half later, the place was neat and organized, like she remembered it. She tied up the last of the kitchen trash and set it by the back door. Then she made her way to the bedroom and turned on the light. The first thing she spotted was the river rock she'd given him a few weeks ago: vibrant blue with red hearts and silver swirls. Had he been as miserable and confused as she'd been these past days? Was that why the place was a wreck? Had *she* done this to him? Pop told her Law had never known what it was like to be loved just for himself.

And what had she done? She'd tossed him aside, questioned their relationship at the first sign of trouble, even when the trouble hadn't been his fault. That was not how a person showed she cared. Ava had a lot of apologizing to do and it was time to start truly trusting again. She slipped out of her jeans and sweater, pulled on one of Law's flannel shirts, and crawled into bed. Minutes later, she fell into a deep sleep...

It was the soft brush against her temple that woke her. She blinked into the dimness of the room, spotted Law leaning over her, his expression unreadable. "I came to see you, but you weren't here... And you didn't answer my calls..." *Where have you been? Did you realize I'm not as perfect as you thought I was? Did you decide I'm not worth the trouble?*

He straightened, stared down at her, looking tired and worn out. "I was on my way back from my uncle's and the roads were horrible. I didn't hear my phone." He lifted a shoulder, fixed his gaze on the strip of flannel peeking from the covers. "I waited three days for your call and figured it wasn't coming." His gaze slid to hers, burned with intensity. "Can't say I blame you. My name comes with a lot of baggage."

She tossed back the covers, sat up and reached for his hand. "I'm sorry. I was so wrong about you. You aren't like the rest of your family. I knew that, but fear made me question it. What happened is not about you, Law." She knelt on the bed, wrapped her arms around his middle, hugged him close. "It's about me and all of my ridiculous insecurities. I've got to learn to trust if we're going to make it, and I so much want us to make it."

"I would never do anything to hurt you, but I can't protect you if you don't let me in." He stroked her hair, his voice gentle. "Caring about another person and opening up leaves us raw and exposed, and I hate like hell to feel that way." He blew out a breath, stroked her back. "But I'm willing to do it to have a chance with you. I've never told any woman that before, but you're worth it, Ava Marie Ventori. Now, it's up to you to decide if I'm worth it."

"You are." She hugged him tighter. "Can you forgive me for not trusting us enough?"

"I'll always forgive you." He tilted her head up, held her gaze. "I love you. I want us to work. But I've got to know that you really want it, too."

There was no sense trying to fight the tears as they slipped down her cheeks, threatened to choke her words. "I love you, Lawson Carlisle—every part of you—and I do so very much want us to work."

He cupped her chin with his fingers, leaned forward and placed a soft kiss on her lips. "Thank you."

She sniffed. "I can't promise I won't do something foolish again, but I'll try not to, and I'll talk to you when the doubts sneak in." She swiped at her cheeks, sniffed again. "I want you to promise to do the same. We're a lot alike, which is good and not so good."

His lips twitched, pulled into a smile, and for the first time in days her heart lightened, filled with hope. She returned the smile, raised a brow. "Now, about the shape of this house. Mind telling me what hurricane hit this place while I was gone?"

He cleared his throat, shook his head. "It was a hurricane all right; her name was Ava. You turned my world upside down the other night and not in a good way. I don't like feeling unsettled and I haven't been so unsure of myself since I was a teenager. Don't walk out on me again and leave me in limbo. If there's a problem between us, we've got to work it out together. No more shutting down, okay?"

She nodded, her chest aching for the pain she'd caused him. "No more shutting you out, I promise. Guess we're going to have to act like responsible grown-ups and talk about things when they bother us...or at least, I will."

"Deal. Thanks for cleaning up the place. I really appreciate it. If it makes me look any better, I *was* planning to clean up in the morning. Living in a mess like this makes me irritable." It was his turn to raise a brow. "More irritable than I already was, and you have no idea what that was like."

"No, but I'd like you to tell me." She smiled up at him. "I'd like you to tell me everything, Law, because I want to be here for you when your days are bad and your mood is dark and your family disappoints you... or I do. I want to be here for you —always."

His fingers trailed from her neck to her cheek, traced her lips. "Okay then. I've got a long story for you and it's not a good one. I'll tell you how I've been blaming my father all these years for something that wasn't his fault." Law sat on the edge of the bed, slung an arm around Ava and pulled her close. "I paid a visit to Harriet Schuster because I wanted to apologize for my past bad behavior with the car incident. Imagine my surprise when *she* was the one who wanted to apologize. Seems poor Mrs. Schuster has been harboring guilt for something she was forced to do."

His arm tightened around her, his voice dipped. "My family blackmailed her to push for my punishment. She didn't want to do it, said all she really had hoped for was that I might learn about tough love: a punishment that didn't include jail or sending me away. But my family blackmailed her to have me sent away. *Who does that to their own flesh and blood?* The poor woman had no choice, not when they threatened to make sure her nephew's employer found out about his drinking problem. He had a wife and kids, a job; he was a good employee. There was no reason to bring up his drinking, but my family was going to use it against him to get what they wanted."

Ava buried her head against Law's chest, tried to take some of the anger and disappointment from him. "It's all so wrong and I should have been here for you. Oh, Law, I'm so sorry."

"I just need to know you'll stick with *us* from now on."

"I will. I promise."

He brushed his lips over the top of her head, let out a quiet sigh. "When I went to apologize to Mrs. Schuster, I never antici-pated there would be a whole other level of deceit tied into that visit."

From this second on she would stand by Lawson Carlisle, no matter what, and she would support him and believe in him. She touched his hand, whispered, "Your father was behind this, wasn't he?"

"I wish it was my old man, but it wasn't him." His voice split open with a raw pain. "My mother was behind all of it, said she needed to protect me, no matter what. Yeah, no matter if it ruined other people's lives... Looks like I've been hating the wrong member of the family all along."

Ava's heart ached for him. "I don't want you to hate anyone. It tears your soul apart and you're worth so much more than that." Ava eased her arms around Law's waist, framed his face with both hands. "We will get through this pain together, I promise you that. Let me shoulder some of this burden." She leaned in, placed a soft kiss on his lips and whispered, "Let me be your family."

When they made love, there was a new honesty and a pure vulnerability that had not been there before. Ava opened her heart to him, offered her soul and a promise to love him forever. There were no words as they joined their bodies, their hearts, their future in a union of hope and new beginnings. As Law lay next to her, his quiet breath fanning her hair, Ava breathed in his scent, closed her eyes and vowed to love this man. No matter what.

CHAPTER 26

Christmas was a time for families, gatherings, and that damn elusive hope. Wasn't that what the cards and movies pushed? Happiness and joy for all? Spending time with loved ones far and near? Families coming together for food and drink?

Right? Not Law's family, but he'd believed this year would be different because Ava Marie Ventori was in it. This year would be about promises and hope and setting new traditions. But he hadn't counted on his brother trying to destroy him and a chance with the woman he loved, and that's why he'd been blindsided when it happened.

A few days before the first Christmas Law was actually looking forward to, Brett showed up at the cabin with a manila envelope in his hands, a too-smug smile on his face. The man really did deserve another punch in the face, but it was Christmas and Law was not going to stoop to his brother's level. *Your brother wants to start a battle with you*, Cal had said the other night when Law told him about the text messages he'd been receiving from Brett the last few days with vague innuendoes about how *change was coming* and *the truth always surfaces*.

He hadn't mentioned it to Ava because he didn't want her to see how really screwed up the relationship dynamics in his family were. Plus, he thought she might confront Brett, which was not going to happen.

It shouldn't have surprised him when Brett showed up at the cabin the next afternoon, acting like he had a big secret to share, one that involved Law, and not in a good way. Of course, the guy couldn't get right to the point in six sentences or less. No, he made Law suffer with his I'm-the-real-victim-here speech and then followed up with talk about Ava.

It was the mention of Ava's name that almost forced Law to toss his brother from the house, but curiosity regarding the contents of the manila envelope in Brett's hand, made him hesitate.

"I've been hearing all about you and Ava Ventori. 'Aren't they a great couple? Meant to be together… Perfect… Wouldn't be surprised if Law ended up running the company…'" Brett's lips twisted, spilled out pure venom. "Even the old man's betting there's going to be a marriage. Ha, what the hell do you know about a wife and a family? It all might look good to you right now because everything's new and fresh, but wait a couple years until the kids start coming and the wife starts bitching and you look at her and wonder how you landed in this place. Do that, Law. See how it changes you when you have to follow expectations and you can't do what you really want to do." He scowled. "You're no different than me, and you'll find out soon enough how it doesn't matter what you want because life gets in the way and takes your choices from you."

"What the hell are you talking about? Why are you here? Why don't you just take your miserable self and leave?" He wanted to add, *Go to your other family, the one you have with Paula Morrisen in Renova*, but stopped himself. Some discoveries were better kept secret, at least for now.

His brother's laugh was harsh, cold. "Fine, I'll leave, but when your perfect world crashes, I want you to know I'm the one behind it." He tapped the manila envelope against his hand. "See if you can work your way out of this one. It's not going to be the same as when you left sixteen years ago. You should have been sent to jail or the detention center for what you did, but they bailed you out instead and shipped you off to Hicksville, Pennsylvania." Another laugh, this one colder, harsher. "Life on a farm with our hillbilly uncle. Yeah, bet that looks good on a résumé." He snickered. "Bet you don't even know what a résumé looks like. Why would you, when you've got no skills and nothing to offer?"

Law closed the distance between them, stopped when he was a punch away, balled his hands on his hips. "Why are you so miserable, and why do you hate me so much? I never did anything to you."

"Because you got away... Because nobody expected *anything* from you, and that made it so much easier to do whatever you wanted. Me? I had to do what was expected of me, what the Carlisle name demanded as the first son."

Was he talking about the business or was he talking about Paula Morrisen? "You think you had it rough? At least they wanted you and didn't send you away. You were the golden son and I was the afterthought who was just too much trouble. But it's up to me to live my life the way I see fit and stop blaming everybody else, including family, for a life I didn't recognize. Maybe you should do the same, Make the tough choice, Brett." His next words were as close as he'd get to mentioning trouble with Katrina. "You don't like where you are or what you're doing, change it. You've got a miserable marriage? Get out. Take responsibility for yourself and don't blame Katrina or the kids or anybody else for your choices."

"Have you been talking to my wife? Did she tell you something? She's got issues and you better not go near her."

"Why don't you want me to talk to Katrina? Is there something you're trying to hide?" Law crossed his arms over his chest, waited for his brother's response. Whatever he said would be a lie, no doubt about it. The question was how big and how deep a lie.

"Yeah, keep that thought, because you're going to need all the psychology you have to figure your way out of this one." He handed Law the manila envelope. "Merry Christmas, brother. And happy New Year. Gotta go." Brett turned to leave and when he had his hand on the knob, he glanced over his shoulder. "Everything that's in that package has already been sent to Roman and Ava Ventori. And if you're wondering why, call it payback for all the years I had to hear how much the old man missed you and how much our mother loved you. I tossed a little something in there for Roman Ventori, too. Bastard had the audacity to interfere with my personal business. Let's see how he likes it when someone does the same to him. Once they read what I sent them, your life is over. They'll never trust you again." He smiled. "Welcome to my world where hell is home."

Law ripped open the manila envelope and pulled out what looked like a contract between a company called Pink Oleander, Inc., and Sal's Market. He scanned the pages, read about the company that wanted to purchase the business with the intent of turning it into a chain grocery store. What the hell? Who was Pink Oleander, Inc.? He'd been working with Sal, looking at the financials and trying to come up with a list of potential buyers. This company wasn't on the list so how had Sal's name ended up on a contract? The man would never sell the grocery store to anybody who wanted to convert it to a chain grocery store. How did Brett get his hands on this, and why had he sent it to Roman and Ava?

With Brett, it was always a game of posturing and position-ing. Maybe he'd been trying to work a side deal with this company and that's why he'd neglected to mention it when Law asked about companies for sale. *What was going on?* Did Montrose know about it? Law's gut said no, that Brett was working alone on this one. But why throw it up in Law's face and tell him it would destroy his relationship with Ava? Did the guy really think Law wouldn't do anything? Brett didn't know the power Law had, but he would...soon enough.

He stood in the living room and read each page, scouring for details that would tell him more about the offer. There were always hidden agendas with people like Brett, and if he was bringing the deal to Law, then he wanted him to know about it. But why? The answer landed on top of him when he reached the final page that listed the names of the involved parties. Principal of Pink Oleander, Inc., Lawson Peter Carlisle.

Law read the contract four times before he called his uncle. "Why would Brett do this? And I mean the real reason, not some BS about wanting me to know what hell is."

A long sigh filled the phone and Law pictured his uncle sitting in his recliner, his weather-beaten face creased in thought. "Isn't it obvious, son? The boy wants you to pay because you have a life: freedom, a woman you love, a future that's not full of lies and deceit. He's so caught up in his own misery that he wants to make everybody else miserable, too."

"But how could he just add my name to the document? Who's the company? I looked for them and they didn't come up on any Internet search."

"The truth doesn't really matter, now, does it? All he's trying to show is reasonable doubt and this contract gives the Ventoris reasonable doubt about your intentions. Face it, you've seen the financials, know the backstory, you're as close to them as a person can get without being family. Ava sounds feisty and emotional enough to question whether your relationship with her was more about getting the store and less about her."

"To hell with that. I love her and she knows that."

"She knows that because you haven't had any more bumps in the relationship. This is a big one, and even for the strongest couples, it could prove a challenge. Throw in the brother who's got to be annoyed that she's even seeing you, considering his history and the false accusation against him that points back to the Carlisles, and he's not likely to believe you're one of the honest ones. Hell, if I were in that situation and Ava were my sister, *I* wouldn't believe you. Does the guy even know you exist?"

Law dragged a hand through his hair, swore under his breath. "Of course, he knows I exist. We're from the same damn town."

"You are but being from the same town and planning a future with the guy's sister are two very different things." His uncle's voice gentled. "This is going to be a tough one, Law. It will test you in ways you haven't faced yet, but you can't give up."

"Give up? Give up what?" When his uncle didn't respond, Law clutched his phone, spat out, "Give up Ava? I'll never give her up."

"It might not be your choice, son. She's going to have a lot of mixed emotions about this, and she'll need time and—"

"Cal, I'm innocent. I don't know anything about this company and I didn't have anything to do with it. I'm not involved."

"I know you're not. I know the kind of man you are, but now you're going to have to hope that Ava knows, too."

CHAPTER 27

W hen the messenger delivered the manila envelope to the store, she'd almost tossed it on the stack of to-be-read mail. But Brett Carlisle's name in the top left corner caught her eye. What did *he* want? She'd run into him a few times since she and Law had gotten together and each time the man stared like she was a freak, not worthy of associating with his family. What did she care what he thought? He was cruel and manipulative with an arrogance that diminished his good looks and turned him into a disgusting example of excess.

She opened the envelope, slid the enclosed document onto her desk, and began to read. Pink Oleander, Inc., and Salvatore and Lorraine Ventori, owners of Sal's Market....

Twenty minutes and two read-throughs later, she stuffed the document back into the envelope, taped it shut, and shoved it into her desk.

Law Carlisle was a liar.
He didn't care about her.
He'd never cared about her.
But why did he want Sal's Market?

He'd offered to help her father find the best buyer for the grocery store, saying he and his uncle were good at this sort of thing. Of course, she'd accepted. Why wouldn't she? There was no reason to refuse the offer. Ava should have consulted her brother because Roman was the business person in the family, and everybody knew that—apparently so did Law.

Law Carlisle was a liar.

He didn't care about her.

He'd never cared about her.

Nothing made any sense and yet in some strange way, everything made sense. Deep down, hadn't she always known Law Carlisle was too good to be true?

When Roman called, he was less kind about the man or his motives. *You and Law Carlisle? Ava, what were you thinking? The guy's a bum, no matter how much money he has. He played you, can't you see that?*

She clung to one last shred of hope. *Don't you find it strange that Brett offered him up? It's like he wants us to go after Law. Maybe Brett's behind this. I wouldn't put it past him. In fact—*

Ava. Stop. Law's name is on the contract. He played you. And as to why one brother sacrifices another? The Carlisles don't know the meaning of family or loyalty, and why you ever thought Law would be any different...

Silly me. Always making the wrong choice.

I'm really sorry.

I thought he was different, Roman. I really did. The tears started then: gut-wrenching, consuming, unstoppable. Law found her an hour later, still sitting at her desk surrounded by wads of tissues.

"Ava?"

She swiped her hands across her cheeks, dragged her gaze to his. "Did we ever mean anything? Was any of it real, or were you just playing me to get my parents' store?" She stared at the man she thought she knew, but all she saw was a stranger.

"Listen to me, Ava. Brett set me up. Think about it. When we met, the store wasn't for sale. That didn't happen until later." He paused, his voice shifting like it did when he wanted to convince her of something. "Do you think I would do that to you? To your family?"

He looked so sincere, his words filled with a desperation that made them seem real... Honest... True. But the Carlisles were liars, every single one of them, including this one. "I told you everything, shared my parents' concerns, their hope for the future of the store. I shared their *financials*." Her voice drifted, filled with dread. "You used me to get what you wanted. It was never about me at all."

"It was always about you, Ava. I love you." Panic sifted through his words as he moved toward her, stopped when he was a touch away. "You know me. I would never do that to you. Please, don't let my brother tear us apart. We're stronger than that. You know that."

But she didn't know that. "I trusted you, believed you were different from them, but you're not. You're worse." Her heart shut down, her brain followed, hope withering with the recall of her brother's phone conversation. *He used you, Ava. That jerk flat-out lied and used you to get what he wanted. That's been the plan all along, and you were the way to do it.* "I want you to leave."

"Leave? Can't we try to sort this out?"

"There's nothing left to sort out. You destroyed that."

Those green eyes sparked with emotion. "You're just going to pretend what we shared didn't matter?" When she didn't respond, his gaze narrowed, his voice turned rough. "Don't do this, Ava. Please."

"If you ever cared about me, you'll leave me alone." More

pain squeezed her chest, forced the words from her lips. "You'll leave Magdalena." She thought she understood heartache after Jordan cheated on her, but this pain was so much worse.

Law's jaw clenched, unclenched. "I'm not giving up. I'll prove I had nothing to do with that contract."

"It's too late, Law. I don't trust you anymore, and if you can't trust someone, what's the point?"

❧

WORD SPUN around town with a heavy snowfall that Lawson Carlisle had done Ava Ventori wrong. Some said it was the bad boy slithering through his veins that crept out and could not be tamed. Others said the man had grown restless. Still others said what could you expect from a Carlisle; once a lying, no-good cheater, always a lying, no-good cheater.

But there were some who guessed Lawson Carlisle wasn't behind the breakup, that it was Ava. The girl had a habit of flitting from this to that. Hadn't she quit nursing school? Hadn't she been trying jobs here and there for years and ended up with exactly what? Nobody could really say.

What did she *do* anyway?

Maybe she'd only been after the Carlisle money and when she realized Lawson Carlisle was getting none of it, she dumped him. A handsome face and a toned body weren't enough to pay the gas bill come winter.

There were a few, closer to the situation, who thought it might have something to do with the grocery store. Hadn't there been rumors that Sal and Lorraine wanted to sell it? And still, okay, hadn't somebody mentioned the Carlisles getting involved with the sale, as in trying to buy it? There'd been no particulars on which Carlisle wanted the store and since Law and Ava's split, everything was hush-hush.

Pop knew the truth behind the rumors, but he didn't share those thoughts with anybody who didn't already know about it. Of course, Sal Ventori *did* know, and that's exactly why Pop had to get to the bottom of this mess and find a way to get Law and Ava back together.

"Don't you think we should talk about this hippopotamus in the room?"

Sal grabbed a pizzelle, studied it like he was examining blossom-end rot on a tomato. "Don't you dare mention that name in my house."

Pop shook his head, bit into one of the pizzelles he'd brought his friend. Pizzelles and homemade Chianti could work out a lot of problems, and he was counting on both for this latest disaster. "You mean Lawson Carlisle?"

"That's blasphemy, Angelo. I invited that man to share sauce and meatballs, watched television with him, even tossed out a few suggestions about a wedding. My daughter and that ponytailed, tattooed scoundrel? Over my dead body."

"Don't you think you're being a little heavy with the drama? The boy says he's innocent and I believe him. Got no reason not to, neither do you, unless you're saying Brett Carlisle's got Boy Scout credentials." Pop scratched his jaw, pondered the older Carlisle brother. "And with the situation between him and Paula Morrisen, I'd say he bears watching."

"It's not right he keeps two families," Sal said. "That poor wife of his. What a shame." He paused, squinted at his glass of Chianti. "Maybe he's trying to do right, and that's why he notified us of the brother's intent to swindle us."

Pop rolled his eyes. Sal could be so gullible. Good thing Pop was around to steer him toward other possibilities. "Or maybe he's a mean, jealous alley cat who wants to destroy his brother and wouldn't mind bringing down Roman's family seeing as it was Roman who found out the truth about Paula."

"Hmm." Sal nodded, finished off his Chianti. "I don't know, Angelo. The truth is buried in there somewhere, but I can't find it, not when all I see is wording about turning my place into a Grocery Time Anytime store. Can you believe it? You think anybody would care if the endive was fresh or the vegetables were local? Heck, they'd probably get rid of endive and substitute spinach. And what happens to the people who can't pay until next Friday? Will they go hungry? Be forced to do without?" He jabbed a stubby finger on the table, spat out, "Of course, they will. You think a damn Carlisle will care if bellies are empty? They won't try to hold on to tradition or memories. All they'll want is money, so they'll look at volume, price, and a way to make a quick buck. It makes me sick to think about it."

"So, what are you going to do about it? Sit there and fuss until you get indigestion and heart palpitations? The document isn't signed by anybody, and word has it the company might not even exist. Oh, I heard all about how maybe the company's too new and that's why it's not listed on the Internet, but I'm not buying it. People put everything on the dang Internet two seconds after it happens. The only reason it's not there is because it doesn't exist except in Brett Carlisle's devious brain." There were a lot of rumors swirling around town about what would happen next, ranging from Sal being forced out of semi-retirement to Roman coming back to Magdalena to run the grocery store. A few even had Ava getting together with a high school boyfriend to buy the place. Pop saw through the holes in those possibilities, every single one of them.

"Roman said it was Law, and my son knows business." Sal puffed out his chest, snagged another pizzelle. "He said the boy used Ava to soften us up."

Pop blew out a sigh, shot back, "He did, huh? Even though he started seeing her before you ever mentioned selling the grocery store? Roman's a good boy, but he's so blinded by the

Carlisle name and the ones who tried to destroy him that he can't consider other possibilities, like Law's innocence."

"I guess with a family like that, they don't care much for hurting each other." He muttered under his breath, shrugged. "If the Carlisle boy was head over heels for Ava, and the older brother wanted to destroy the relationship because of jealousy and because he hated Roman, I could see where he might think up the fake company idea."

"Yup, my point." Sal could sure lose sight of the real issue and it was Pop's job to redirect him, like he was doing now. "You know, since my cataract surgery, I'm seeing a lot better, and thanks to my dear Lucy, I can see what most people don't." His wife had always had a knack for telling what was in someone's heart, or what their intentions were, sometimes even before *they* knew. It was a gift she taught him from years of living together, and one he cherished. "Ava and Law belong together, like garlic and olive oil."

His friend remained silent for a long time, and if Pop could poke around inside Sal's head, he bet there'd be a lot of confusion, maybe even a little regret over this whole situation. The man was a black-and-white problem solver who'd grown up surrounded by two choices, right and wrong. No half right, half wrong. But maybe Pop could help him see that situations weren't always just right or just wrong. "Ava's never going to find another one like Lawson Carlisle, and I'm not talking about his bank account."

"Ha! You mean his father's bank account. That boy's a hard worker but if he clears enough to pay for that beat-up truck he's driving and a place to live, I'll bet he goes in the hole every month."

Goes to show appearances didn't always tell the story. Neither did impressions a person left. "Guess again, Sal. The boy's got money, and none of it came from his father. Of course, you're too busy staring at the ponytail and the tattoos and thinking about the Carlisle name to listen to the man. I'm disappointed in you, thought you were better than that."

Sal scrunched his nose, scowled. "Angelo, stop dancing around with your fancy words and tell me what you're talking about. Are you saying the boy's rich? Last I heard he was a farm hand at his uncle's place."

Pop shook his head, let out a healthy sigh. Some people could not see past their own nose. "How about he's not *just* a farmhand? Goes to show what you don't know." The huffing and puffing started next, and Pop did not want to agitate the man's heart, so he spilled. "The boy's got plenty enough to pay for ten trucks, a house the size of the Carlisle mansion, and a new linoleum floor for you." Pop chuckled, added. "Plus, a lot more than that."

"He does? How? With lying and cheating involved? Gambling maybe?"

"One more word like that and I swear, Salvatore Ventori, I will tell Lorraine you've been sneaking pizzelles and Chianti since the heart attack and then see how much you're going to judge others."

CHAPTER 28

A good drunk never solved anything, and it usually left a person with a blasted headache and a heap of regret. But right now, Law needed that good drunk, craved it so he didn't have to think about his situation. How had it all gone so wrong? *Trust* was a dicey word. And love? Who even knew what that meant? Family was supposed to love you, weren't they? Family was supposed to be trusted, weren't they? And what about a woman? Law took a healthy swallow of dark ale, thought on that. Sure, a woman you thought was part of your life should be somebody you could trust when life got jumbled up and you couldn't find your way out.

He'd thought Ava Ventori was that woman, thought he'd finally found someone who understood him, accepted him, wanted to be with him. But he'd been wrong. Whatever he'd shared with Ava had been short-term, until the rocky parts surfaced, and the doubt crept in that said she didn't want it enough, didn't trust him enough to look deeper than what looked like truth. Hadn't she told him from the beginning she wasn't looking for permanent? And later, when she admitted—not without hesitation and confusion—that maybe he was more than short- term, hadn't she acted like she wasn't happy about it? She'd found a reason to dump him and act as if he'd never mattered to her, act as if they weren't real...and maybe for her, that was true.

But not for him, and that's why he was on his way to a mind-numbing drunk, a bad choice he'd regret in the morning. Law stared at his beer bottle, tried to block out the music in O'Reilly's bar. He'd snuck in here years ago, a month before he got shipped out of town, and downed half a beer before Old Jack Finnegan spotted him, told him to get his skinny butt out or he'd drag him to his father's house. No one was going to kick him out tonight or care enough to ask what he was doing drinking all by himself. He had nothing to worry about except finding a way home since he didn't plan to drive.

Law was three beers deep toward feeling sorry for himself and the pain-in-the-ass situation he called life when Cash Casherdon slid into the booth opposite him and plunked down his beer. "That look says you're in bad shape and working on getting in worse shape." He eyed Law as though he already knew the problem but was going to make him admit it anyway. "So...trouble in paradise?"

"You mean trouble in hell, don't you?" Half the town knew about the split, and the other half guessed as much when they didn't see Law and Ava strolling down Main Street or sharing coconut cream pie at Lina's Café. Who cared what they thought?

"It's not like we haven't all been there, some of us more than once." Cash lifted his beer, took a swig. "So, what are you going to do about it?"

At least the guy didn't come out and say her name. There was comfort talking *around* the name, like neither wanted to bring it up: easier that way, somehow less painful. But Law should have known with a guy like Cash Casherdon that dancing around the subject would only last so long. "Not sure there's much I can do that I haven't already tried. If a person doesn't want to listen to reason, what's a guy to do?"

"That sounds like a pity party, and you didn't seem like the kind of guy to feel sorry for himself." Cash shrugged. "Maybe I was wrong. Maybe you are one of those who gives up, or maybe you didn't care about her as much as we all thought you did."

Law clenched and unclenched his jaw, forced the words to fall out: smooth, even, no emotion. "Yeah, maybe." They both knew that was a damn lie and Cash wanted him to admit it, but what was the point? Ava Marie Ventori thought he was no better than pond scum, and she'd been pretty clear about that the last time he saw her.

Cash opened his mouth to respond when Ben Reed, the cop in town, interrupted. "Hey, mind if I join you?"

Cash slid over, grinned. "Thought you were going to stand me up. What happened? Did your wife give you five more chores to finish before you could leave?"

The cop laughed, his broad shoulders filling up the rest of the booth. "No, we were wrapping Christmas presents for the kids." Law stared at the cop and Cash, his childhood idol. Despite the muscles and stories about being tough guys, they didn't sound so tough right now. Nope, in fact, they sounded pretty mild-mannered—like husbands in love. He pushed the thought aside, nodded at Ben Reed. "How's it going?"

"Good. Actually, great." Ben paused, his blue gaze narrowing. "I'm sure a whole lot better than you're doing right now." He shook his head, let out a long sigh. "I don't wish discontent on any man, especially where his woman's involved. Makes life pure miserable, and it's not a good place to be."

"You sure missed the fireworks, Law." Cash grinned, toyed with his beer bottle. "Ben could tell you a few stories that would make your situation look like nothing."

"Hey, can we just leave that one alone?" The cop's sigh was

louder and longer than Cash's. "I don't like to recall my stupidity and bad choices. Worst time of my life, and I'm not going to forget it."

Cash nodded, tossed a smile Ben's way. "Can't fix stupid."

"You should know." Ben scowled at him. "It's not like you didn't have your own share of stupidity and bad choices, and don't try to deny it just because we have company."

Red inched up Cash's neck. "Point taken. Law here's in a bind and I'm betting he thinks he's the only one who's ever screwed up. I'm not big on sharing what we've done, but we can give him the highlights of our time in the bad choices and worse choices arena. What do you say? I'll spill if you do."

Ben Reed's face paled, his brows pinched together, and he frowned. Law didn't care if the man didn't want to divulge his less-than-stellar past. What was the point? It's not like Ava was going to change her mind about him. She'd been pretty clear about never wanting to see him again. "Hey, don't worry about it. It's not like telling me is going to change my situation. Save the stories for someone you can help."

Cash settled back in the booth, crossed his arms over his chest, and stared until Law looked away. "Finding the right woman is never easy; keeping her is even harder, so you have to figure out how much you want to fight for it."

"And it's going to be one hell of a fight," Ben added. "Most of it with yourself."

"Isn't that the truth?" Cash nodded, sipped his beer. "So, here's what you do. Picture your Ava—"

"She's not *my* Ava," Law snarled, shooting him a look.

"Okay, my bad. Picture *Ava*," Cash corrected, those whiskey-colored eyes narrowing on him "—in someone else's bed. How's it feel? Make you want to puke? Or puke after you flatten the guy?"

"Both."

"Okay then. Now we're getting somewhere."

Cash Casherdon might be a former bad-ass who was still one of the coolest guys Law had ever known, but his strategy for winning back a woman was pointless. What the guy didn't understand was that it took two people to *want* to be in a relationship; not one in and the other all the way out. Maybe for a cooler-than-cool guy like Cash, it really was that simple.

But the guy's next words said the opposite. "Nobody's screwed up worse than me, and more times, but I was not going to give up, even if Tess thought I was a loser and a worthless piece of crap."

Ben laughed. "And an idiot. I think she called you that a few times, too."

"Yeah, don't get me started on *your* brilliant maneuverings in the relationship department. Why you'd ever think it was cool to share your life's-passing-me-by worries with a woman who had no business touching you, let alone hearing your secrets, is what I call idiotic. And the whole hospital bed deal?" It was Cash who laughed this time. "Yeah, that was real smart."

"Shut up." Ben nudged his arm. "Just shut up."

Cash ignored his buddy, turned to Law. "It sounds worse than it was, but it was pretty bad. The woman was a physical therapist who wanted to take care of more than his knee."

"Cash—"

"Okay, okay. Just relax, Ben. I'm not going to let Law think you took Little Miss Let Me Show You How to Feel Young Again up on her offer. Ben opened his eyes, but there was a lot of damage control to do, and with Gina Reed, building trust again was one uphill battle."

Ben blew out a long sigh. "Which is why I'm not going to do anything to upset the peace in my home."

Law listened to these two tough guys and realized their women were just as strong, maybe stronger, when it came to holding the family together. His parents had never had that sort of relationship, and while his aunt and uncle may have, he'd been too angry to look for it. What did he know about making long-term work? Hell, he'd never used the term *girlfriend* before, no matter how many times they'd shared his bed or where he'd taken them. Greece, Italy, Spain. But Ava had been so much more than a girlfriend; he'd wanted her for keeps. He opened his mouth and the truth spilled out. "I wanted to marry her."

It was Ben who responded. "Yeah, we all kind of figured that. Nate said you'd propose by Christmas. I bet you wouldn't make it to Thanksgiving."

"I see." So, they'd been betting on his love life. Guess they all lost. "And you?" He eyed Cash. "What did you say?"

The man who'd been his idol met his gaze head-on, no backing down, and smiled. "I laid odds your family was going to blow it all up and you'd be left in the ashes. Wish I'd been wrong, but from what my wife says, Ava's been calling you all kinds of names, none of them good."

"I told you it was over." The beer wasn't numbing his senses fast enough. He needed another one, and he needed it now. "I appreciate the support, but a guy's got to know when to step aside and call it quits."

"Call it quits?" It was Ben Reed's turn to stare. "Why would you do that?"

What did these two not understand? Maybe they were so knee-deep in love that they thought with a little effort and an apology, everyone else could be in love, too. Well, it didn't work that way. At least, not for Law and Ava. "Look, she's not interested in anything but seeing me leave town and she was pretty clear about that request."

"That's where you're wrong." Cash's smile spread. "If she's still calling you names and can't get two sentences out before she's cussing you, then you've still got a chance." More smiling, this time accompanied by a laugh. "Crazy as it sounds, it means she still cares."

"I agree." Ben reached for his beer, took a long pull. "All you have to do is prove you weren't involved in the scheme to buy the store, and then let the laws of nature do the rest."

CHAPTER 29

There comes a time in a child's life when she's got to face up to the past, including her parents' perceptions of who they think she is. Since her breakup with Law, Ava had been hiding in her room to paint or sneaking to the office early to work on the river rocks. Several times, her mother had found her and commented about what she considered odd behavior. *Where did you get that blue smudge on your hand? And look, there's a pink smear on the desk. How did that happen?* Withholding information became a true challenge and after the tenth comment, Ava decided she needed to tell them the truth.

She waited until they finished dinner, fixed her father's coffee, handed her mother a chamomile tea and the plate of pizzelles Pop had given her yesterday. The Godfather of Magdalena had become a cheerleader, confidant, and someone she considered a friend. She sank onto the couch, tucked her stocking feet underneath her, and turned to her parents. "Mom, Dad, there's something I need to tell you."

Her father made the sign of the cross, clutched a pizzelle so hard it crumpled between his fingers. Her mother sprang from her chair to pick up the pieces of pizzelle and brushed them onto the plate with a *tsk-tsk*. "There's more?" Sal asked. "How much more?"

Her mother stepped back, clasped her hands to her chest. "I do hope this is not about the grocery store situation. Or…the other."

By *other*, they meant Law. So, they couldn't say his name. She didn't blame them because she couldn't either—at least, not without tears. "This is about me and something I've been hiding because I wasn't sure what you'd say, but most of all, because I was too unsure of myself and what I wanted. I'm not anymore." She reached into her sweatpants pocket, pulled out a river rock. "Here, this is for you." Her father took the rock, held it between his large hands. "I like that shade of green. It says Christmas." He squinted, read aloud, "I love you, Mom and Dad, Ava."

"It's beautiful, dear," her mother murmured. "Thank you."

"And thank that artist. She's something else," her father said, his voice gruff. "A real talent."

Ava stood, moved toward them. "Actually, the artist is who I wanted to talk to you about. You see…" She cleared her throat, opened her mouth, closed it.

"We're going to get to meet her, aren't we?" Sal's expression lit up, his voice simmering with excitement. "Wait until I tell Angelo that I got to meet the artist behind the river rocks. I can see his face now… He'll want to finagle a meeting, no doubt about it. And then he'll have two hundred questions, but you're going to keep it a secret, aren't you, Ava? We'll be the only ones who are going to meet this artist, right?"

"Pop's already guessed who the artist is. Besides, I think everyone should know. This person has a gift and shouldn't keep it hidden."

"Ha." Her father scratched his chin, stared at the river rock. "Angelo knows? He never said anything to me."

"Oh, Sal. Angelo would never betray a confidence; you know that." Lorraine took the rock from her husband's hand, smiled. "I'd love to meet this artist. This person has a way of bringing people together and helping them see what's important —" her voice gentled as she traced the lettering on the rock "— and also helping us realize what matters in our lives, like family, love, forgiveness."

"Uh-huh." It had taken losing Law to make Ava understand the true meaning of love, forgiveness, and trust. "Mom, turn the rock over and read what's on the other side."

She held her breath as her mother lifted the rock, read the back. "This river rock was created by artist Ava Ventori. Ava?" Her mother's voice wobbled with emotion. "*You're* the river rock designer?"

"I am. I've been doing this for a long time but I never had the confidence to share them with the world. And then..." She thought of Law and the support and encouragement he gave her —right up until he betrayed her.

"Don't you give up, Ava." Her father's voice cracked, split open. "This story isn't over yet."

LAW WAITED until he knew Brett was out of the office before he showed up. Interesting how people aligned themselves with you once they knew who had the real power. The blonde guy who'd almost tossed him out the first time he saw him was a decent spy and must have realized Law could make things happen for him, while Brett was just talk. When Law entered the dealership, the blonde-salesman-turned-spy descended on him in a flurry of designer clothes and whispers. "Your brother left twenty minutes ago and won't be back until late this afternoon. He does that twice a week." More whispers, lower, "Your father's in his office."

"Thanks, Jeffrey." Law made a point of knowing people's names, knowing their weaknesses, too. He shook the young man's hand, smiled. "Good job." Sometimes people just wanted to be appreciated.

"Thank you, Mr. Carlisle."

Mr. Carlisle. Interesting. He headed to his father's office, knocked on the frame of the open door. "Got a minute?"

Montrose glanced up from the papers in front of him. "Law, what a pleasant surprise. It's good to see you."

The man almost leapt out of his chair to get to Law and acted as if he wanted to hug him, but Law stepped back. "We need to talk."

"Sit, please." His father sank into the chair next to Law, not the big leather one, but the straight-backed match to Law's, intended for visitors and potential clients.

"Is this about Ava? I heard... So sorry. What a lovely girl. I hope you can work things—"

"This isn't about Ava, though she's collateral damage. I guess we both are." He rubbed his jaw, studied the man he'd hated for almost half his life. "Did you know Brett fabricated a company with me as the principal owner?" A person couldn't fake that kind of shock, which meant his father didn't know. What else didn't his father know?

"He did? Why would he do that?"

"So he could make it look like I wanted to buy Sal's Market. Imagine what Ava and Roman thought when Brett sent them the dummy contract with my name on it saying I planned to turn the place into a Grocery Time Anytime."

Shock morphed into confusion, spread across his father's face. "You mean the chain store?"

"Yeah, I was surprised, too. My guess is he didn't like my

comments about his personal life, or the fact that I was with Ava. Misery wants company and all that. And it wasn't just that I was happy, but who I was happy with..." Law homed in on his father, studied him. "I'm sure he didn't like that Ava was Roman's sister, you know, because of the whole deal with Paula Morrisen." The look on Montrose's face said guilt, and lots of it. "So, why don't you tell me what you had to do with that whole situation and if you have any hope of a relationship with me, it had better be the truth, and it had better be all of it."

Montrose Carlisle, the figurehead of wealth, authority, and privilege, crumbled before him, his eyes filling with tears, shoulders slumped. "I'm so sorry. So sorry. I knew it was wrong, but your mother...." His voice cracked and split open with pain and regret. "God forgive me but I could never say no to her."

CHAPTER 30

"So, you want to tell me what's going on between you and Ava Ventori, or should I just start guessing?" Pop rubbed his jaw, squinted through his glasses. The cataract surgery improved his vision, but his years walking this earth gave him a bead on what was going on inside the boy's head.

"You mean the whole town hasn't already told you? Give it a few seconds; I'm sure you'll hear all about it. Then you can draw your own conclusions."

Oh, the look on that boy's face said *hurt* and *in pain*. Pop had seen it enough times to recognize it. "I'm not interested in what anybody has to say but you. I like to go to the source, and you and Ava Ventori are the only sources I'm interested in." Pop sat forward, narrowed his gaze on the young man. The town had tossed him aside as irresponsible, reckless, and a hoodlum. "What's really going on, Law? What happened between you and Ava?"

"She thinks I used her to get close to her parents so I could buy their store. It's crazy, but my name's on the unsigned contract, listing me as the principal in a company that doesn't exist. This is all my brother's doing; payback for poking around in his personal affairs and calling him on it."

"I see." No doubt this had to do with Katrina and her sad circumstances. Pop knew all about Brett Carlisle's wife, but the woman wouldn't leave him. Maybe she thought she couldn't. He'd have to think on that and see what could be done... For now, he had to concentrate on Law and Ava before they let anger and hurt destroy their chance for a future together. "Your father wasn't involved in the deal?"

Law shook his head. "He swore he wasn't and I can't find anything that indicates he was."

Well, at least there was only one bad egg in this mess and it wasn't Montrose. Pop felt a pang of sympathy for the man who'd been willing to sacrifice himself to please his wife. No person should ask that or expect it of another. "Some people will do anything to protect their own. Others, will say anything to see their agenda served." He thought of Gloria Blacksworth and her many disastrous attempts to destroy people, including family. The woman had been pure evil, and yet she'd always considered herself a victim. But Montrose Carlisle was more victim than perpetrator here, forced by his wife's demands that he protect family, no matter what. Did the boy know that? "Ava needs time to process this, but I believe she'll come around, and that will open the opportunity for conversation."

The look Law gave him said there would be no talking *or* understanding. "She was pretty clear she didn't want anything to do with me. Called me a liar and said I betrayed her." Pain smothered his next words. "I knew deep down it was only a matter of time before she realized she was too good for me, that I didn't deserve her."

Oh, but the boy was hurting bad. "You really believe that bunch of malarkey? You think you and Ava Ventori don't belong together? I've been observing you and watching with keen eyes, and what I see is a couple in love... A couple destined to be together."

"I think you're mistaking me for somebody else. Or maybe you're seeing something you want to be there that isn't."

He spoke as though he'd considered the options too many times and come up with nothing but empty. "Why do you want everybody to think you're nothing more than a ruffian, no better and no different than you were in high school?"

Those green eyes sparked, glittered with an emotion that looked a lot like misery. "Because maybe I *am* a ruffian, not worthy of somebody like Ava."

Pop scowled, shook his head. "Now you sound pure pitiful. You got to get out of your own way, Lawson Carlisle. Open your eyes and your heart, and trust that other people see the good in you, the *real* you that's nothing like your brother. Stop pretending and stop being afraid to trust."

Law shifted in his chair, slid him a look. "You know, I remember you from back in the day. You weren't afraid or intimidated by anybody, not even my father."

"Nope, I wasn't. You know the only person who intimidated me?" Pop smiled, glanced at the portrait of his dear sweet Lucy. "That woman right there: my wife. Lucy was the only one who saw me for what I was, a man unworthy to wipe the mud from her shoes and loved me in spite of it." Pop sniffed, swiped a tear. "True love sees us for who we are and loves us anyway."

"For the first time in my life, I found someone I wanted to hold onto...someone who made me believe I deserved to be happy." Law's voice turned rough. "And now she's gone."

Pop slid back in his chair, clasped his hands over his belly, and let out a long sigh. "I know, trust me, I do know. It's going to take some work, but you and Ava belong together, heart to heart, and I'll help you get there."

Ava checked the inventory on the spreadsheet, flipped the page. Tomatoes would be in tomorrow, followed by the cauliflower and the broccoli. She'd have to go through them three more times to make sure she hadn't made a mistake. It was difficult to focus when all she saw was Lawson Carlisle and his lies. *Stupid, stupid, stupid.* She'd trusted him. How could she have been such a fool?

When the office door creaked open, she thought it would be Sammy with news of the next delivery. She never expected to see her mother limping in, followed by her father. "Mom? Papa? What are you doing here?"

"You got a minute?" Her father stood a few feet away, his stocky frame next to her mother.

Ava pushed back her chair, made her way to them. "Sure, come in and sit down. Can I get you something to drink? Coffee, tea? Water?" *Why were they here?*

"No, dear, we just need a few minutes." Her mother's soft voice covered her like flannel pajamas on a chilly night.

Sal cleared his throat, spoke in a voice that crackled with emotion. "We got something to say, and we want you to hear us out." His dark eyes grew bright behind his black glasses. "Just listen and don't say a word until we're done. Okay?"

She nodded, sank into her chair, and leaned her elbows against the worn desktop. "Okay, what's the matter?" She darted a glance from her mother to her father. "Is there something going on with one of you? Please just tell me. Is it Angie and the baby?"

"It's none of those." Lorraine offered a gentle smile, placed a hand on the desk. "This is about Lawson."

The name snuffed the oxygen from the room. "What about him?"

"He came to us last night, Ava. Told us something we thought you should know."

What could Lawson Carlisle tell her parents that she could possibly want to hear? *I lied but I won't lie again. I'll take good care of your grocery store and I promise not to turn it into a Grocery Time Anytime? Oh, and I really do want to be with your daughter?* Right. "I don't know what he could say that would change anything."

"We misjudged him, you more than anyone." Her father's voice shifted, filled with sadness and remorse. "He's a good boy, Ava. Honorable, kindhearted, loyal."

"Good for him. Maybe you should tell Roman and see what he thinks about him. I'll bet he won't be as forgiving as you."

"We did talk to Roman and he's the one who suggested we come here."

Ava stared at her mother, trying to comprehend her words. "Roman said that? He wanted you to come here and talk to me?"

Her mother swiped her cheeks, nodded. "He did. You see, Law talked to Roman yesterday and I don't know what was said, but your brother gave the go-ahead for us to work with Law to find a buyer. Seems Law's pretty good at negotiating deals and he must have impressed Roman and you know that's hard to do."

"Roman's okay with all of this?" That didn't sound right.

Her father nodded. "Absolutely. He said it's good to have someone close by who can answer questions and make sure we're not getting taken advantage of... Not that we would, but you know your brother worries."

"I don't understand." Nothing made sense anymore, least of all her brother trusting a Carlisle. Fear that he'd try and persuade her to break off with Law had kept Ava from telling him about their relationship. Who would have thought Roman would be okay with it?

"What's to understand?" Her father sat up straighter, clutched the arms of the chair. "I might be old and crotchety, but even I can see the truth in this one." Sal studied her, said in a gruff voice, "We misjudged him. He's a good boy, an honest one, too. You could do worse than setting your sights on him, but you better have a big apology ready because he deserves it."

Ava didn't hear the rest of her father's speech because she kissed her parents, grabbed her jacket, and ran out the door. As she drove to the cabin, she thought about how much she had to apologize for and hoped Law wouldn't shut her out. She *had* misjudged him and not trusted him when she should have. All she wanted was a chance to tell him how sorry she was, how she wouldn't make the same mistake again. Would he listen to her?

Don't give up on us, Law. Please. She recited the words into the emptiness of the car as she drove toward the cabin, snow pelting the windshield. *Please, don't give up on us.* When she reached Law's driveway, she parked behind his truck, said a prayer, and trudged through the snow to his front door.

She knocked, sucked in a breath, and said another prayer. Three prayers later, he eased open the door. "Ava? You shouldn't be out in weather like this."

The dark expression said she shouldn't be out at all, certainly not risking her life to get to him. Was it already too late? She eased the hood of her jacket from her head and forced a smile. "I need to talk to you. Can I come in?"

He hesitated. "You should have called first and I would have told you to stay home." He glanced past her at the heavy snow. "It's bad out there. You took chances you shouldn't have taken."

"And I also didn't take chances I *should* have taken. But it doesn't matter now, does it? I'm here and I need to talk to you. You can kick me out when I'm through, or if you're so worried, I'll call for a ride and pick the car up in the morning. Either way, I'm not leaving until I say what I came to say."

The sigh said he knew she wasn't going to listen to him. He

stepped aside and Ava entered, shrugged out of her jacket, and waited for him to step aside so she could follow him into the living room. She did not expect him to block her way, arms folded across his chest, lips flat, gaze narrowed. Law had shut her out and shut her down. Well, she could share what was in her heart from the tiny entranceway to the cabin she'd come to love.

"I hurt you, I didn't trust you, and I'm sorry. You deserved so much better than what I gave. I heard what you're doing to help my parents and how you and Roman spoke. No idea what you two said and doubt my brother will spill. I'm grateful you're going to help them. Only an honorable man would care so much, especially after the way my family treated you." She paused, sipped air. "I love you, Law, and I should have told you a long time ago, but I couldn't get the words out. I was too afraid and that fear hurt us, hurt what we shared and what we could be together. I don't know if you can forgive me, but I'm asking you to try, or at least think about giving me another chance." She cleared her throat, wishing he'd jump in and profess feelings for her as well, but he didn't.

What was he thinking? What was he feeling? Her heart couldn't tell. Was there no forgiveness left? Had she hurt him so badly he didn't *want* to forgive her—or couldn't? "Law, please, say something."

Those lips she'd tasted so many times, opened, spilled emotion that consumed her. "I never wanted a woman like I wanted you. I'm not talking about the physical part. I mean the raw need to be with you, even if it was just to talk or feel your presence. It was like nothing I'd ever felt before, and I wanted more." His voice turned rough. "I wanted all of you—for keeps. I'd never told any woman I loved her before, but I told you."

Her heart filled with hope. Maybe he would forgive her...give her another chance... "We belong together," she whispered.

"I thought so, I really did." Those beautiful lips pulled into a frown. "But you don't trust me, Ava, and you didn't trust *us*—not enough to build a life around. What's going to happen the next time we're faced with some sort of challenge? Will you call me a liar and a cheat, tell me to leave town and never see you again?"

"No, I will *never* do that again. I promise you." *He had to believe her.* "I'm so sorry." Her voice dipped, fell to a whisper, "I trust you, Law, and I trust us...today and always."

His gaze narrowed on her, grew so bright she almost had to look away. "But you see, Ava, I don't trust you, us, none of whatever we shared. Not anymore."

CHAPTER 31

The small box arrived at Law's doorstep late one afternoon. He had the radio on while painting trim in the bedroom and hadn't heard the vehicle, but the tire tracks and the box said someone had been here. The tracks were too large for Ava's car, not that she would try to see him again. He'd been pretty clear about where the relationship was going, as in nowhere. How many times was a guy supposed to let himself get burned before he shut it down and said enough? Ava Marie Ventori was more volatile than gasoline in a candle shop. And trust? Hadn't she promised to stand by him, no matter what? Yeah, she'd stuck with him as long as there were no issues, no questions, and no complications. He picked up the box, stared at it. But once there was one little problem, it was game over. She was done with the promises and not interested in hearing anything but her own ill-founded assumptions.

He tossed the box on the kitchen table, his gaze darting to the empty spot where she'd eaten and worked on her river rocks. Their relationship had been sparked by passion, hope, and the need to believe they deserved a chance, but the relationship had been as combustible as the woman. Sure, she wanted to apologize—*yet again* when she realized how wrong she'd been. Well, not this time: no more chances, no more do-overs, no more *anything*. Pop and Cash might think Law and Ava belonged together, but they were wrong.

The house would be finished in a few months, and by then, the grocery store should have a buyer. He'd promised Roman he'd guide his parents through the process and he was not going back on his word—even if it meant staying in Magdalena and risk running into Ava. He could be civil, work on the niceties of casual conversation: *How are you? Been busy? I like the latest river rocks.* He just needed practice so he could pretend she didn't affect him, pretend she didn't *matter*. Let her think he'd been more con than real, that his words had been manufactured...let her think whatever she wanted.

He'd only cared about two women in his life: his mother and Ava, and they'd both broken his heart. For years. Law blamed his father for pushing him away, but it had been his mother and her desire to protect family that had caused the real destruction. How would he ever reconcile himself to that? And his father? Could he call a man's obsessive love for his wife a weakness that drove him to compromise himself and his principles? Law didn't know, didn't want to know, but he'd been awfully close to pledging his life to Ava, and come Christmas, he'd planned to propose.

That was done. Over. Saved by the devious actions of his unscrupulous brother. Maybe Brett had done him a favor. Why would he want to live a life where another person owned his happiness? Nope. Not worth it. He refused to think about Ava's smile, or the way her laughter lightened his mood, or how he'd never felt such peace until he met her. The risk was too high and the woman was too volatile.

Life would move on and he'd move on with it, decide what he wanted to do, which might not even be with Cal's business.

Hell, he didn't know anything right now, other than maybe he really was meant to be alone. Maybe his family wasn't the only place he didn't belong. Maybe he didn't belong anywhere. Law snatched the box, untied the string and opened it. There, nestled in a bed of cream tissue paper was a river rock with a bold message painted on it: *Harry's Folly. Tonight. 7:00 p.m.*

AVA ARRIVED at Harry's Folly fifteen minutes early and ordered a glass of red wine. She clutched the river rock in her left hand, tried to calm herself. *Harry's Folly. Tonight. 7:00 p.m.* She'd memorized the bold silver lettering. Who else but Law would write that? But even as her heart hoped it would be him, her brain asked why? Harry's Folly was a public place and he'd made it clear they were done. He didn't trust her anymore, didn't trust *them* anymore. Yes, she remembered every word and the lack of emotion that went with them. But hope had forced her to come tonight because she could not give up on the possibility that he'd changed his mind.

Harry Blacksworth had eyed her with sympathy and something close to pity when he led her to the secluded booth in the back of the restaurant. *It's nice and quiet here.* He'd smiled, patted her shoulder. *Nobody will bother you, especially the busybodies.* And then his lips had pulled into a smile and he'd leaned close and said in a low voice, *Good luck.*

What did the man know about tonight? Lawson Carlisle was not one to confide in others, especially strangers. Had he told Harry the truth behind the breakup? Men didn't share, and if they did, it was usually with the woman in their lives. Ava sipped her wine, checked her watch, and when it was 7:05, told herself the dinner guest wasn't coming. Of course, the guest had been Law and no doubt someone had put him up to the invitation and he'd rethought his position. She closed her eyes, rubbed her temples, and knew she was to blame for losing the one man who mattered to her.

"Hey."

Ava opened her eyes, squinted past the dim lights silhouetting the man who stood next to the booth, hands shoved in his pocket, expression grim. *Law.* Wounded. Untouchable. "Hi." She clutched the rock tighter, waited.

Those green eyes burned her and she swore they saw right inside her soul. He shrugged out of his jacket and slid into the booth, his gaze never leaving hers. "So..."

Was he angry? Annoyed? Curious? Hard to tell. "When I received the invitation, I hoped it might be from you, but..."

His brows pinched, his lips pulled into a frown. "Invitation? What invitation?"

Oh, dear Lord, no. She eased her hand onto the table, opened it to reveal the river rock. "You...didn't send this?"

He reached for the rock, took it from her hand, studied it. The frown deepened. "I didn't send it." Law dug into the pocket of his jacket, removed a river rock that said *Harry's Folly. Tonight. 7:00 p.m.*, and set it on the table. "And I'm guessing you didn't send this."

"No, I didn't." She picked up the rock, traced the lettering. Someone had sent a message using *her* river rocks. "Who would do this?"

Law shook his head. "Somebody who didn't like the current situation between us." Pause. "Somebody who made it their business to get us here."

Harry Blacksworth took that exact moment to appear, a broad smile plastered on his face and the slightest pink creeping over his cheeks. "River rocks, huh?" He leaned closer, read, "Harry's Folly. Tonight. 7 o'clock." He let out a laugh. "Great advertising.

I like the idea. I'm going to have to include it in my marketing program."

"You do that, Harry. In the meantime, why don't you tell us what you know about these." Law's voice matched his no-nonsense expression. "The truth, Harry. Who did this?"

The man with the fifty-dollar smiles and the fancy clothes darted a glance between them. "Okay, I'll confess. I was the facilitator, but it wasn't my idea."

Law raised a brow. "Whose idea was it?"

Dread snuck through Ava. "It was my parents, wasn't it? Did they talk you into this?" Sal and Lorraine Ventori might not have been fans of the long-haired, tattooed man she'd fallen for, but they'd certainly changed their mind along the way and didn't hesitate to tell her.

"Sal and Lorraine are innocent. Let's just say the involved party believes in giving people a second chance. She's about love, happiness, and finding the right match, and she says there's a perfect match for everyone." Harry leaned closer. "She thinks you're made for each other and convinced me this was the way to get you together. She was so damn certain if you got in the same room together, you'd be able to work it out." He straightened, rubbed his jaw. "It's not like your situation is the worst we've seen in this town. Trust me on that, but things have a way of working out once a couple opens their eyes and gets past their wounded pride."

"Save it, Harry. We're not going down that road again." Law snatched up the rock, shoved it in his pocket. "I'm out of here. She likes the fried calamari and mushroom ravioli." He grabbed his jacket, slid to the end of the booth. "I'm sorry." He held Ava's gaze seconds before he stood and shrugged into his jacket.

"Wait! Wait! You can't leave before you have dinner." Lily Desantro rushed toward them in a red turtleneck and green slacks, her blue eyes bright with tears. "Please, Law. Don't leave just yet. Sit down and have a meal with Ava and if you still feel the same way by the time you finish your chocolate lava cake, I promise to never bother you again about getting back with Ava." Those eyes turned brighter, the voice wobbled. "But I know you love each other because I know what love looks like. I've seen it with Nate and Christine, Cash and Tess. And Ben and Gina."

She glanced at Harry, smiled up at him. "Uncle Harry has the biggest heart of all for his wife, Greta, and all of their children. Even their dog, Cooper, who is a rescue and steals sandwiches from the counter." She sniffed, swiped a finger beneath her glasses to stop a tear. "Pop says true love is hard and messy and it only comes around once in a person's lifetime. And if you're too stubborn or too hurt to see it, it will get away and then you'll spend the rest of your life wondering how you let it go." Her lips pulled into a tiny smile, and she pointed to Ava's rock. "I painted those because sometimes people don't have the words to say how they feel. But the river rocks say it all. They're what Pop calls conversation starters, and once the first word comes out, the second follows and before you know it, you've spoken a whole book's worth of words."

Harry placed a hand on Lily's shoulder, pulled her to him. "I couldn't have said it better myself, Lily." He glanced at Ava and Law. "I'd like to invite you to enjoy your meal. Lily's picked it out for you and apparently has done some careful studying of your likes and dislikes. I didn't ask how she knew or where she determined any of this, but this girl's instincts are as good as Pop's, so I trust her. Guess the only question left is, will you trust her, too...even for a little while?"

Ava slid a glance at Law, waited for his answer. If he declined, there'd be no hope for them. But if he agreed to have a meal with her, then maybe he'd agree to another meal, and another after that. And then who knew what might happen? She could have an opportunity to show him that she wasn't the same fretful, impulsive, and untrusting woman who'd turned him away, but a woman who, if given one more chance, would spend the rest of her life showing him how much she loved him and how much they belonged together.

"Well?" Harry eyed them. "I've got a kitchen to manage and the calamari's not gonna wait for you. Either it's a go or a no-go; which will it be?"

Law eased out of his jacket, settled into the booth, and reached for his wineglass. "Okay, Lily," he said, directing his gaze to her. "Let's check out this menu and while we're at it, maybe your uncle can fill my wineglass."

"Yes!" Lily's ponytail bobbed up and down as excitement slithered through her words. "Yes, to all of it."

CHAPTER 32

"So...this is awkward."

"A little." Mortifying was what it was. Ava hadn't missed the dread smothering his face when Lily Desantro started talking about love and meant to be together. No guy wants that thrown in his face, especially with witnesses, including the ex-girlfriend who dumped him, using words like *liar* and *cheat*. "I'm really sorry about all of this. I had no idea..."

"Hey, it's fine." He settled back against the leather cushions, worked up a half smile. "That girl is some kind of salesperson. And a very creative marketer."

"She is, but then Lily sees things most of us miss." *Like how we're meant to be together...how we love each other...*

"Yeah, I guess."

Obviously, he did not want to dwell on anything Lily said. "Did you finish the living room?" He'd been working on it when their relationship blew up. *It's going to be something else*, he'd told her. *Wait until I stain the mantel and bookshelves. It'll make the whole room pop.* Well, she'd never know if it "popped" unless he invited her to the cabin again, which at the moment, didn't seem likely.

"I did finish it." He hesitated as though uncertain what or how much to say.

There'd been a time when they hadn't needed to sterilize their words or thoughts, when it all spilled without effort or censorship. "And did the stain make the room pop?"

Law eyed her, lifted a shoulder as though he hadn't been excited about the living room project. "It did."

Ah, he didn't like the reference to a past conversation they'd shared. Now, why was that? Was he going to pretend they were strangers? That she'd never stepped inside his cabin, shared secrets, a bed, I-love-yous? Great. He really wasn't going to give her another chance, no matter who orchestrated the meeting. The stingy phrases, the unsmiling lips, the tense body language. This wasn't happening and Ava had been a fool to think it might. "Okay, well, I think I'll be going." She gathered her handbag and jacket, slid to the end of the booth. "Enjoy the meal and tell Harry and Lily thanks."

"You're leaving?"

Was that surprise splashing his face? "Yes. I'm leaving." She thrust an arm into the sleeve of her jacket.

"You're not going to see what Lily's conjured up for us? She had to have gone to a lot of trouble to set this up." Red slithered from his neck to his cheeks. "I think the least we could do is stay and eat."

The man hadn't said that many words since he sat down. Ava narrowed her gaze on him, forced her breathing to remain even, the irritation to remain hidden. "Oh, so you want to share a meal. Together?" Dang but the irritation snuck past her good intentions. "Or would you prefer I move to the next booth so you won't have to talk to me?"

He stared at her so long that she didn't think he planned to answer. And then, those lips she'd tasted so many times turned at the corners, spread. "Why don't you stay here? Lily won't like it if she finds you in another booth, and I can't disappoint her."

She didn't want to, but Ava couldn't help herself. She smiled. If she'd had a thousand dollars, she'd have bet the night would turn out with them on the way back to where they'd been...a start...a chance...a sleepover...maybe a whole new beginning.

And she would have lost.

After a dinner filled with a bottle of red wine, calamari, Caprese salad, mushroom ravioli, chocolate lava cake, and enough catch-up conversation to make her think she'd have doubled-down on the bet if possible, Law walked Ava to her car, clasped her hands and said, "Thanks for tonight."

He's going to ask me to stop over...I see the way he's looking at me...any second now... "I had a good time. I've missed this." *I've missed you...I love you...I want to be with you...*

"Yeah, me too." He released her hands and stepped away. "Take care, Ava." And then he turned and walked away.

CHRISTMAS CAME and went with Midnight Mass, a dusting of snow, a video chat with Roman and his family, and a homemade offering of stuffed shells, salted cod, antipasto salad, cannoli, and of course, pizzelles. But no Law. He was noticeably absent from every conversation. Ava's mother told her there was an interested party for the grocery store and Law was handling the details, and then she added, *We think it's better if we don't mention him. Your father and I can't stand the sad look on your face when we say his name. We're so sorry it didn't work out.*

Yes, she was sorry, too. When she learned he headed back to Pennsylvania the day after their dinner at Harry's Folly, her heart ached. He could have told her and yet he'd stayed silent. *He'll be gone three weeks, that's all I know*, her mother said. *Now, no more questions about Lawson Carlisle.*

Three weeks meant Law wouldn't be back in Magdalena until the middle of January. Now what? She could sit back and feel sorry for herself, or she could make one final plea to Law for a second chance. He might say no, but what if he didn't? It was the small hope he wouldn't that made her pack a bag, gather her art supplies, search out her parents in their tiny living room that night as they watched their favorite sitcom. "I'm going to stay at Law's cabin until he comes back. Then I plan to have a conversation that will either humiliate me for the rest of my life or make me the happiest woman in the world. It could go either way. All I ask is that you please don't tell him what I'm doing." She'd expected her parents to insist she hang onto her pride, but they didn't. Her mother and father gave her their blessing and promised to keep her plan a secret.

"God be with you," her father said.

"And the angels, too," her mother added.

When Ava arrived at the cabin, she slid the key he'd given her weeks ago into the lock and opened the door. He'd never asked for the key back and while she'd intended to give it to him, she hadn't. Something stopped her, and right now she thought of that *something* as destiny. The cabin smelled of evergreen and Law and after the first tear fell, the second followed, then the third until her vision became obliterated with tears. What would he say when he returned home in a few weeks and found her here? Would he listen to her final plea, or would he stare, stone-faced, and ask her to leave? Only God and the angels knew the answer to that one.

Ava unpacked her bag, set her art supplies by the kitchen table, and searched for the cookbook Law had started for her listing basic recipes like baked chicken, chili, spaghetti sauce, meatloaf. *These are go-to recipes. I'll teach you the basics and we'll build from there,* he'd said, his voice soft, his green eyes intense. Filled with love—she'd seen it, heard it in his voice. And she'd destroyed it. Ava found the cookbook, pulled it out, and sat at the kitchen table reading each recipe. Tomorrow she'd buy ingredients and then she'd start cooking. It was a way to feel close to Law, remember what they'd shared, what they could have had, maybe what they could still have.

Ava curled up in Law's bed wearing one of his flannel shirts and hugging another to her chest. "I love you," she whispered into the darkness. "I love you, Lawson Carlisle. And I miss you."

The days passed and Ava spent them between the grocery store and the cabin, cooking in Law's kitchen, sleeping in Law's bed, creating more river rock memories at Law's kitchen table. Her heart wept for him and as time passed, her heart healed, filled with hope. Each river rock she created spoke of forgiveness, joy, and never-ending love. The solitude of the cabin didn't bother her because she felt Law's presence and it calmed her, gave her hope they still had a chance for a future filled with happiness and love.

Two weeks after she moved into the cabin, Law's uncle showed up. The second she opened the door, she knew the tall, rangy older man had to be Calvin Beaumont. The look he gave her said he'd identified her as well. "Hello, Ava." He tossed her a crooked smile, said in a gruff voice, "I'm Cal Beaumont, Law's uncle."

Ava smiled up at him. "Come in, please." The man stepped inside, clasped her hands. "The boy hasn't been the same since this whole mess. He needs you, Ava, but he's too darn stubborn and heartbroken to admit it."

"I need him, too, and I'm not too proud to admit it."

Cal touched her shoulder, gave it a gentle squeeze, his

weather-beaten face a mix of sadness and empathy. "He loves you, no doubt about it. You two belong together and I've come to see what I can do to make that happen."

CHAPTER 33

"This is excellent chili. Law must really care about you to give you his secret because he doesn't share his chili recipe with just anybody." He shot her a look, his lips pulling into a slow smile. "But you're special, Ava, and he knows that, even if he doesn't want to admit it."

She'd heated up the chili she made yesterday and fixed cornbread for their meal. Spending time with Law's uncle was almost like having Law here. Cal shared bits and pieces of Law's life, the angry boy he'd been, to the young man he'd become *before and after* Ava, including the closed-off, distant one Cal saw after the breakup.

"He used to cook for me while I worked on my river rocks. I sat right here painting and sketching while he fixed our meals. We talked and laughed, and the hours went by so fast. Law was the one who gave me the confidence to share my work. He said I had a gift and I should let others see it. I don't think I would have done it if not for him. He gave me so much and I caused him such pain. What an unfair bargain for him." Ava stared at a slice of cornbread, heard Law's voice as he instructed her on how to cook the cornbread. *It's all about the time,* he'd said. *Too short and it falls apart... Too long and it crumbles.*

"You're wrong there, Ava. You gave that boy plenty. It wasn't often that I saw a real smile from him, but when you came into his life, I heard it in his voice when we talked on the phone. The first time I saw him after you two got together, he said there was somebody in his life." He rubbed his jaw, shook his head. "'I'm kind of seeing someone,'" he said. Yup, I think that's how he put it, but I could tell it was a lot more than kind of, and I told him I was happy for him."

He blew out a long sigh. "Law's never had a lot of people in his corner, loving him for himself, asking nothing in return. I loved my sister who was his mother, but she played games with people's lives, thought she could control the universe and everybody in it. I was never a big fan of Montrose Carlisle, but you got to feel sorry for someone who knows the pain of loving too much. She loved him, too, but she never understood what give and take meant. For her, it was always about take and that's hard to admit because she took a lot from me, too. We shouldn't have let her... We should have told her it wasn't okay to use other people even if you think you're doing it for something good. But you see, Evelyn needed us and we never wanted to disappoint her, so we made excuses for her demands; people got hurt. I take responsibility for a lot of Law's issues, and when I heard there was a woman in his life that he really cared about—even loved —well, that gave me hope that maybe God would forgive me for not taking a tougher stand when I should have."

"This is not all on you, Cal. He needed me to believe in him and I didn't. I was so caught up in my own anger that I'd been done wrong, yet again, that I refused to listen to him. I wanted to punish him for what I thought he'd done and I wanted him to feel my pain." Ava rubbed her temples, tried to block out the horrible things she'd said to Law, but they bombarded her with their cruelty. "How will he ever forgive me?" She blinked hard, bit her bottom lip. "And maybe the bigger question is, do I *deserve* that forgiveness? He used to say I was too good for him, but maybe he was too good for me, and maybe he's finally realized that. Maybe I'm just too much trouble."

Cal reached for her hand, squeezed it. "There's where you're wrong, Ava. That boy's heart beats for you, and he needs you. Like I needed my Maddie. You make him human... You make him care... And no matter what's happened before, all that matters is what happens now. Follow your heart and go after him before he convinces himself he's meant to live his life alone. Do that, Ava. Go find your happiness and make my nephew see that you can give him his."

~

WHEN CAL GOT something in his head, he would not give up. Like now. Why did the guy insist Law head back to Magdalena to have a face-to-face conversation with the Ventoris when Law had been in touch with them almost daily?

They depend on you, son, Cal had said. *You can't rely on phone calls when there's a potential offer on the way. The Ventoris might get jittery and lose sleep with questions, and it's up to you to calm them. Didn't the husband have a heart attack a few years back? You want to carry that one on your shoulders?*

Of course not, but they seem fine. I've talked to their son and Roman's cool with everything. I told him I'd be back in Magdalena by the end of next week.

Not good enough. I raised you to stand by your word and that means in person. Tomorrow.

Damn it. Cal tossed out ten more reasons why Law needed to have a face-to-face conversation with Sal and Lorraine Ventori and didn't stop until Law agreed. What choice did he have?

None, unless he confessed the real reason he didn't want to head back to Magdalena. Of course, his uncle was a crafty one and had no doubt figured that out before they had the conversation.

Yup, Cal knew the stalling and excuses had to do with Ava, but at least his uncle didn't call him on it. Law guessed that should count for something, though right now not much. It was late, it was snowing, and he was tired. Damn tired. Did he have any beer in the fridge at the cabin? Any food in the freezer? He guessed he'd have to make a grocery run tomorrow since he'd promised Cal he'd stay in Magdalena for a few days. *Until you get a real offer from the buyer*, Cal had said. That could mean three days or three weeks, and at least three grocery runs—to the grocery store in Renova since there was no way he was walking into Sal's Market.

Ava might be there. He couldn't risk seeing her again. The night at Harry's Folly had almost done him in. He'd been three seconds from caving and telling her they belonged together.

And then what? She'd be great until the next time doubt crept in and then she'd slam him with the liar, cheater, get-out-of-my-life crap. Who needed *that*? She wasn't worth it. *Not. Worth. It.* But he was only fooling himself and he knew it. Maybe that's why he was so damn annoyed right now because even though she'd gutted him, he'd been ready for another round of let's-try-again.

By the time Law reached the cabin, he was annoyed with himself, Ava, Cal, the world. And then he spotted *her* car in his driveway. What the hell? His pulse tripled, his breathing escalated, and he jerked the truck to a stop, hopped out, and ran to the front door.

Ava Marie Ventori, the woman who'd torched his soul, was inside.

Was this why Cal had insisted he make the trip back today?

Law pushed the numerous possibilities aside and fit his key

into the lock, stepped inside. At least she'd remembered to lock the door. The place smelled of cinnamon, apples, and was that a hint of vanilla? Ava didn't cook, but maybe she'd been lighting candles or heating potpourri. In his house. Without his permission. Ava Marie Ventori, squatter. He'd have to talk to her about the definition of trespassing.

Or not.

He shrugged out of his jacket, unlaced his boots, and headed down the hall toward his bedroom. It was after midnight, so if she were here as the car in the drive suggested, she'd be asleep. Law eased open the door, moved toward the bed and the lilac scent. The small nightlight illuminated the figure curled up in his bed. Wearing his flannel shirt, hugging another one...

Ava. He let out a whoosh of air, took in the sight of her, and knew an instant calm. *Ava.* The truth clawed its way from his heart to his brain; he would *never* be over her. He loved her, would always love her. Law kept his gaze on her as he unbuttoned his shirt and stripped out of his jeans and socks. If she needed ten do-overs, he'd give them to her for a chance to share a life with her. Their life. Their future. He crawled into bed, wrapped an arm around her waist, and pulled her close. "Ava," he breathed against her neck.

She stirred, snuggled closer to him, let out a sigh that ended with "Law."

"I love you," he murmured, placing a soft kiss on her neck. "I've missed you so damn much."

"Law?" Ava turned to him, squinted into the darkness. "I thought you were a dream... I thought... What are you doing here?"

Only Ava would ask that question. "You mean, what am I doing in my house, in my bed?" He trailed a finger along her jaw. "I could ask you the same question."

"I've been waiting for you." She inched closer, touched his

cheek. "Waiting, and hoping...and learning how to cook. I found the recipe book you started for me and I can make a pretty decent chili." She paused, her voice filling with a hint of humor. "At least your uncle thought so."

"Cal was here?" Now it all made sense. His uncle's absence the other day for a supposed business meeting with a customer Law had never heard of before. And then the insistence that Law head back to Magdalena because he'd *given his word.*

Ava nodded, said in a soft voice, "He shared a lot with me...about you."

Law tensed, thinking of all the *sharable* possibilities. "I'll bet he did."

"He loves you, Law, and he wants to see you happy. He told me that it didn't matter what happened before; all that mattered was what happened now. And he said I should follow my heart and go after you because you might get some lamebrain idea that you were meant to be alone."

"Lamebrain?"

Her laughter warmed his heart, made him smile. "That was my word, but you get the gist."

"Yeah, I get the gist. My uncle and you were plotting behind my back."

"I wouldn't exactly call it plotting." She brushed her cheek against his hand, kissed it. "I'd call it working together for the common good." Another kiss, a flick of her tongue. "You and me. Us."

He liked the sound of that. "So, did you have a plan to come after me?"

She lifted her head, whispered, "I did. Do you want to see it?"

"Do I?"

"I hope so." Ava sat up, turned on the lamp and opened the top drawer of his nightstand. "Here," she said, handing him a small box similar to the one he received a few weeks ago with the invitation to Harry's Folly.

"Huh." Law eyed the box. "Another invitation?"

She bit her bottom lip, nodded. "Of sorts."

"Now I'm really curious." Law untied the blue ribbon, lifted the box, and stared at the shiny black rock inside. "Marry me," he read, his throat clogging with emotion. "Marry me," he repeated.

Another nod, a gentle "I know it's pretty bold, but your uncle said I needed a plan and—"

Law pulled her to him, eased her onto the pillow, and held her gaze. "Yes," he murmured. "Yes, I'll marry you. I love you, Ava. You're a part of me, now and always. Let's build a great life together."

"That sounds absolutely perfect."

"What do you think about six weeks? Is that do-able?" She could be Ava Carlisle by then...

She reached for his T-shirt, lifted it over his belly. "Four weeks is better."

Four weeks. He liked the sound of that. Law pulled the T-shirt over his head, tossed it on the bed, and placed a soft kiss on her mouth. "Now that we've gotten that business out of the way, how about a little pleasure?"

His wife-to-be laughed, stroked a hand down his back. "Now *that* sounds absolutely perfect."

CHAPTER 34

Four weeks later: Law and Ava's wedding

Law heard the comments from his new father-in-law and Pop Benito as they drank Chianti in Law's living room. Correction: Law and Ava Carlisle's living room. Neither man had a quiet voice and what they considered a whisper was hardly a whisper.

Where's Father Reisanski? Sal asked. *Whoever heard of a ceremony in the snow? What kind of ceremony was that anyway? Writing their own vows? And that minister...was he a minister?*

Pop raised a brow, stared at Ava's father. *Does it really matter who wrote the vows or where they're exchanged or who presided over the ceremony as long as the message is true and the hearts are loyal? You want a big fancy wedding and a husband that will cheat with the first woman who looks at him sideways? Be happy for them, Sal. Can you do that?*

It just doesn't feel normal or natural. And those rings aren't even rings. Sal made the sign of the cross, took a gulp of Chianti. *They're tattoos!*

But not just any tattoo, Sal. Those are called infinity tattoos; at least that's what Ava told me. They mean everlasting love. Kinda nice sentiment, don't you think?

Everlasting love, huh? Sal scratched his chin, nodded. *That is kinda nice, and those two do look keen on one another.*

Keen? That's called love.

Sal's eyes misted, and his voice grew louder. *I know. It's just... Where's the flowers? I thought he had money. Why is she dressed like she just came off the set of* Dr. Zhivago? *Why is she wearing a dress that looks like a coat? Is that a coat? And no veil? Why no veil?*

Thankfully, Lorraine stepped in. *Sal, would you stop your complaining? Our daughter just married the man she loves. Be happy with that and maybe if we're lucky, we'll enjoy time with them and our grandchildren.*

Grandchildren? You mean... Is she...?

Lorraine Ventori shook her head and pointed a finger at her husband. *Not that I know of, but if and when the announcement comes, you will not comment other than to congratulate them. Understand? If they announced their new child has four legs and a soft black coat, you will congratulate them.*

That comment made Pop laugh. *Love is a funny thing and something tells me there's room in Law and Ava's heart for two-legged and four-legged children. But Lorraine's right, when the time comes, no comments. Not even if they want to name their child Wednesday or Happiness...*

Huh? Sal scratched his head, squinted at his friend. *What are you talking about?*

Lorraine patted her husband's hand, smiled at Pop. *One thing at a time, Angelo, one thing at a time...*

The Ventoris were an interesting family and Law's gut told him life with them would never get boring. He slid a glance at Roman who stood in the corner talking to his sister and Nate Desantro. The guy sure knew how to own a room and while Law wasn't intimidated by many people, this guy and Nate Desantro were exceptions. Roman and Desantro took turns eyeing him, not bothering to disguise the hidden message in their expressions: *Do not hurt Ava or you will answer to us.*

Law hadn't looked forward to the face-to-face with Roman Ventori and thought his wife's pregnancy issues might prevent him from attending the wedding. But he should have known a guy like Roman was not going to skip his sister's wedding, even if it meant a whirlwind visit to Magdalena. Plus, he'd agreed to sit in on a meeting with Sal and Lorraine tomorrow morning, where Ava and Law would deliver a shocker offer. *Surprise, we want to buy the grocery store! And with your permission, we've got ideas to expand it.* Law would even sweeten the deal and get his hair cut if that would persuade Sal to say yes.

Who would have ever thought Law would want to stay in Magdalena, would marry Ava Marie Ventori, and actually look forward to a relationship with his father? Not Law, no way, but it had happened, and stranger things continued to happen.

Like right now, Cal and Montrose were sipping bourbon by the fireplace and…were they laughing? Sure looked like it. Montrose seemed happier, more relaxed, and no doubt part of his new demeanor had to do with shipping Brett off to work at the dealership in Renova and removing his name from the company bank accounts. Montrose said a father could only be cheated so many times before he took a stand... Rumor had it he and Katrina were talking, which meant Brett better get used to the idea of divorce because it was coming.

Before he returned to Magdalena, Law hadn't thought it possible to actually *want* to share more than an occasional night and "surface talk" with a woman. And to find a woman he'd care about enough to call it love? Doubtful. He hadn't believed one existed who could ever make him feel differently. And then he met Ava. His gaze landed on his bride, caught her watching, eyes bright, lips pulled into a soft smile. He moved toward her, anxious to reach her side, touch her. She was his one and only, his heart and soul—his true happiness—today and always.

Many thanks for choosing to spend your time reading *A Family Affair: The Proposal*. If you enjoyed it, please consider writing a review on the site where you purchased it.

If you'd like to be notified of my new releases, please sign up at http://www.marycampisi.com

ABOUT THE AUTHOR

Mary Campisi writes emotion-packed books about second chances. Whether contemporary romances, women's fiction, or Regency historicals, her books all center on belief in the beauty of that second chance. Her small town romances center around family life, friendship, and forgiveness as they explore the issues of today's contemporary women.

Mary should have known she'd become a writer when at age thirteen she began changing the ending to all the books she read. It took several years and a number of jobs, including registered nurse, receptionist in a swanky hair salon, accounts payable clerk, and practice manager in an OB/GYN office, for her to rediscover writing. Enter a mouse-less computer, a floppy disk, and a dream large enough to fill a zip drive. The rest of the story lives on in every book she writes.

When she's not working on her craft or following the lives of five adult children, Mary's digging in the dirt with her flowers and herbs, cooking, reading, walking, or, on the perfect day, riding off into the sunset with her very own hero/husband on his Harley Ultra Limited.

If you would like to be notified when Mary has a new release, please sign up at
http://www.marycampisi.com/newsletter.

To learn more about Mary and her books…
https://www.marycampisi.com
mary@marycampisi.com

facebook.com/marycampisibooks

twitter.com/MaryCampisi

instagram.com/marycampisiauthor

amazon.com/author/marycampisi

bookbub.com/authors/mary-campisi

OTHER BOOKS BY MARY CAMPISI

Contemporary Romance:

Truth in Lies Series

Book One: *A Family Affair*

Book Two: *A Family Affair: Spring*

Book Three: *A Family Affair: Summer*

Book Four: *A Family Affair: Fall*

Book Five: *A Family Affair: Christmas*

Book Six: *A Family Affair: Winter*

Book Seven: *A Family Affair: The Promise*

Book Eight: *A Family Affair: The Secret*

Book Nine: *A Family Affair: The Wish*

Book Ten: *A Family Affair: The Gift*

Book Eleven: *A Family Affair: The Weddings, a novella*

Book Twelve: *A Family Affair: The Cabin, a novella*

Book Thirteen: *A Family Affair: The Return*

Book Fourteen: *A Family Affair: The Choice*

Book Fifteen: *A Family Affair: The Proposal*

Book Sixteen: *A Family Affair: Bonus Scenes*

A Family Affair Boxed Set: Books 1-3

A Family Affair Boxed Set 2: Books 4-6

Meals From Magdalena: A Family Affair Cookbook

Park Bench series:

Book One: *A Family Affair Shorts: Destiny*

Book Two: *A Family Affair Shorts: Regret*

Book Three: *A Family Affair Shorts: Love*

Book Four: *A Family Affair Shorts: Heartbreak*

Book Five: *A Family Affair Shorts: Peace*

A Family Affair Shorts Boxed Set

NEW: Small Town Perfect series

Small Town Perfect Boxed Set 1

Small Town Perfect Boxed Set 2

Small Town Perfect Boxed Set 3

Small Town Perfect Boxed Set 4

Small Town Perfect Boxed Set 5

Small Town Perfect Boxed Set 6

Reunion Gap Series

Book One: *Strangers Like Us*

Book Two: *Liars Like Us*

Book Three: *Lovers Like Us*

Book Four: *Couples Like Us*

More to come…

That Second Chance Series

Book One: *Pulling Home*

Book Two: *The Way They Were*

Book Three: *Simple Riches*

Book Four: *Paradise Found*

Book Five: *Not Your Everyday Housewife*

Book Six: *The Butterfly Garden*

That Second Chance Boxed Set 1-3

That Second Chance Boxed Set 4-6

That Second Chance Complete Boxed Set 1-6

The Betrayed Trilogy

Book One: *Pieces of You*

Book Two: *Secrets of You*

Book Three: *What's Left of Her*: a novella

The Betrayed Trilogy Boxed Set

The Best Intentions

Book One: *The Sweetest Deal*

Book Two: *The Perfect Deal*

Book Three: TBD

Regency Historical:

An Unlikely Husband Series

Book One - *The Seduction of Sophie Seacrest*

Book Two - *A Taste of Seduction*

Book Three - *A Touch of Seduction*, a novella

Book Four - *A Scent of Seduction*

An Unlikely Husband Boxed Set

The Model Wife Series

Book One: *The Redemption of Madeline Munrove*

Young Adult:

Pretending Normal